SCORED FOR LIFE

A Die-Cut Mystery Series

JUDITH DICKENSON ACKARET

JAT Trax Studios

Published by JAT Trax Studios
PO Box 230151, Tigard, OR 97281-0151

First printing, October 2018
Second printing, January 2020

Cover design by DLR Cover Designs
Etsy.com/shop/DLRCoverDesigns

ISBN-13: 978-1-7328821-1-9

eISBN-13: 978-1-7328821-0-2

This book is dedicated to my beautiful sister, Donna,
the inspiration for the character Marie,
And
To my wonderful husband, Jerry,
encouraging me to keep writing.

Acknowledgments

If my mom had not been so creatively talented and had the attitude to 'just go out and try it', I probably would not have written a book. So I must first thank my mother, LaVerne, for instilling in me the drive to try anything...within reason of course. Mom, I love you now and forever.

My husband, Jerry, was my rock through this whole ordeal of writing a first book. He did countless hours of research, not so much for the content of the book, but how to edit, publish, and market the end result. I love you more than can be put into words.

Then there is my sister, Deborah, who was the catalyst for me to open up my laptop and type out those first few words. When she announced she wanted to write a book, I suddenly realized I too have always wanted to write a book. Debbie and I constantly encouraged each other to keep writing and not listen to what people say, just focus on the material. By-the-way, you must read her book 'Uniquely Stella', under the pen name of Deborah M. Menenberg. Love you, sis!

A big thank you to my dear friend (since grade school), Dr. Sue Stoller, who has been my cheerleader and support throughout this entire project. She was gracious (or brave) enough to be the first to read my book, even staying up until two-thirty in the morning to finish. Love you, my friend!

A special thank you to Dan Kelly, retired homicide detective, who gave me the information I needed to describe a crime scene. I hope I made it real enough for this book. As I refrained from the actual details of a messy murder, I will keep the detailed notes and maybe use some it in another book. You are a wealth of information!

Before I got too far into my book, I wanted to research certain ideas, one being the urn which contained the ashes of two victims. For that I turned to Ron Rohde, Holman-Hankins-Bowker & Waud Funeral Service in Oregon City, Oregon. Thank you, Ron, for answering my questions so I could design the urn I needed for this story.

Author

Judith has been writing from the moment she learned how to put letters on paper. In grade school she wrote and directed plays, created comic books, and teamed up with her friend to write short stories. Her passion was to work behind the scenes in the police field and after some years in the accounting world, Judith was hired by a police department, spending the majority of her career in the Criminal Investigations Division as a Records Technician. In that position, she became a Composite Artist, transcriber, and a youth peer court advisor. Judith's love of paper-crafting has exploded from a small desk area to a full blown two-room studio. (Some of you can relate!) A line of vintage greeting cards and love of box designing is her current distraction from writing.

Along with their three adorable cats, Judith and Jerry (husband and Systems Reliability Engineer) spend a lot of time watching whales from their home on the Central Oregon Coast in the Pacific Northwest.

Judith Dickenson Ackaret

CHAPTER 1

Monday

The Oregon Coast air was calm and the sun all too inviting for day-dreaming the day away. That's what Annie Weston thought as she sipped her coffee at the kitchen counter of her mother's home overlooking the Pacific Ocean at 5:30 AM. The sun was just coming up over the mountain from the east, shining on the waves like an oil painting Annie had seen so many of in the galleries on the coast. The light refracting in the water caused a beautiful, almost translucent, turquoise color to appear below the white foamy waves of water hitting the rocks. As the sun moved across the sky the effect was short-lived, but the memory of the image stayed with Annie. It was almost spiritual.

It was a Monday morning, and like all Monday mornings before, Annie wanted to get to her shop early. She loved the quiet, peacefulness of mornings in her paper craft supply shop. This was a time she could ponder new ideas, dream up new paper box projects, and create greeting cards for customers to make and take. Her table set-up in her shop encouraged sales when customers could use the tools to create their own cards. Many came back over the course of their stay at the local time-share resort, as they found an appetite for crafting at the coast. There was something in the ocean air that brought out the creativity in people. Some people she would see back often to try out new tools of the craft trade. Annie had a website where customers could read about new designs and order supplies from her to be shipped to them. It was also a good source of income during the winter, when the tourist trade slowed down.

Annie's paper craft shop, Ocean Loads of Paper, was situated in a cozy cove of boutique shops in the quaint, but touristy town of Bridgewater Harbor. A section of shops sported two entrances, one on the street side and one on the ocean side, where a boardwalk lay between the shops and ocean wall. During the summer, tables and chairs were placed in various locations for the tourists to spend time and hopefully money in the shops. On the south end next to Annie's shop is a bakery/coffee shop where Annie swears she supported the bakery in coffee and baked goods all through last winter and spring. It was her favorite place to buy chocolate chip croissants, chocolate iced donuts, coffee cake drizzled in dark chocolate, and of course a dark chocolate mocha coffee drink. Not all at the same time...heavens, no. She spread it out over the day, especially long days in the summer.

Annie took a long deep breath and stood to stretch. She carried her coffee mug to the kitchen sink, where she washed and then dried the mug with a kitchen towel. She placed the mug in the cupboard, closed the door, and checked the counter to make sure she cleaned up after herself.

Annie's mother, Stella, would be up in an hour or so, and Annie knew she liked to wake up to a clean kitchen in the morning. A clean house was her mother's spiritual view. Smiling at the thought, Annie went to shower and dress for work.

After a quick dry with the hair dryer, Annie fluffed the bangs of her light brown hair, sprayed the bangs with hair spray, and pulled her shoulder length straight hair into a ponytail high on the back of her head. This was her usual style, she did not like hair falling into her face while working on crafts. It was also helpful when outside due to the Oregon coast getting quite windy.

Grabbing her purse and jacket she headed out toward the front door. As she opened the door, she was caught off guard by the sight of police cars parked across the street at Helen's house. Helen was a friend and neighbor of Annie and her mother. Helen was also guardian to a twenty-four-year old woman with Down Syndrome. Sudden fear filled Annie.

◆ ◆ ◆

Annie did not know how she got there. When she crossed the street, Annie felt herself in a dazed state at the opened front door looking in at the body of Helen Harper, a sixty-five-year old, sweet, loving, caring, person...her friend...her mother's dear friend. Crouching next to the body of Helen was a familiar face to Annie.

Detective Dan Surely was someone she had grown up with, although he was a couple of years ahead of her in school.

At the young age of five, Dan's father abandoned him when he ran off with another woman, leaving his mother in despair and broke. Within months after Dan's father left, his mother turned to alcohol. Annie's father, Richard Weston, had been at the Surely household on numerous occasions as a police officer following disputes between Dan's father and mother. Bridgewater Harbor was a small town, so when Dan's mother was arrested for drinking and neglect for the third time, she asked if there was any way to keep her son in town and not become a ward of the State.

Rich and Stella, Annie's father and mother, agreed to foster Dan and soon he came to live with the Weston family. Although Dan's mother did see him often, she thought it best that he live with the Weston's, and they in turn, became friends. Eventually, Dan's mother was able to stop drinking and get a job for meager wages. She was able to support herself, but Rich and Stella feared that if she were to have Dan back full time, she might regress into drinking. They felt she was not able to handle the stress in her life. So it was, that Dan would remain at the Weston house until he turned 18. Even then, he was always welcome to come 'home' anytime he wanted.

At the age of twenty-two and straight out of college, Dan began employment at Bridgewater Harbor Police Department as a police officer. Dan moved to Portland to join the Portland Police Bureau when he turned twenty-six. He had been there for twelve years, seven of those years in criminal investigation.

Annie heard through her mother Dan Surely moved back to Bridgewater Harbor to find a quieter way of life. He loved his career, but did not enjoy the long days, the late-night call outs, and the many times he had made plans only to be canceled by a rape, murder, or some other major crime of sorts. Yet, Annie thought, he started work yesterday and here he is at 6:00 AM crouching over a dead body...her neighbor.

Shaken, Annie called out to Dan by his last name. "Surely", she said in a hoarse/tearful whisper. "It's Detective Surely," Dan replied in an authoritative tone, then turning his head to see the person standing by the front door. He recognized Annie, the only girl who he sometimes hated, but most of the time liked. Dan was the big brother Annie never had, and while she would have preferred a sister, she would call Dan by his last name to torment him as siblings sometimes did. They would often disagree on choices Annie made, but Dan was always there to provide emotional support to Annie after her father passed away.

Annie's father, Captain Richard Weston, worked with Dan from the time Dan joined the Bridgewater Harbor Police Department at the age of twenty-two, until he left to move to Portland. They had a father-son relationship, when Dan's father left his mother and never came back. Richard Weston was the guiding influence for Dan working in law enforcement.

"I'm sorry, Annie. I know Helen was a friend of the family," Dan said apologetically. Although, Dan really never knew Helen, he knew that Stella and Helen were good friends.

Dan stood to his full height of 6'01" and even with a trench coat on, Annie could tell he kept to his sleek body frame. Who wears a trench coat anymore, Annie thought to herself. Thoughts often popped into her mind at inopportune times.

♦ ♦ ♦

Annie noticed Dan turn his attention toward the kitchen, which was uncluttered and so clean one could eat off the floor, not that Annie would eat off the floor. Her heart still pounding in her head, Annie looked at Marie. Marie! Poor Marie! She was quietly sobbing, rocking back and forth from her waist in the white wooden kitchen table chair. Annie started to move inside the house toward Marie, but Dan's sharp look stopped her.

"I want to talk to Marie," Annie said in a brave, don't mess with me, tone.

"This is a crime scene. I can't have you walking all about. Let me bring Marie to you. I will need to talk with her soon, so don't go anywhere. Sit on the front porch chairs for now," Dan directed. He turned and went to Marie's side. He lowered his body to her eye level, and spoke in quiet tones, letting her know Annie was there and wanted to talk with her on the front porch. Marie rose from her chair and froze when she saw a man placing plastic bags over the hands of Helen's body. Tears flooded her face again. Dan walked the sobbing and terrified Marie to where Annie was sitting. He then disappeared into the house.

Annie sprang up from the wicker love seat, stylishly arranged on the covered front porch of the large two-story bungalow. Wrapping her arms around Marie they hugged so tightly that Annie felt she could not let go. Speaking words of comfort to Marie, she finally pulled apart from their embrace and looked Marie in the eyes.

"What happened?" Annie said in a soft voice.

Marie began to sit down. Detective Dan Surely returned with a box of tissues and offered it to Marie. Annie reached for the box and set it on the table in front of the loveseat. Pulling out a few tissues, she handed them to Marie. She then pulled out a few tissues for herself. Detective Surely sat in a cushioned wicker chair across from Annie and Marie.

"Can you tell me what happened?" Detective Surely asked Marie. He pulled out a ruled yellow pad and searched his pockets for a pen. He found a pen in his upper right-hand pocket.

"I..., I...saw the light on in the kitchen", said Marie, "It was really early." Marie stopped talking while looking for a tissue that fell on the floor of the porch. Picking up the found tissue, Marie continued.

"Aunt Helen does not get up this early. I do. I like to get up early. I can see the sun shining on the water between the houses across the street. That's why I get up early. I go to bed early." Marie explained.

Marie blew her nose and handed the tissue to Dan. He looked perplexed at the tissue and then at Annie. Annie grabbed the tissue and set it on the glass-topped table next to the tissue box.

"Go on," said Detective Surely.

Annie listened closely as Marie told Detective Surely of how she got dressed and went to the back door. Marie showed both Annie and Dan the two keys she kept around her neck on a wide pink heavy ribbon-like band. Marie explained that one key was for her apartment above the garage, and one key was for the door of her Aunt Helen's house.

It was at this point that all three were interrupted by the medical examiner and paramedics removing the covered body by gurney through the front door to an awaiting transport vehicle. Detective Dan Surely stood up, turned to Marie and Annie and said, "I'll be right back. Please stay here."

Marie stood and tears began to flow as her guardian left the house, never to return.

♦ ♦ ♦

Annie jumped from her seat as she spotted her mother, Stella, dressed in a blue fluffy robe and blue embroidered slippers. Stella quickly walked across the street, toward the gurney, past the firemen preparing to leave. Dan met Stella and grabbed her by the shoulders.

"Helen?" Stella cried questioningly.

"Yes," Dan answered.

"Marie! Where is Marie?" Stella continued to question.

"She's with Annie on the porch. Why don't you go see her?", Dan said, hoping not to answer further questions about the current situation.

The gurney carrying the black bag of Helen's body passed by Dan and Stella on its way to the ambulance.

"No! Helen? No!" Stella's sobs were softened by the arms suddenly wrapped around her. Dan held her close, the same way he did when he had to deliver the news that her husband, Annie's father, passed away of a heart attack while on duty fifteen years earlier. As the gurney was being loaded into the coroner's van, Dan walked Stella to the front porch, where Annie and Marie stood, tears again flowing, hearts aching, and sounds blurring in the background.

The fire trucks, police vehicles, and coroner's van all began to drive away. Marie, Annie, and Stella all watched as the last vehicle turned and disappeared out of sight. All seemed serenely quiet. They stood, not knowing what to do next. Annie realized she was holding her breath. She finally inhaled deeply and slowly exhaled.

♦ ♦ ♦

After interviewing Marie and taking Marie and Annie on a walk-through of the house, Detective Dan Surely told the women to go back to Stella's house and get some rest. He would remain at the house with the crime scene officers gathering evidence, photographing the scene, and securing the house. Dan looked at Marie and asked that no one enter the house for any reason until he released the crime scene to the attorney of Helen Harper. Knowing that Marie would comply, he did not bother to ask for the key to the house that she hung around her neck. If it gave her comfort to keep it, he was okay with that. On the other hand, he wasn't so sure about Annie or what she would do, but felt somewhat secure in the feeling that she would at least call and bother him about going into the house before she attempted to enter.

Marie grabbed the box of tissues, hiked the straps of the canvas bag she always carried with her over her left shoulder, and followed Annie to cross the street to Stella's house. It was just past nine o'clock in the morning, and Marie was at a loss of what to do now. Following Annie to Stella's house seemed like a safe thing for her to do at this moment.

Annie turned and noticed her mother still standing on the sidewalk, staring down the street in the direction of where the coroner's van took Helen's body. Annie walked back across the street and hugged her mother. She then gently guided Stella back to her house. Stella wrapped her robe tightly around her body, as she suddenly felt the coolness of the coastal morning.

Stella was sixty years old and had retired from the county library as the Librarian a few months before and was collecting her state employee retirement fund. She loved the library and was a voracious reader. Her eclectic reading material included books on Physics and History to Romance novels. Stella was a feisty person all of five feet tall and had a wonderful sense of humor. Everyone loved visiting the library, because Stella was there to direct them to stretch their reading desires to various genres.

Now, Annie thought, Stella seemed small and fragile at this moment. She had never seen her mother in this light. It made Annie see how old her mother was. Yes, sixty was not that old at all, considering her grandmother was in her late seventies. Her mother was still a very active person who even drove a little blue sports car!

As the three women entered the house through the medium blue-colored door, Annie realized that many hours had passed since she originally walked through this very door to go to work. The gray cedar-shingled one-story house had white trim and a beautiful garden of flowers in the front yard. A tall pampas grass bush grew in the south corner, stretching its branches far over the short white picket fence that wound around the property line. A small porch with pots of daisies invited people to the front door.

Annie, Marie, and Stella stood in the front entrance, taking in the occurrences of this morning. They were all thinking the same thing. What was next?

♦ ♦ ♦

Annie then realized that she needed to contact Lizzy, her shop employee, to open the store this morning, as Annie wanted to stay with her mother and Marie.

Lizzy had become a dear friend and valued employee of Annie's. She had a Master's degree in Business Administration and in the shop her talents were in inventory purchasing, stocking and displaying products, and web design. Annie, who had a Bachelor's degree in Accounting, actually used her best talents in designing, crafting, and bringing people together to create beautiful cards and paper crafts. Although Lizzy never liked the crafting of paper herself, she would spend time on the computer learning how to use the various products she and Annie ordered. When a customer would ask about the product, Lizzy was the person to go to for answers. Lizzy even sold more items just by demonstrating what she had learned from watching the instruction videos on the internet.

The shop had a small demonstration area on the counter by the cash register for last minute questions and quick instructions of new product that had just arrived in the store. Lizzy's next project was to make instructions for each product for the customers to take home and try out their new purchases. She was organized and clever, Annie thought. The two made a great team.

"How about I make a late breakfast?" Stella asked heading to the kitchen.

"Sure." Annie said, "Let me just make a call to Lizzy to open the shop this morning."

Marie remained quiet. Annie thought how scared Marie must be right now.

"It's going to be okay." Annie told Marie. "Mom and I will take care of you."

"No!" Marie shouted, "I don't want you to take care of me. I don't want you to die."

"Die?" exclaimed Stella, "We're not going to die."

Annie, understanding what Marie meant, said, "Marie, just because your mother passed away and then Helen died this morning does not mean we are going to die too."

"Aunt Helen was murdered!" Marie cried.

CHAPTER 2

Tuesday Early Morning

Sounds of tapping thundered in her head. Annie was dreaming about people and animals dying all around her. Her mother was dying, her friends and neighbors...all dying and disappearing. All she could hear was her heart pounding, pounding, and pounding. She had difficulty breathing. There was a tremendous weight on her chest. Was she having a heart attack and dying too?! Sounds of tapping kept coming.

"Meowww!" said Callie, Annie's Maine Coon long haired calico cat. The weight on Annie's chest was actually her fifteen-pound cat, whose polydactyl front paw was lightly patting her cheek.

There it was again, the sounds of light tapping. Annie realized that someone was at her bedroom door. She picked up Callie and set her down on the bed. Callie meowed again as Annie tossed the blankets over her unhappy cat while trying to crawl out of bed. As her feet hit the floor, Annie's left foot stepped on her slipper. Leaving her slippers on the floor, she wasted no time in heading for the bedroom door. Annie opened the door to find Marie who was standing there dressed in a borrowed nightgown and robe from Stella.

"Marie. Is everything alright?" asked Annie in a whisper.

"There is a light on at Aunt Helen's house." Marie answered.

A light, Annie thought. But all the lights were off when she looked out the living room window before going to bed. She remembered how cold and dark the house looked then.

"Show me", Annie directed and led Marie back to Marie's bedroom. The lights were on in Marie's room and the window facing the street stood with the curtains opened. Annie turned off the lights and walked to the window. She stepped to one side and motioned Marie to step to the opposite side. They then turned their heads to peer out the window to the house across the street. They quickly backed their bodies up against the bedroom wall almost in unison. Annie took a deep breath. 'Calm down', she told herself. She looked at Marie and gave her a weak smile. They then turned and looked out the window again. Sure enough, a small light appeared to be shining inside the living room area of the house. It almost seemed like someone was using a flash light, but the light was not moving at the moment. Annie motioned for Marie to follow her to the hallway.

"I am going to go get dressed and sneak over for a look in the window." Annie whispered to Marie. "You stay here and keep the lights off."

Marie nodded.

Quietly closing her door behind her, Annie quickly dressed. She jumped as Callie gave a loud "Meow!" when Annie sat on the bed to tie her tennis shoes, disturbing the cat's sleep. Giving Callie a quick pet and moving off the bed, she searched her night stand looking for a flashlight. She unplugged her phone from the charger and stuffed it into her front pocket. Standing up, Annie leaned back toward the night stand to search for her pepper spray. She was going to be prepared.

Sneaking out the bedroom door, Annie nearly ran over Marie, who was fully dressed and ready to go.

Annie whispered, "Marie, you can't go with me. It might be dangerous."

"Detective Dan said you cannot go in the house. He told us that." Marie stated.

"You're right, but I was just going to sneak over and look in the windows. I won't go inside the house." Annie offered.

"No. You should call Detective Dan." Marie said.

◆ ◆ ◆

"Alright. Alright." Annie said as they walked down the hall to the front door, "Let's go to the front door so we don't wake up Mom." Annie pulled her phone out and looked up Dan's cell phone number from her contacts list. She pressed the number and heard the familiar ring begin.

A few rings later, Dan sleepily answered, "Hello?"

"Dan, there's a light on at Helen's place." Annie whispered into the phone.

"Who is this? Speak up!" yelled Dan into the phone. Dan was awoken from a fitful sleep. Something was just not right. The Helen Harper case was not adding up. The house was immaculate. No sign of struggle. No known threats to Helen. Yet when he walked into the house, something was off. He could not ditch that nagging feeling.

He was not happy being called on the second night he had been working at Bridgewater Harbor Police Department. Was this going to be a continuous occurrence? He could have stayed in Portland and gotten more sleep.

"This is Annie. There is a light on at Helen's house."

"Annie? Did you call 9-1-1?" asked Dan.

"No. I was just going over to the house and peek in the window. I wanted to let you know in case there is someone inside."

"Call 9-1-1. I am getting dressed and will be there shortly. DO NOT go over there. Do you understand?" came the all too familiar authoritative tone in Dan's voice. He often got frustrated with Annie's impulsive nature to just jump into the middle of things. She was like that all the time he had known her. Nothing had changed. "Stay in your house", he demanded. "I will be there shortly."

"We will watch the house from Mom's porch." Annie whispered.

"We? Who is 'we'?"

"Marie is with me. Marie is the one who saw the light on in the house and woke me up. I went to her bedroom and saw the light through the window." Annie explained.

"Call 9-1-1, and stay inside your house." Dan hung up.

♦ ♦ ♦

Annie called 9-1-1 and gave Helen's house address and a brief description of what was happening. She told the dispatcher that she had to hang up, and that Detective Dan Surely was on his way. Annie hung up and put the cell phone into her pants pocket.

"Dan wants us to stay inside the house, but I think we can see better from the porch. Maybe if we just sneak out onto the porch and hide behind the potted trees, we will be fine." Annie explained to Marie.

Marie was getting excited. This was an adventure. She never got to be involved in an adventure. She will do as Annie says and hide behind the tree. Marie quietly followed Annie out the front door. She stopped and realized it was dark outside. She reached up and turned on the porch light, which illuminated Annie, who was already standing outside on the porch.

Annie, startled by the sudden bright light, jumped back, nearly knocking over Marie, and wildly grabbed for the light switch. Turning the light off, she grabbed Marie's arm and pulled her outside. She closed the front door behind them and signaled for Marie to hide behind the tree. Annie hid behind the potted tree on the opposite side of the stairs leading down to the sidewalk in the yard.

Helen's house went dark. Whoever was in there saw the light turn on at the house across the street. Annie chided herself for allowing Marie to follow her. If anything happened to Marie, Annie would not be able to live with herself. Annie suddenly seemed very protective of Marie since learning of Helen's death. What was happening to her? She never had kids with her first marriage, which thankfully ended in divorce after six months.   The whole baby thing never appealed to Annie. It was enough to clean a kitty box daily, wipe up the occasional hairball throw up, and clean bedding weekly in the various sleeping nooks of her cat Callie. A baby would be so much work and she had a shop to contend with daily. At the age of thirty-six, Annie figured that the "kid" thing was never going to happen anyway. She had no prospects of dating at this point, let alone marriage.

Moments later, Annie and Marie spotted a dark figure coming from behind Helen's house, down the driveway to the street. Annie motioned to Marie to stay down and be quiet. Pushing limbs of the tree apart, Annie was able to get a better view, but the dark figure walked briskly to a vehicle parked in front of Helen's neighbor's house. Annie and Marie quickly jumped out from behind the trees and ran to the picket fence gate. Annie was trying to see what looked like an older model truck. While the truck was not close enough to see the letters on the license plate, she did notice that the license plate was in an odd place on the truck. It was attached to the truck's tail-gate. The truck moved quickly out of its parking spot. No lights were turned on and as the truck roared around the corner, the driver did not signal or brake.

The vehicle was out of sight just as a patrol car pulled up in front of the neighbor's house on the other side of Helen's house. Annie ran down the sidewalk and crossed the street to signal the officer. Marie was close at her heels. The officer listened to a quick description of the vehicle and radioed dispatch as he ran back to his police vehicle. Seconds later, the police cruiser disappeared around the corner.

Detective Dan Surely arrived in his unmarked police vehicle. He shook his head in a disappointed manner when he saw Annie and Marie on the sidewalk. He pulled up next to them.

"I thought I told you to stay in your house!" Dan said as he exited his vehicle.

"We saw someone come from the back of the house and get into a truck." Annie said breathlessly.

Another police vehicle pulled up in front of Helen's house. Two officers alighted from the patrol vehicle. Detective Surely walked over to meet them. Annie strained to listen to the conversation, but could not distinguish a word the three men said.

The two officers turned and walked to the back of the house. Detective Surely watched the front. Lights went on in the house as each room was searched. Minutes ticked by until an officer came to the front door and announced the house was all clear. Detective Surely motioned for Annie and Marie to follow him inside Helen's house.

As Annie approached the threshold of the front door, she was taken aback by the sight of the living room. Sofa cushions were strewn across the floor, papers were scattered all about, books tossed carelessly from a small bookcase under a window, paintings tilted on the wall, and small knick-knacks lay broken on the floor. Helen would have been devastated to see such a mess, Annie thought.

The officers took photos of the crime scene, and then the three men had a conference in the kitchen. Annie was not even trying to listen this time, as she was in such disbelief that anyone would cause such damage to another person.

Dan called Annie to the kitchen. He pointed out the broken glass from the kitchen door. This was how the burglar got inside the house. Small shards of glass were all over the floor. Annie instinctively went to the broom closet and retrieved a broom and dust pan. As she began to clean up the broken glass, Dan and the two officers went outside to the garage. They returned with a small piece of plywood, a hammer, and nails to temporarily secure the kitchen door.

Annie cleaned up the last of the glass and tossed the glass in the trash bin under the sink. She put the broom and dust pan away in the kitchen broom closet. A quick look around the kitchen was next to see if anything else had been touched. Everything seemed in order. She then looked into the living room to find Marie putting books into the small bookcase. Marie knew the order in which Helen kept the books. She lovingly placed each book back in its place. Annie watched, leaning up against the counter in the kitchen. What will happen to Marie, Annie pondered.

It was 1:30 AM when Annie and Marie walked through the front door of Annie's mother's home. They silently walked to their respective bedrooms. Annie stopped at her door, looked down the hall at Marie, and said, "Goodnight, Marie. We will get this all figured out in the morning. But we need to get some sleep right now."

Marie nodded and entered her room, closing the door behind her.

CHAPTER 3

Tuesday Mid-Morning

Morning came way too soon for Annie. She opened her eyes, yawned, and stretched in bed. Noticing that her cat was not in bed with her, she turned over to look at the clock on her nightstand.

"Eight o'clock!" Annie gasped. She sprang out of bed, grabbed her robe, and hurriedly went to Marie's room to wake her. The door was open, the bed was made, and the room was neat and tidy. Annie suddenly smelled bacon, coffee, and pancakes. She followed the beckoning aroma down the hall, through the family room, and into the kitchen. There she found Marie at the breakfast bar eating three pancakes smothered in whipped cream, drizzled with chocolate sauce, and nuts. Next to the pancakes sat three slices of bacon. Stella was adding scrambled eggs to Marie's plate.

"Good morning. Would you like some breakfast?" Stella asked as she poured Annie a cup of coffee.

"No," Annie answered. "I'll just have coffee," her eyes lingered on the bacon, "and maybe a slice of bacon!" Annie took one slice of bacon. Taking a bite convinced her she needed more, so she grabbed three more slices off the plate on the counter attached to the breakfast bar.

Annie sipped her coffee as she turned and looked out over the ocean. It was going to be a nice day, although windy, the sun was shining and that was a great start for a coastal day. Her thoughts wandered to Marie working at the shop part-time. There were many things that Marie was perfectly capable of doing. She was not sure how Marie was with money handling, but thought with time and training, Marie would be able to help with cashing out customers. Annie was willing to make it work for Marie's sake. Marie needed something to fill her life now that Helen was gone.

"Marie, would you like to go to the shop with me today?"

Marie looked up with a big smile. "Oh yes. I can help you. I am a good cleaner. I can straighten things up. I always helped Aunt Helen with the housework. I helped her keep her house nice. I can help you now in the shop."

"Then it is settled. You come to work in the shop with me today." Annie grabbed her coffee and headed to her bedroom to get ready for work.

After Annie showered, dried her hair, and dressed in a nice casual outfit of blue slacks, a plain white top, and a light blue button-up sweater, she donned her socks and shoes and headed for the door. Her thoughts were of Marie's comments of keeping Helen's house neat and tidy. Annie picked up her purse, turned to look at her messy bed, set the purse down and made a quick clean-up in her room. She could learn a lesson or two from Marie, she thought.

Marie was standing at the front door with a jacket on and her canvas bag slung over her shoulder. Marie's light blond long straight hair was the perfect style for her beautiful round face. Marie's light brown eyes crinkled when she smiled. It was a smile that melted Annie's heart. Marie was like an unexplained angel in her presence. She never had a harsh word to say. She was kind and innocent.

♦ ♦ ♦

Walking to town consisted of two blocks south and one block west toward the ocean. Ocean Loads of Paper, Annie's shop, was on the north point of the boardwalk. Next to her shop, on the north end, was a painted furniture and upholstery shop called "Hermitage Furniture". A young woman by the name of Lynda Hermitage owned and operated the shop. She specialized in painted furniture, but did a fair amount of upholstery of older furniture, an art form she learned from her father and grandfather. Lynda was married with two kids in grade school. Her husband had a business in yard maintenance and worked the entire county with contracts through vacation home owners.

On the south side of Ocean Loads of Paper was Ione's Bakery and Coffee Shop. Ione Landon owned the shop and it proved to be the most popular of all the shops on the boardwalk. Ione served not only incredibly delicious baked goods, but she served soup, salads, and sandwiches, as well as expresso coffee drinks. Her sandwiches were always made with bread freshly baked by her each morning.

Next to Ione's Bakery and Coffee Shop was Ocean Waves Gift Shop, owned by Lois Bookman, where tourists could purchase knick-knacks and t-shirts in various ocean themed designs. The shop also had postcards and small stuffed ocean creatures, like crabs, dolphins, and whales.

No coastal town would be complete without a candy shop, and Bridgewater Harbor had the best. Not only did Old Salty's Candy Shop make their own salt water taffy in every flavor possible, but they specialized in Carmel Corn, chocolates, and caramels. One side of the shop was set up with soda shop style chairs and tables. Old Salty's Candy Shop was the place to go for ice cream, sodas, and burgers. It began as a candy shop and later expanded into the space next door and added the ice cream and burgers.

Natural Seas, a natural fiber clothing store stood next to Old Salty's and was run by a woman named, Joyce Hindersen, who worked in a top accounting firm in Portland, but tired of the pressure of deadlines and decided to move to the coast and open up a small shop. Annie loved her dresses, which made her slightly overweight figure look slim. The shop was small, but large in inventory.

An art gallery stood next to the clothing shop. Local artists of all venues displayed their works for sale in Spencer's Art Gallery. The shop was bright in color and offered a variety of pieces in varying prices. It was a fun place to wander around and spend time admiring the works of art.

With so many dogs now vacationing with their persons, a pet boutique was housed in the second to the last shop on the south side of the building. Pet owners could purchase anything from chew toys to bedding and clothing. The boardwalk was a good place to have a pet shop.

On the far south side of the building stood a favorite shop of both town people and visitors. It was Debbie's Quilt and Yarn Shop. Debbie's fabrics were unique and beautiful. Debbie Walker, the owner, offered classes in quilting and various yarn techniques like knitting, crocheting, and such. Annie often wanted to learn to quilt, but with so little time in her busy schedule she was never able to begin. She often window shopped the wonderful display of fabrics on her way to the shop owner dumpster area beyond at the end of the boardwalk.

♦ ♦ ♦

As Annie unlocked her shop door, she heard her cell phone begin to ring. She signaled to Marie to turn on the lights while she struggled to pull her cell phone out of her purse.

"Hello", Annie answered the phone she held to her ear.

"Annie, this is Dan."

"Hello, Surely!"

"It's Detective Dan Surely to you!" Dan announced, sounding exasperated. He took a breath. "I have some good news for you. I have been in contact with Helen's attorney. His name is Charles Conklin. He will be calling you today."

"Oh. Is it okay for us to go inside the house to finish cleaning it up?" Annie asked.

"No. I'm afraid not."

Dan explained that the attorney wanted to contact Helen's heir to her estate first. He also wanted to contact Annie today. Annie assumed it was to discuss Marie, as Marie was now staying at Stella's house, and Dan probably discussed Marie with the attorney as Helen was Marie's legal guardian.

Annie felt an uncomfortable twinge in her stomach. Even though she had not spent a lot of time with Marie in the past, she heard about her through her mother, Helen's best friend. Helen and Marie would frequently be at Stella's house when Annie arrived home from the shop at night. Annie was so busy trying to make her shop profitable with work during the day and classes she taught at night, that she spent little time with her mom. She felt bad about that. Things had to change.

Annie realized that Dan had stopped talking. Did she hear all that he was saying? She should really pay more attention when he talked to her, she thought. Was it the sound of his voice that caused her to drift off to other thoughts?

"Annie? Are you still there?" Dan questioned.

"Um, yes. Can I take Marie over to her apartment to get her clothes and personal things?" Annie asked.

"Sure," Dan replied. "But wait until you talk with the attorney first."

Annie asked Dan for the contact information of Charles Conklin. She entered the information into her phone contacts list.

CHAPTER 4

Tuesday Afternoon

Hanging up the phone, Annie told Marie what Dan had said. Marie was happy she could get back to her apartment over the detached garage in the backyard of Helen's house.

"Well, I am waiting for a call from Helen's attorney before we can go there, so in the meantime, let's get the shop ready to open."

Annie showed Marie all of the light switches and display lights she would turn on in the morning. She noticed Marie beginning to straighten up areas of the store to make things look tidy. While Marie was puttering about the shop, Annie took their jackets and went to her office behind the counter.

Annie hung up the jackets on the antique white hooks on the wall just to the left of the door as she entered the office. Her desk was up against the wall to the right. Next to it stood a small two door cabinet about the height of the desk. On her desk stood a desk top computer, two monitors side-by-side, a telephone, a Disney coffee mug, two water glasses filled with pens, pencils, highlighters, marking pens, and a letter opener. Stacks of papers, not the decorative kind, stood to both sides of her desk, creating an organized, but cluttered look. Annie set her purse on top of her desk.

It was nine-thirty in the morning and the shop opened at ten. Annie took her keys and unlocked the cabinet doors next to her desk. Opening the doors revealed a small safe. She punched in the safe code and extracted a register drawer. She closed the safe and took the drawer to the cash register in the shop, where she quickly counted out the money and made a notation on a daily log.

Lizzy walked into the shop. She had become fast friends with Annie from the moment she walked into Ocean Loads of Paper to ask for a job. Lizzy was taller than Annie, about five foot-seven, long dark brown naturally wavy hair past her shoulders, and always stylish in the clothing she wore. Annie loved Lizzy's ability to be direct, organized, and get on well with customers. With the cheer she brought to the shop, they were the perfect team for a paper craft store.

"Good morning!" Lizzy said in an attempted cheery voice. Gossip spread fast in this town. She set down coffees and a bag of pastries. Unbuttoning her black, waist length puffy jacket, she tossed it and her purse on the counter.

Noticing Lizzy with two coffees and a pastry bag, which could only mean chocolate croissants, Annie returned the cheery "Good Morning". Marie walked up to the two women at the counter and smiled at Lizzy.

"Oh, I didn't know Marie was coming to the shop this morning or I would have picked up more pastries. Let me go back and get more. Would you like a coffee, Marie?" Lizzy said grabbing her purse off the counter.

"No, thanks." Marie said, "I can go to the bakery and get something."

"Well, okay, but it's my treat. Here, take this and get whatever you want." Lizzy said handing Marie a ten-dollar bill from her wallet.

"Let Ione know you now work with me at the shop and she'll give you a discount." Annie told Marie. Ione was great about giving shop owners a discount. Annie reciprocated with shop owners on the boardwalk as well.

Marie looked at Annie and smiled. When she left the shop, Annie quickly began telling Lizzy about the murder, Dan being in town again, and what was going to happen to Marie. She took a bite of her chocolate croissant and washed it down with her coffee before answering questions that Lizzy asked.

"First of all, Marie found Helen on the floor. Helen was wearing the red dress that she had on the day before. Dan told me he thinks she was murdered sometime the night before." Annie took another bite of the croissant, which caused flakes of the pastry to fall on her white shirt. She casually brushed them off. Picking up her coffee in her other hand, she took a couple more sips. She set the cup down on the counter.

Annie continued to tell Lizzy about the burglar in Helen's house, the old truck parked on the street, how the living room was tossed about, and the broken-out kitchen door window. Lizzy listened intently while drinking her coffee.

"What about Dan coming back into town? Tell me about that?" Lizzy questioned, tucking her hair behind her ears.

"According to Mom, Dan wanted to come back, because he was missing small town life, and got tired of being called out in the middle of the night on major crimes."

"Wow, and then he gets called to investigate Helen's murder the day after he comes back to work here." Lizzy commented. "Is he seeing anyone?" Lizzy diverted her eyes to appear uninterested, but Annie could sense Lizzy had definite interest!

Annie chuckled. There goes Lizzy being direct. "I simply don't know what you mean?"

"Oh, come on, Annie. You know what I mean. I just want the gossip, that's all." Lizzy said picking at her croissant, trying not to look Annie in the eyes.

"I have not talked to him long enough to find out any details. I can ask Dan if you are interested."

"No!" Lizzy said jerking her head up to look at Annie. "I was just making conversation."

"Well, on another topic, Marie has been staying with Mom and me until we can get things straightened out. I was thinking Marie would be a good fit in the shop. She is a bit of a neat freak. I could use that here. You and I are so busy with our separate duties. It would be nice to have someone here to do clean-up, sorting, sweeping, helping customers find what they are looking for, and maybe even help with classes. She would be perfect for helping to organize the kits for the classes. What do you think?" Annie asked, taking another bite of her croissant.

"I think we should give it a try. I noticed when Marie and Helen would come to the shop, Marie was the one picking out the product for the projects. She seemed to know quite a bit about crafting. Was this something she often did with Helen?"

"Yes. Helen encouraged Marie to learn new skills. Mom and Helen would often include Marie in their senior activities. I wonder if Marie was lonely for someone her own age!" Annie laughed.

Lizzy, being the business person behind the shop slapped her hand on the counter and said, "Let's get Marie's paperwork filled out for employment and talk with her about job duties."

Marie walked into the shop with her canvas tote slung over her left shoulder, carrying a hot chocolate and a chocolate iced donut wrapped in a waxed paper sheet. Something Annie would have chosen herself. Both Annie and Lizzy stopped talking.

◆ ◆ ◆

It was late in the afternoon and constant customer traffic kept the ladies busy. Marie proved to be an excellent employee by helping customers with product selection and referring them to Annie's creative table to try out new product before finishing their purchases and leaving the store. Marie was all smiles, courteous, and excited to talk about a product. Annie could not believe how fortunate she was to have Marie working in her shop.

Annie walked into the office when she was able to take a break. She had just sat down when her cell phone rang. The caller-ID showed it to be Charles Conklin, Helen's attorney.

"Hello?" Annie spoke softly into the phone.

"Hello. My name is Charles Conklin, attorney for Helen Harper. Is this Annie Weston?" Mr. Conklin stated.

"Yes. Detective Dan Surely told me you would be calling." Annie slid her chair up to the desk. She got a pen and paper just in case she needed to take notes.

"First of all, let me just say how sorry I am to hear of Helen's death." Mr. Conklin said. "It was disturbing to find out someone had taken her life."

"We are still in a bit of shock ourselves. My mother was friends with Helen. She is not handling it well at the moment."

"Until the murderer is caught there can be no healing." Mr. Conklin said.

Charles Conklin was in his late fifties with his own law practice specializing in estate planning in the neighboring town of Newport, Oregon. Helen's husband, Dr. Robert Harper, had hired Mr. Conklin over ten years ago to handle their Living Trust. After Robert's death, Helen had made several changes to the Living Trust. Mr. Conklin was the attorney Robert had entrusted with his business legal matters as well personal matters.

Charles Conklin continued, "I am sorry to need to bring this up now, but I located the heir to the Harper Estate yesterday. I would like to meet with you, your mother, and the heir tomorrow morning to read the Will and to set forth the wishes of the Living Trust. I understand Marie is in your care at this time. Would you be willing to bring her with you?"

"Yes, of course. Marie is staying with my mother and me at this time. I just hired her to work in my shop part-time. This has all been so hard on her. Dealing with Helen's death is probably bringing back memories of her own mother's death. She is scared about being left alone." Annie rambled on, nervous for Marie's sake.

"I understand and it will all be addressed tomorrow." Mr. Conklin stated, "I will see you then tomorrow morning at my office."

"Yes."

Charles Conklin gave Annie the address and phone number of his office. They agreed to meet at 9:00 AM.

Annie opened the door of her office and entered the main shop area. Lizzy and Marie were both busy with customers. Annie caught Lizzy's attention and told her that she was going next door for a coffee and donut and she needed to make a call to her mother. Lizzy nodded and turned her attention back to the customer.

The sun was shining brightly and many people were on the boardwalk watching the ocean for whales spouting periodically in the small bay. The migrating whales would spend some time at this location due to the food source available. Every year twenty-thousand gray whales would head to Baja California to breed. In April through June, the whales migrate to Alaska. Approximately eight hundred break from the migration and spend their vacation on the Oregon Coast and Washington Coast. It is on the Central Oregon Coast that the whales discovered a tiny shrimp delicacy. They feed on this food until around November, when they merge into the whale highway heading south again.

Leaning on the rock wall facing the ocean, inhaling the salt air was calming for Annie, her head now reeling with thoughts. She was happy to accompany her mother and Marie to the reading of the Will, but it all made her so tense and nervous. She did not realize until this moment how strong she was being for Stella and Marie. It must have been frightening for Marie, and so sad for her mother. She had no idea how much they grieved for their friend. They were both keeping up stoic fronts. At least that is what Annie thought. Maybe she just wasn't aware of how they were dealing with anything. She really needed to pay special attention to them to help them through the next few weeks.

The cell phone in Annie's hand rang and vibrated at the same time. Annie noticed it was her mother's phone number.

"Hello, Mom." Annie answered with as much cheer as she could muster. She turned to look out at the ocean.

"I just talked with Mr. Conklin, Helen's attorney. He wants us all to meet him at 9:00 AM tomorrow morning. Can I ride with you?"

"Yes, that will be great. Have you heard anything about a relative coming to handle the funeral arrangements yet?" Annie inquired.

"No. Helen only spoke of a brother of Robert, but the two never got along. I believe Robert's brother and wife had a son, who would be a few years older than you. I do know that Helen wanted to be cremated. Robert was cremated and Helen told me she wanted to have her ashes with Roberts. I don't know anything more than that. She really did not like to talk about it."

"I am assuming the attorney will have all that information tomorrow." Annie suggested. "I think Marie and I will close up the shop early and head home soon. Lizzy is going to leave at four." Annie quickly ran a list in her head of things to be done before she could leave today.

"Okay, dear." Stella added, "I'll see you at home then. We'll plan something comforting for dinner tonight."

"That would be great. Should I stop by the store and pick up something?" Thinking the grocery store was only a few blocks out of the way.

"No. We have plenty." Stella said, and then said her good-bye.

♦ ♦ ♦

It was almost four and Annie gave up the notion of coffee and walked back to the shop. She told Lizzy she was closing up early, as she wanted to discuss the events of tomorrow with Marie. Annie also mentioned that her mother was making comfort food and invited Lizzy to join them. Lizzy begged off as she had an appointment. She did offer to accompany the three to the attorney in the morning as moral support, but Annie asked if she wouldn't mind opening the shop on her own instead. Lizzy agreed knowing that otherwise Annie would just worry about the shop not being open during the busiest time of the year. Lizzy was a great friend, Annie thought with a smile.

Annie began closing proceedings. Marie closed and locked the front door on the ocean side of the shop. She turned the "Open" sign to "Closed" and began turning off lights on the displays. Lizzy had earlier closed and locked the door on the street side. Marie went to the back room and came out with a broom and dust pan. She began systematically sweeping the floor.

As Marie swept, Annie opened the cash register to count out the day's receipts and cash. She made her tallies, set up the cash drawer for the next day, and placed it in the safe with receipts to deal with tomorrow. Marie came into the office and took her coat off the hook. Annie noticed Marie's canvas bag. It looked like she was carrying a large box or something of the kind.

"Marie," Annie asked, "What are you carrying in your canvas bag?" She pointed to the bulge in the tote bag.

"The photo book," Marie answered. "It has pictures of my mom inside. It was Aunt Helen's photo book. She let me look at it when I was in the house." Marie took the photo album out of her canvas tote and showed it to Annie.

"This is Helen's photo album?" Annie questioned, opening the book and turning the photo pages. She noticed photos of Helen and Marie's mother.

"Yes. I have kept it with me since she died."

"Oh, Marie," Annie exclaimed. "You can't keep that. It belongs to Helen's relatives now," holding the album out to Marie.

"But it has my mother's pictures in it. I don't have pictures of my mother." Marie took the photo album and placed it back into her canvas bag.

"Let's do this. Let's return it when we get home. You still have a key to the house, right?" Annie said, devising a plan in her head.

"Yes."

"Good. Then I will go inside just long enough to place the photo album back where it belongs and then get out." Annie planned.

"I will go too. I know where it belongs." Marie stated.

"I don't think it would be a good idea that we both go inside. We really don't have permission." Annie was wondering if she should do this under the cover of night.

Then Annie decided that it would not be a great idea to go to the house at night, as the burglar could be there at that time as well. No, she would go in the house right after she got home from work and it was still daylight outside. She would ask her mother to watch from her house just in case something happened. Yeah, that seemed like a good plan.

On the walk home, Annie explained about the meeting with the attorney tomorrow morning. Marie was silent. She stayed silent the rest of the way home. Annie tried to reassure Marie that all would be okay.

CHAPTER 5

Tuesday Evening

I t was a little bit past five when Annie opened the front door of her mother's house and announced she and Marie were home. Stella came from her bedroom and Annie could see that her eyes were red. She hugged her mother and tried to give her comfort. The three of them went to the kitchen and Annie made tea for herself and her mother. She made hot chocolate for Marie. They talked about all the good memories of Helen. Some were so funny they all laughed for the first time since Helen's death. They were beautiful memories, Annie thought to herself.

Spying the canvas bag on the floor in the kitchen, Annie stood from her chair at the breakfast bar and told her mother of the plan she had to get the photo album that Marie had taken back to Helen's house before the 'heir' arrived. Stella was worried that Annie might be breaking the law by entering the house, but she agreed to watch from the living room window in case something happened to Annie.

Annie asked Marie for the album and Marie got up from her chair to retrieve the photo album from her canvas bag. She handed the book to Annie. Annie asked for the key to the house, which was around Marie's neck on a ribbon.

"No." Marie said, stepping back and shaking her head. "I am the one to open the door. I am not allowed to give the key to anyone. Aunt Helen told me that." Marie announced.

Annie sighed. She did not see a reason why Marie could not unlock the door and Annie would slip the book inside and close and lock the door. It was daylight outside. What could happen...right?

Stella stood by the living room window inside her house and watched Annie and Marie cross the street to Helen's house. At the front door, Annie motioned for Marie to put the key in the lock. Bravely, Marie pulled the key from the ribbon around her neck and slipped the metal device in the lock. She turned the key and Annie slowly pushed open the door. They walked in quietly, Annie listening for any sound of movement in the house just in case the burglar had come back.

Marie walked into the living room, pulled the photo album from her canvas tote and placed it reluctantly in its proper place in the bookcase. She stood looking at it then turned and began to walk toward Annie, who stood at the bottom of the stairs leading to the second-floor bedrooms.

The house had not yet been completely cleaned up since the burglary and as Marie walked through the room, she stumbled and fell forward into Annie, who in turn went crashing into a small round table standing at the side of the stairs. A white colored ceramic statue of a mermaid went crashing to the floor with a loud bang.

Annie picked herself up just as a light went on in the upstairs hallway and a man...a very broad-shouldered, muscular, good looking man wearing only a dark blue towel wrapped around his waist appeared at the top of the staircase. His light brown short hair was damp from being towel dried and looked quite sexy all ruffled up, Annie thought. She must have stared for what seemed like hours. She just could not look away. It was like a train wreck, but a really great looking train wreck. Marie giggled, and without closing her mouth or looking at Marie, Annie placed her left hand over Marie's eyes. Marie giggled again.

Donald Harper, nephew of Helen Harper, descended the stairs and came face-to-face with Annie and Marie, as Annie kept her hand over Marie's eyes.

"Hello", Donald said, tightening the towel around his waist. "Are you a burglar? Should I be calling the police to arrest you?" He smiled warmly at Annie and she smelled the intoxicating fragrance of his after-shave lotion. She began to swoon.

Annie took a sudden deep breath, realizing she actually was a burglar. She turned Marie's body around so Marie could not see this man standing there in almost all of his glory. She held her hand out in a polite introduction.

"Hello", Annie said shaking his hand. "I am Annie Weston and this is Marie. I just want to convey my condolences."

Marie turned to say hello, and Annie quickly turned her back around. Marie giggled again.

"Nice to meet you...I think." The half-naked man said smiling, "I'm Donald Harper, Helen Harper's nephew. I was getting dressed to walk into town for dinner."

"Very nice to meet you," Annie said smiling. "We obviously interrupted your shower, so we'll just be going now."

"Oh! Sorry about my appearance," Donald said. "It is not exactly the first impression I wanted to make." Donald tightened his hold on his towel and continued explaining that he flew to Portland and hired a town car to take him to his Aunt Helen's house. He had just arrived about an hour ago and decided to shower, change, and make contact with the detective who had called him. He told Annie that he really did not know where to begin. He knew no one in town.

"Do you want to eat dinner with us?" Marie said without turning around. "Annie is going to make us all a comfort dinner and we are going to watch a movie."

"Oh, yes." Annie jumped in. "Please join us across the street at my mother's house for dinner. Helen and my mother were very close friends. We can catch you up to date on what has happened here."

"Dinner and a movie, I am all yours." Donald said, smiling and looking intently at Annie.

Annie blushed, stepped sideways, and bumped into Marie. She put her hand on Marie's shoulder and moved her to the front door. Marie took a quick glance at Donald, giggled, and went out to the porch.

"Come over when you have finished dressing." Annie said. "We are right across the street." She closed the front door.

♦ ♦ ♦

When they reached the house across the street, Annie raced to her bedroom to change into something clean and a bit more casual than her work clothes. She decided that a bit of make-up would help. She was trying to not get too excited about this handsome man she had just met, but she thought she caught an attraction between them. Maybe it was only her having the attraction. Maybe she was making it all up in her mind. Why was she getting butterflies in her stomach? Calm down, Annie, she told herself. When she came to the kitchen, she found Stella and Marie discussing what had happened.

"Maybe I should have gone with you two over there? Marie tells me you found a naked man in Helen's house," Stella said with an amused expression on her face. "Please, give me details!"

"He had a towel wrapped around his waist." Annie said in defense. "He was in the process of taking a shower when he heard me breaking a statue of Helen's."

The statue! I should have offered to clean it up, Annie thought. It's not like he doesn't already have a mess to clean up from the burglary. Annie decided she would offer to help clean the house tomorrow after the attorney appointment. He might even need help in dealing with all of Helen's things as well. She figured he would be selling the house. That meant that Marie would need to clear out her belongings in the apartment over the garage. Annie was suddenly depressed. Tomorrow was not going to be a happy day for any of them.

♦ ♦ ♦

It was no more than thirty minutes and Donald Harper appeared at Stella's door step ringing the doorbell. The three ladies jumped from their chairs, but only Annie went to the door.

Annie greeted Donald and led him to the kitchen to introduce him to Stella. The evening went off comfortably as Donald told them of what he knew about his Aunt Helen, and Stella told Donald stories about Robert and Helen.

Donald spoke about his engineering job in Palo Alto, California. He worked as a Reliability Engineer for a top computer company. He tended to work from his home office and spent most of his days in teleconferences with co-workers from around the world. Working from home gave him more time to concentrate on projects at hand, and less time socializing in the hallways going back and forth to meetings in conference rooms. It was the perfect working situation for him. Since he worked all day with statistics, he needed time alone.

When Stella asked about his parents, he said that they were both still living in Palo Alto, California, but retired. Donald's father, Randolph, was a doctor, like his uncle Robert. His mother, Patricia, was a retired florist. When asked about the disagreement between the brothers, he told them he never really understood the argument.

Donald said he would make a note to ask his father, as he was now curious.

Donald asked about Annie and what she did as a career. Annie excitedly told him about college, a brief marriage, various places she had worked, and moving back to Bridgewater Harbor after her dad passed away. She told him about her father's career as a police officer and later captain of the police force. Annie glanced over at Stella, who appeared a bit saddened. She decided to move on to her current career as a shop owner.

Donald seemed interested in Annie's shop and asked if he could come see it while he was staying here. Annie had a hard time not showing her excitement, as her heart was thumping out of control. He was definitely taking an interest in her!

Annie began preparing dinner by finely chopping up some onion and garlic, putting it in a fry pan with extra virgin olive oil to sauté just long enough to send off a delightful scent throughout the kitchen. Stella placed a large pot of water on the gas burner next to the fry pan. She turned on the gas and waited for the water to boil so she could get the spaghetti cooking. Annie added a mixture of lean ground beef and mild Italian sausage to the frying pan to brown.

As the meat mixture began cooking on the stove, Annie used a potato masher to break down the chunks of meat into fine crumbles. She then added chopped carrots and zucchini. Both were chopped finely enough that Marie would not mind eating them. Marie commented that she did not like vegetables. Annie was going to take that as a challenge, she thought as she placed spaghetti into the pot of boiling water.

Donald was helping Stella choose a suitable wine for dinner. Stella asked Donald if he would mind opening the wine. She handed him a cork screw and Donald masterfully popped the cork. Annie reached into the upper cabinet to the right of the stove and pulled down four wine glasses. Marie quickly ran to the refrigerator and pulled out a soda pop to pour into her wine glass. Donald poured the wine into three glasses for Stella, Annie, and himself.

Donald and Stella were busy talking at the breakfast bar while Annie stirred the meat mixture. Marie asked what she could do to help, and Annie gave her the task of buttering the sliced French bread.

Annie chopped garlic and grated Parmesan cheese for Marie to add to the slices before wrapping the loaf in foil and placing in a hot oven to heat up. Marie finished her task and walked the loaf of bread to the oven. Annie opened the door and Marie carefully placed the bread on the rack. She closed the door and set the time for ten minutes.

Annie then sipped the wine from her glass and stirred the pan on the stove. It was ready for the can of diced tomatoes and a can of tomato sauce. Marie helped by opening the cans and pouring them into the pan. Annie stirred carefully, so as to not spill any of the sauce on the stove or worse yet, splatter tomato sauce on her shirt! Annie tended to be a messy cook, and she really did not want to make a mess in front of Donald.

Donald turned to Annie and asked, "Would it be okay if I rode into Newport with you, Stella, and Marie tomorrow morning? It was late when I arrived today, and I haven't had a chance to rent a car. I understand the meeting begins at 9:00 in the morning."

"Yes," Annie said, adding, "It takes about a half an hour to get there, so we might want to leave about 8:15 or so to make sure we can be there on time."

Donald said he would walk over at 8:15 AM and meet them by the garage. Stella then insisted that he come for breakfast at 7:30 AM, and they would all be ready at the same time. She said he needed to have a good breakfast before meeting with the attorney. He agreed.

Annie added heavy cream to the tomato and beef sauce and let it cook for a few minutes. After it simmered, she poured the rich red sauce into a bowl. Donald stood from the tall chair at the breakfast bar and offered to help strain the spaghetti in the boiling pan. Annie tested the spaghetti and stood aside as Donald, gloved in oven mitts, picked up the pot and headed to the sink. Annie turned off the burner. Marie was busy placing dishes of sauce and bread on the table that she had earlier set for dinner.

Having enjoyed a wonderful dinner and even more delightful conversation, the group moved to the living room, where Stella and Marie walked in with trays of iced tea and chocolate cupcakes with chocolate frosting. Annie, stuffed from dinner, contemplated the cupcake and thinking twice about indulging even more, but it was chocolate and how could anyone resist dark chocolate! She drew a deep breath and stretched her arm out to grab a cupcake. Stella smiled at her daughter, knowing the temptation was too much.

It was nine o'clock when Marie announced she was going to bed. After saying 'goodnight', the group fell silent as Marie left the room and went to her bedroom.

Donald turned to Annie and said, "Why is Marie staying here and not in her apartment?"

"She was afraid of the burglar coming back, and I think she enjoys living in a house with people around. It must have been lonely for her all by herself in that apartment." Annie said.

Stella then spoke up, "Actually, when Robert and Helen were alive, Marie really did enjoy her independence in the small apartment, but now I think she is scared of being left alone. She did spend a lot of time with Helen in the house after Robert's car accident. Most of the time she just went to the apartment to sleep."

"It is really none of my business. I was just curious." Donald said, "I should be heading back to the house. We have a long day ahead of us tomorrow. "

Donald placed his cup on the tray, thanked Annie and Stella for a great dinner, stood and headed for the front door. Annie followed. Stella gathered up the cups on the tray and took them to the kitchen.

"We will see you tomorrow morning at seven-thirty then." Annie said, as she reached for the front door knob.

"Yes. I really enjoyed dinner and the conversation was fun. I thought I was going to be alone up here in Oregon while settling my Aunt's estate. You make it shamefully enjoyable." Donald remarked as he headed out the door.

Annie was grateful for the dim lighting, as she was sure she was blushing from the compliment. Was it her imagination? Was he sending signals to her? This was not a good time to be thinking such thoughts when Helen, his aunt, was not even buried yet. He could just be a nice guy. She didn't even know if he was married, had a girlfriend, or both! Stop thinking about this, Annie thought and closed the front door.

Walking back into the living room, Annie picked up the second tray and walked into the kitchen where she found Stella washing up the pots and pans. Annie placed dishes and glasses in the dishwasher, added soap, and pressed the start button. She then grabbed a towel and began drying the pots and pans in the dish rack next to the sink.

"What is your impression of Donald?" asked Annie.

"I think he is a very nice, intelligent, man...who I think likes you." Stella answered back.

Annie paused. She looked directly at her mother and said, "Mom! I just met the guy. He plans on returning to California after he settles his aunt's estate."

"Maybe," Stella returned.

Stella dried her hands on a kitchen towel and walked out of the kitchen. "I am going to lock up and go to bed. Would you turn the lights off when you are finished? Goodnight."

"Goodnight, Mother!" Annie said.

CHAPTER 6

Wednesday

It was barely light outside at five thirty in the morning. Fog was thick and rolling up the coastline. The ocean was gray and the waves were crashing on the rocks that jutted outward into the water. Through wisps of fog, Annie could see brightness on the horizon.

"Could that be a sign?" Annie said to Callie, who was sitting in her cat tree by the window in the corner.

"What sign?" Marie appeared, sleepy-eyed, hair disheveled, wearing a pair of Stella's pajamas and slippers.

"You are up early." Annie sat up straight and smiled at Marie.

"I like to wake up early and watch the ocean. It makes me feel good." Marie said as she sat down next to Annie.

"It makes me feel good, too. I like to think about my day ahead, while sitting here watching the morning sun rise. We seem to have something in common."

Marie smiled and reached over to hold Annie's hand. Annie looked at Marie's hand on hers, and then looked up and smiled at Marie.

"Everything will work out. Don't worry." Annie said, knowing how today must weigh heavily on Marie's mind. This is the day Helen's Will is read and Marie's future currently lies uncertain. Annie vowed to herself though, that she would watch over Marie.

At six o'clock, Stella quietly walked into the kitchen and stopped suddenly when she saw Annie and Marie sitting at the breakfast bar looking out over the ocean. Her heart melted at the sight of Marie holding Annie's hand.

"Well, we'd all better get dressed and get breakfast started before Donald arrives." Stella announced.

"You two go get dressed and I will start the breakfast meat, then we can trade off." Annie said getting up from her tall stool at the counter.

"That sounds good to me." Stella said, "Marie, I have a lovely pink skirt with a white sleeveless sweater for you to try on and see if it fits. You can wear it if you like."

"I like pink."

As Stella and Marie left the kitchen, Annie made herself another cup of coffee from the pod coffee maker. She gathered breakfast meats from the refrigerator and began cooking. It wasn't long before the aroma of breakfast was wafting through the house. Annie could hear Marie coming from her bedroom, and Marie soon turned the corner into the kitchen. She immediately went to the dish cupboard and gathered plates to set the table. Shortly after, Stella came into the kitchen.

"Go get dressed!" Stella ordered Annie, "He'll be here in thirty minutes."

Annie looked at the clock on the wall. Good grief! Where had the time gone? She raced into the bedroom, laid clothes to wear on the bed, and hurried to the bathroom to shower. It was a quick shower. She toweled dried her hair, donned her robe, and hurried to the bedroom to dress. She then ran back to the bathroom to dry her hair and apply some make-up. Normally she would not bother with make-up, but since Donald was riding to the attorney's office with them...well, let's face it, since Donald was there...period! Boy was she falling for him. She wanted so much to stop thinking about him since he was going back to California to live his own life. There was a sound of a motor vehicle racing down the street. A short time later, Annie could hear the doorbell.

Stella, dressed in a dark blue and white floral-patterned dress, opened the front door. There before her stood a man in a light beige sports jacket, a light blue, tan, and cream-colored cotton shirt that buttoned down the front, a light blue tie, tan colored cotton slacks, and brown casual dress shoes. Stella greeted Donald and they walked to the kitchen dining table. Annie raced into the kitchen just in time to be seated with the group.

"You look nice." Donald said.

Stella and Marie looked at each other and grinned.

"Thank you!" Annie said. She was wearing a dark blue pants suit with a white cotton shirt and black slip-on shoes with a slight heel.

As they were sitting down, Donald said, "I just about got run over by an old truck while crossing the street. He came around the corner driving like a mad-man. Good thing I was able to jump out of the way."

Both Annie and Marie looked at each other in concern.

"A little early to be drinking, don't you think?" Donald said jokingly as he passed a plate of pancakes to Annie.

"Did you get a license number of the truck?" Annie asked.

"No, but I noticed it was mounted up high on the tail-gate."

"What color was it?" Annie questioned.

"Maybe a yellow or gold color at one time, it was fairly rusted and banged up, hard to tell." Donald responded looking at Annie.

"Did you see who was driving?"

"No. Just that it was a man." Donald said, "Why all the questions?"

"Before you came here, Helen's house was burglarized by a man who ran to an old truck down the street. It was too dark to really see the truck in great detail, but it was old and the license plate was attached to the tailgate, just like you described." Annie explained as the others listened intently, "I think I should call Dan and tell him that the same truck may have tried to run you down."

"There is really nothing to report. I didn't see who it was, could not swear to the color of the truck, and don't even know if the guy was trying to run me down. I could have been in the wrong place at the right time."

"But we both saw the license plate attached to the tailgate of the truck. That is a clue as to the identity of the burglar, and possibly the murderer of Helen!" Annie stated excitedly.

"Well, I can't get too excited about it with very little to report." Donald said reluctantly. "Let's just keep our eyes open for the truck in the area from now on. If we see it, then call the police."

Annie was a little frustrated with Donald's response and decided she would call Dan later today to tell him what Donald related. Stella eyed Annie and knew exactly what Annie was thinking. She knew Annie would not let this bit of information pass without telling Dan.

♦ ♦ ♦

After the breakfast dishes were placed in the dishwasher, the group headed out for Annie's SUV. Annie drove with Donald in the front passenger seat. Stella and Marie sat in the back. Marie was once again quiet. She looked down at the canvas bag on her lap and fiddled with the straps. Stella reached over and patted her on the hand. Marie looked up at Stella. Marie had tears in her eyes.

The thirty-minute drive to the attorney's office seemed to fly by, or was Annie speeding? She did not remember. In fact, she did not remember much about the trip. Donald did most of the talking, and that may have been his way of coping with the unbearable silence.

The group entered the office area of Charles Conklin and while Annie announced their arrival, the others sat in comfortable chairs in the reception area. At exactly nine o'clock a young woman escorted Annie, Stella, Marie, and Donald to a glass walled meeting room with a large table and chairs. They were asked to take a seat and told Mr. Conklin would join them in a moment.

Marie positioned herself to sit next to Annie, Donald sat across from Annie, and Stella sat next to Donald. They left the chair at the head of the table for Mr. Conklin, who entered with a storage box with a lid and set it on the table. Donald stood to shake hands with Charles Conklin and then sat down. The attorney introduced himself and shook hands with Annie, Marie, and stretching across the table he shook hands with Stella. He then asked if anyone wanted refreshments. All declined.

Inhaling deeply, and exhaling, Charles Conklin began to speak, "Let me first say how deeply sorry I am to hear of Helen's passing. It was quite a shock when I was told by Detective Surely. Frankly, I didn't even know Detective Surely was back in town."

"He was called out on his second day on the job." Annie stated.

"He was probably hoping to have a little more time adjusting before being thrust into a homicide." Mr. Conklin continued turning pages of a notebook, "Helen's autopsy report has not been completed yet. As per her wishes, she will be cremated and her ashes will be placed in the sculpture urn, the compartment next to her husband,

Robert. She has spelled out what she wants done with her and her husband's ashes. That information is enclosed in a letter for Stella."

Stella's eyes teared up. It was final, or at least will be soon. Her dear friend...gone. She would, of course, follow any wishes her friend had. Stella felt honored to be the person to handle such a responsible job.

"As you all know, Helen was the legal guardian of Marie." Mr. Conklin went on, "It is Helen's suggestion that Annie Weston become Marie's legal guardian. Helen fully supports this arrangement and asks that Annie seriously consider the position."

Annie was momentarily shocked that Helen had thought of her to watch over Marie. Excited, Annie turned to Marie and gave her a big hug. Marie was smiling from ear to ear with relief. It took a few minutes for everyone to calm down and continue.

Mr. Conklin continued, saying he would be willing to make the arrangements and complete all necessary paperwork for Annie to apply for guardianship of Marie in court. Both Annie and Marie agreed. Annie would be the representative of Marie's trust as well. Annie thanked Mr. Conklin.

"There's more." Mr. Conklin stated, "Helen left her house, contents, and land the structures sit on to Annie Weston. It is Helen's wish that Marie continue to live at the property listed, with Annie as the home owner and caretaker of the property. Helen has also bequeathed the downtown building to Annie."

"Downtown building?" Annie and Stella questioned in unison.

"Yes, the building and the current boardwalk are owned by Helen." Charles Conklin stated looking over his paperwork.

"That building is owned by RH Enterprises. I pay rent to RH Enterprises for my shop." Annie stated skeptically.

"Yes, Robert and Helen Enterprises own that building. I have a list of shop owners and business records pertaining to the businesses currently leasing space. Have you ever been curious as to why you pay so little rent compared to the other shops?" Mr. Conklin queried.

"No. I really never asked anyone what they were paying. It never came up. I guess it might be that I have been there for a long time?" Annie replied in a questioning manner.

"Helen always knew she wanted you to take care of Marie in the event of her death and also because she was such good friends with your mother, Stella."

Annie was a bit taken aback by the generous gift she was given. She didn't know what to say. She was in shock. She was expecting to fully take care of Marie. She had no idea Marie had her own trust or that Annie would now be the owner of a house and a building in town. She was definitely going to need her friend and co-worker Lizzy to help her out. Lizzy was brilliant in business matters, considering her Master's degree was in business.

Charles Conklin was continuing through Annie's deep thoughts. Marie nudged her in the side and Annie suddenly sat up and paid attention to the next bequeath of Helen. A large envelope was handed to Stella with a letter inside and several files. Helen had left Stella with her personal stock portfolio. Helen was always trying to get Stella interested in purchasing stock of her own, but Stella never got around to it. She just felt like she never knew enough to keep up with the stocks themselves. Now she had no choice but to learn about the stocks and how to deal with them. Fortunately, Mr. Conklin advised that an investment company handled the investments for Helen, and Helen received a quarterly payment as a result. Mr. Conklin said he would handle the paperwork to change the ownership to Stella. He asked that a meeting be scheduled between the two later in the week to make the arrangements.

It appeared that Helen had a sizable fortune, which was left in part to Donald, as her only living nephew, bypassing his parents. This visibly shocked Donald, as he was only expecting to sell properties and liquidate assets. He really had no idea his Aunt Helen thought so much of him. He had not seen her in decades. Except for exchanging of birthday and Christmas cards, he really never talked with her. And now she leaves him with a fortune.

Each person in attendance was handed a personal hand-written letter from Helen. The letters were to be read at the receiving person's leisure.

Various charities were left sizable sums, specific jewelry pieces were left for the women, special original paintings were left for Stella, and various collectible belongings of Robert's were left to Donald.

Donald was interested to see what of Robert's possessions were left to him. It was all contained in the letters.

After the reading of the Will, Annie, Stella, Marie, and Donald all walked to Annie's SUV in total silence. It was all shocking to say the least. Annie still could not wrap her head around being a property owner. She would now move into Helen's house and Marie would move back to her apartment over the garage. It occurred to her that Donald would move out. Suddenly she was sad. She did not want Donald to leave, but she certainly could not ask him to live with her. That would be weird. She didn't know him. Who was Donald Harper anyway?

As the car maneuvered into Stella's garage, Stella announced that they should all meet at Helen's house and have some lunch. She would make sandwiches. Annie thought that would be a great idea, but wanted to change into jeans and a t-shirt first. There was clean-up from the burglary to do at that house across the street.

Donald crossed the street and entered Helen's house. Annie, Stella, and Marie entered Stella's house through the garage door leading inside to the kitchen area. They all went directly to their rooms to change.

CHAPTER 7

Wednesday Afternoon

Annie and Marie stood at the front door of Helen's house. Marie rang the doorbell. Annie had to start thinking of it as her house now. Hers and Marie's, Annie thought. They were going to be a family now. Annie felt comfort in believing she, Marie, and Stella were going to be near each other. She wondered if her mother would feel lonely without her in the house. She had been there for a number of years. Certainly, her mother would have some feelings about Annie moving out. It was only across the street Annie kept telling herself.

Donald answered the door and motioned for the two women to enter. As Annie walked into the open floor plan, she noticed that the living room had all been cleaned up. Donald smiled at her when she looked at him in surprise.

"It was the least I could do for you allowing me to stay here."

"Allowing you to stay here? I honestly believed you were inheriting the whole estate. Thank you for cleaning it all up." Annie said.

Annie announced that Stella would be over shortly with sandwiches and suggested they get the table set. Marie walked over to the bookcase to make sure the photo album was still there. Finding that the album was still in its place, she offered to run back over to help Stella. Donald gave a questioning look at Annie.

"She is attached to the photo album. I am going to give it to her when we get settled." Annie informed Donald.

Annie and Donald set about finding a table cloth, and setting dishes and glasses in four place settings. There was an uncomfortable silence as they worked.

"After lunch I will pack my things and check into a hotel before I go back home." Donald offered.

"I was hoping you would be able to stay until the estate is completely settled. I could continue to stay at Mom's house. You can stay here."

"I really don't want to be in your way." Donald responded.

"You would not be in my way at all. In fact, it would be a tremendous comfort knowing you were here, since the burglar has not been caught."

"Would you feel better if I stayed in this house?" Donald asked.

"Yes, I would definitely feel better if you stayed in this house." Annie replied, repeating what Donald had said.

"Then I will stay here until you are ready to move into the house." Donald said, "I can set up my laptop in the office and work from here."

"That will be great. Thank you for helping us out." Annie said, placing napkins around the table.

"I have one condition though." Donald said, "You should be able to come and go in your own house as you wish. Please don't feel like you need to ring the doorbell. I will make sure I am always dressed."

They both laughed, Annie thinking back to when they first met. She would not mind seeing him with only a towel wrapped around his waist again. Maybe even less than a towel! Annie felt her cheeks warming.

"I am off for the rest of the week," Donald said, "I may want to ask for an extra week off from work to help out around here."

"Only if you feel you have the time off to spare. I don't want to keep you from anything or anyone important." Annie said, then regretting she said the word 'anyone', as if she was being nosy about his personal relationships.

Donald moved next to Annie as he was setting down a fork next to a plate and, not looking directly at her, smiled slyly and said, "I am not with anyone at the moment."

Oh great! Annie thought. He understood what she was asking. Then again, he did answer right away. Maybe he wanted her to know that he was not dating anyone. Annie's stomach tightened. She realized she was holding her breath.

"Are you dating anyone at the moment?" Donald asked.

This was bold of him, she thought, but then again, she asked first.

"No." She said, dragging out the "...oh."

♦ ♦ ♦

Stella entered through the front door of Helen's house, now Annie's house, carrying a tray of sandwiches covered with plastic wrap, and a shopping bag containing various chips, veggie sticks, and fruit dangling on her arm. Marie followed with a pack of soda pop. They entered the kitchen and set the food on the table and the soda pop on the kitchen counter. Marie quickly retrieved glasses from the cupboard, handing them to Annie, who added ice from the ice dispenser in the refrigerator. They all sat down and began to enjoy the meal.

"Donald and I have been talking," Annie announced, "And we have decided that Donald will stay in this house while he is helping to settle Helen's estate, and I will stay where I am at for now."

"Oh, how long are you thinking of staying, Donald?" Stella asked.

"I have through this week off. I was thinking of asking for another week off." Donald replied. "If I need to work, I might be able to use the office to set up my laptop and work from there during the day."

"Annie," Stella said turning her attention to Annie, "We really need to begin clearing out Helen's belongings and making plans for an estate sale or something. Can you take some time off from the shop?"

Take time off from the shop, Annie thought. She had taken so little time off since she opened the shop years ago. In fact, she had taken so little time off that she never moved out of her own mother's home. Her stay was only meant to be temporary until her shop got off the ground. Her mother never indicated she wanted Annie to move, so Annie continued living there. It just never occurred to her to move.

"Annie?"

"Oh. Sorry Mom." Annie said, "I was just thinking about how to keep the shop open while sales are good and work on clearing out this house." Annie was also thinking she should be at the shop now. She had classes to prepare for and it took time to plan and prepare the materials.

"I can help." Marie broke into the conversation.

"And I can help too." Stella said. "Let's make a schedule of times when Marie and I can help Lizzy at the shop during the times you need to be here. We'll work this out. I don't want you to close the shop during the summer. I know you need those sales to make it through the winter months."

"Thanks, Mom. Marie, I will definitely need you to work with Lizzy and me at the shop in the afternoons. Maybe we can spend the mornings on this house. Mom, you can fill in where needed."

"That sounds like a plan then." Stella said. "Now, Donald, if you don't mind us girls barging in and out of this house while we get things sorted and cleared, we can begin today."

"I have an idea that will work better." Marie said.

All eyes turned to Marie. With a look of determination and satisfaction, she explained an idea that left everyone amazed at how perfect the plan was for all. Marie told the group that she should move out of the apartment over the garage and into the house with Annie. Donald could live in the apartment and use the guest cottage in the backyard as his office. He could then stay as long as he wanted. Marie and Stella looked at each other, and Stella gave her the head nod of approval. The longer that Donald stays, the better the chances that Annie and Donald realize they share feelings for one another.

"But you love your independence in that apartment." Annie said to Marie.

"Aunt Helen and Uncle Robert built that apartment for me when my mother passed away and they wanted me to live here. I would rather live in the house with you. I get lonely sometimes." Marie stated, "Do you want to live in this big house by yourself?"

"Well, now that you mention it, no." Annie replied.

Turning to Donald, Annie said, "We can clear the apartment out tomorrow, paint, and clean and decorate the way you would feel comfortable."

"Annie, you already have so much to do with clearing out this house." Donald said, "Please let me take care of the remodeling. I will interview and schedule contractors and make all the arrangements. I will even pay all the costs. It just so happens that I recently came into a lot of money."

Everyone laughed, and then suddenly became sullen by the reason why they were all there. Donald raised his glass and made a toast to Helen. All joined him while clinking their glasses in memory of Helen.

"Wait a minute." Annie spoke up, "Marie, what guest cottage?"

"The small house in the backyard," Marie said, "It is covered in roses.

"I had forgotten about the guest house." Stella remarked, setting her glass down.

"There is a guest house in the backyard?" Annie questioned. "I recall the backyard looking a bit overgrown recently, but I don't remember a house back there."

"I can show it to you. Come on." Marie was getting up and heading for the back-kitchen door.

Annie looked at Donald and stood to follow Marie. Donald and Stella followed. They entered the backyard which, as Annie recalled, was a bit overgrown and needed a good cleaning up. It was once a beautiful yard with roses, bulbs, blueberry bushes and a variety of flowering bushes. Stepping stone and concrete pathways led to lovely sitting areas. There, standing in the far corner, almost out of sight, stood a small building covered in rose vines and ivy. It had a small covered front porch and a wide wooden front door with a four-panel window at the top. Beautiful wood framed windows flanked the front door. The horizontal siding might have once been painted a light yellow, but it was difficult to tell now due to age and being covered in rose vines and ivy.

"Do you know where I can find clippers? I would like to take a closer look." Donald asked Marie.

"The clippers are in the garage. Come on, I will show you where to find them."

Stella explained to Annie that this building was originally built as a guest cottage, but Dr. Harper decided to use it as an office away from his office in town. Which is why Marie did not move into the cottage, but instead Helen and Robert built her an apartment above the garage in the backyard.

Annie looked at her watch. It was already two in the afternoon. Lizzy was by herself and Annie really wanted to get to the shop and help out, but she also wanted to see this cottage. Stella noticed her daughter's worried look and said, "Why don't I go to the shop and help Lizzy out. She can take a break and I will hold down the fort."

"Mom, it would be great if you would not mind going to the shop! I really appreciate it. It will give me the time to figure this all out."

Annie said gratefully. "I will call Lizzy and let her know you are on your way."

"It will be fun to help out at the shop again."

"Thank you!" Annie said giving her mother a kiss on the cheek. Stella left the backyard. Annie pulled out her cell phone and called Lizzy to find out how things were going and let Lizzy know that her mother was coming to help.

Donald and Marie returned with a clipper, gloves, and a rake.

"Shall I?" Donald said holding the clippers up and turning toward the cottage covered in vines.

"Be my guest." Annie half-heartedly laughed. She stood aside, next to Marie, as they watched Donald expertly cut through the vines.

It took about thirty minutes to clear enough of the vines to make a decent pathway to the front door. Helen had really left this part of the yard get overgrown. Annie wondered why, as the rest of the backyard was very nice looking. The tiny little house appeared to be a faded yellow in color with horizontal wood siding and white trim. It was once a charming cottage, Annie thought.

Donald made progress to the front door, and motioned Annie and Marie to come forward. Cautiously they stepped through the tangle of vines and gingerly walked up to the front porch area. An old wooden chair could be seen through the thick curtain of vines sitting next to the front door. It must have been picturesque at one time. She vowed to make it that way again.

As they approached the windows, they cupped their hands to peer inside. A large room came into view. Boxes were stacked up high and covered nearly all of the floor space. It was difficult to see what the actual design was of the cottage. Annie tried the door knob. It was locked.

Annie looked at Marie and said, "Do you know where a key might be for this cottage?"

"Aunt Helen said she would not use the cottage ever again." Marie said sadly. "She never told me where the key was. I don't know."

"We can get a locksmith out here to open the door." Donald said.

"Let's look in the kitchen first. She had keys hanging in the cupboard." Annie said, "Maybe one of those keys fits the lock."

Annie made a mental note to go through Helen's office as soon as possible. She wanted to make sure utility bills were paid and to figure out all the financial responsibility she just inherited. She also wanted to check on Marie's trust and how to handle the financial end. Annie realized this place was going to cost her money she did not have.

Annie suggested they move on to Marie's apartment. Marie needed to pack some clothes anyway. This would be a good time to get that done. The three walked up the apartment stairs to the front door. Donald stepped in front of Annie and Marie and said, "Let me go in first. You haven't been here since the burglary. I want to make sure everything is okay first." Marie handed a key to Donald. Donald first tried the doorknob without inserting the key. The door opened. Annie looked at Marie. Marie looked scared and took a step back. Annie stepped back with her.

As Donald apprehensively entered the apartment, the first thing he noticed was how very pink everything was. Off to the right was a kitchen with pink cabinets and white appliances. There was a small white refrigerator, small white toaster, and a two burner stove top. A small white dishwasher sat beside the kitchen sink, which was also white. Pink and white had a theme going on here as Donald walked forward into the pink living room.

On the far wall was a white brick fireplace. In it housed a nicely arranged display of battery type candles. It was at this time that Donald realized that Annie was directly behind him. When he turned to see Annie, he saw Marie standing in the doorway behind Annie. Donald continued to the bedroom area of the studio apartment. The pink walls paled to the pink satin comforter on the bed. The bed had not been made. Slippers were on the floor next to the bed.

Donald walked to the left and opened a closet door. With no one inside, he walked to the bathroom and switched on the light. The, yes pink, bathroom was nicely clean. No sign of a burglary.

"It all looks good." Donald said. "Maybe Marie left the door unlocked the last time she was here. I doubt the burglar even came up here."

"It was really early when I left here and went to Aunt Helen's house. I never came back that day." Marie offered.

Annie suggested Marie pack a bag of clothes to take to Stella's house, as with the burglar on the loose, she did not want Marie staying alone in the apartment. Marie agreed and pulled a suitcase off the top shelf in the closet. Annie walked over and made Marie's bed. She then helped Marie pick out enough clothes to last a week. They locked up the apartment and all went down the stairs. Crossing the patio area, they entered the house through the kitchen door.

Annie made some iced tea and they all sat down at the kitchen table to make plans for the clearing of the house and a possible estate sale. The remodeling plans now included not only the apartment over the garage, but Marie's new bedroom. Even Annie's room, the master suite, was planned for a make-over. Donald said he would handle all the contractors and try to get the job done quickly so they could all get on with their lives. Annie wasn't sure how to take that comment "get on with their lives", and realized she was suddenly tired from the stress of everything. She could not stop now. There was so much to do.

CHAPTER 8

Wednesday night

It was five-thirty in the evening when Annie and Marie walked to Ocean Loads of Paper. They left Donald at the kitchen table drawing up plans, organizing the notes he took while asking Annie questions of how she would like the master bedroom remodeled, colors, textures, etc. Marie picked out the room upstairs that she wanted to occupy and only said that she liked pink and princesses. Annie, on the other hand, wanted something calming such as light turquoise walls, pale grays, and white trim. Other than that, she was not concerned how it all turned out. She never spent a lot of time in her bedroom. She worked late hours, got up early, and was happy with a bed and dresser. Annie was easy to please, according to Donald.

Lizzy and Stella were not really surprised to see Annie and Marie. About six customers were presently shopping. Stella was helping a couple, and Lizzy was ringing up an elderly lady.

"Annie," the elderly woman said when she saw the shop owner walk in, "I heard about Helen. We all understand if you need to cancel tomorrow morning's class. In fact, we expect you to cancel the class."

Annie never thought of canceling a class, but now had second thoughts about it. She really could use the morning to get things done at the house. This was a difficult time for her and it was so thoughtful of her senior crafting group to understand.

"Did you talk to the other ladies?" Annie asked the elderly woman. "Are you sure they would be okay with me canceling this one time?"

"Certainly," the woman said. "I will take care of canceling the class for you and letting everyone know. I am happy to be able to help out."

"Let everyone know that the next class is free." Annie said, "I feel bad for letting them down, but I will make it up to them."

"Nonsense," the woman said, now grabbing her purchased items and heading toward the door. Annie followed the elderly woman to the door. The woman stopped and said, "Life happens or should I say death happens? Just bring those great cookies to the next class." She gave Annie a pat on the arm.

As Annie watched the woman leave through the doorway, she spotted the old truck slowly drive by. The man in the vehicle was wearing a black hooded sweatshirt jacket. When he looked at her, he turned his head straight forward and roared off down the street. Chills ran through Annie's body.

Annie walked to her office and closed the office door. This was something she never did, but she needed to make a private call to Detective Dan Surely. She grabbed her cell phone from her purse sitting on the desk and called his cell phone number.

"Hello Annie. What's up?" Dan said, noticing the caller ID.

"Dan, I called to ask about the investigation of Helen's murder. How are things going?"

"Not as well as I would like. Helen had no enemies that I could find. No fingerprints, except those of Helen, Marie, Stella, and you." Dan explained, "No one saw anything suspicious."

"I have something suspicious to tell you that might be related to Helen's case." Annie informed Dan. "At least it may be important regarding the burglary."

"Let's hear it."

"Remember the old truck with the license plate that was attached to the tailgate? Marie and I saw the man in dark clothes leaving Helen's house the morning after her death and get into this old truck."

"Yes."

"I believe that same truck tried to run down Donald Harper, Helen's nephew, this morning. Donald is staying at Helen's house until he settles the estate."

"I will want to talk to him. Did he happen to see the driver?" Dan asked.

"No." Annie continued, "He just thought it was a wild driver coming around the corner."

"And..." Annie said excitedly, "I just saw the truck drive slowly by my shop. I happened to be at the door. The driver was wearing a black hooded sweatshirt jacket. He had the hood over his head. He was looking at me, and then when I tried to get a good look at him, he quickly drove off in the truck. The tailgate was down, so I couldn't get a license number."

"This doesn't make sense, Annie." Dan said, "He burglarized a house that you don't own, tried to run down a person you don't know, and is now stalking you at your shop."

"Actually, Dan, I do own the house." Annie said, "I just found out this morning that Helen had left me the house and the contents. I know that news travels fast in this town, but I don't know how anyone could have known about the Will in advance."

"It would be a good idea to get some security cameras installed in Helen's...I mean, your house." Dan said.

"I can do that. In the meantime, Donald is staying in the house until it can be cleared out and redecorated."

"Good." Dan said, "Having someone in the house should deter the burglar. I'll let patrol know about the old truck. Let me know if anything else suspicious happens.

"Thank you, Dan." Annie said softly, "Welcome back."

"Yeah, right," Dan laughed sarcastically.

◆ ◆ ◆

After closing up the shop for the day, the four ladies stood by the counter and talked for about twenty minutes. Lizzy said she needed to go grocery shopping, and even though Stella invited her to dinner, she said she had been putting off shopping for food much too long. She thanked Stella for the invitation and said she would take a raincheck. Lizzy grabbed her jacket and purse and left through the street side of the shop, locking the door behind her.

Annie asked her mother if they should pick up Chinese food at the restaurant across the street for dinner. Stella liked the idea, and Marie chimed in asking for appetizers. They discussed asking Donald over for dinner. Annie said she would call Donald and ask him to meet them at the restaurant to help carry the take-out home.

Annie dialed Donald's cell phone number and waited for him to answer.

"Hello," said the voice on the other end.

"Hi, Donald, this is Annie." There was a pause on the other end of the line. Annie continued, "Mom and I were picking up Chinese food for dinner. Would you like to come over and eat with us?"

"Oh, Annie, I knew it was you. I was just picking up papers off the floor when you called. Yes, Chinese food would be better than the can of chili I was going to open for dinner. Can I bring anything?"

"No, we have enough here. Just bring yourself. We should be home in about fifteen minutes."

"See you in fifteen minutes."

Annie checked her email and straightened up the shop a bit before walking across the street to the Chinese restaurant to meet her mother and Marie. She arrived just in time to help carry the food home.

As the women approached Stella's house, Annie saw Donald sitting on the front porch of Helen's house. He stood and walked up to them to help carry the two large bags of food into the house.

Marie and Annie quickly set up the kitchen table with plates and utensils, while Donald opened a bottle of wine that Stella handed to him. Stella placed the food on platters and filled bowls with fried rice and white rice. It seemed like a lot of food for just the four of them. Annie filled glasses with water. Marie was sitting down already dishing up the crab puff appetizers and rice. It was a wonderful family feeling, Annie thought to herself.

After dinner, Stella told Annie and Donald to take their wine out to the patio and she would join them after she cleared the dishes and started the dishwasher. Marie wanted to go out on the patio with Annie and Donald, but Stella convinced her to help in the kitchen.

Annie walked to the patio and sat on the loveseat facing the ocean. Donald sat down next to her. They chatted about their lives, living in Bridgewater Harbor, their careers, and hobbies they wanted to pursue at some point in their lives.

Marie's face was in the window watching Annie and Donald when Stella moved her away and distracted her with ice cream and television in the family room. Stella closed the curtains so as not to disturb the two outside. Donald noticed the curtains closing and smiled to himself.

Annie realized her mother had not walked out to the patio yet. She looked at her watch and discovered that two hours had passed. It was almost nine o'clock at night. The air was warm and the sound of the ocean was calming.

Annie fidgeted in her seat and Donald moved to be seated a bit closer to her. He was so warm and inviting that she wanted to snuggle up next to him. Donald stretched his arm out across the back of the loveseat. Annie instinctively moved closer to him. He then moved his arm across the top of her shoulders.

"Are you cold?" Donald asked pulling her closer to him.

"I was, but now I feel quite cozy."

They sat and talked another two hours, when Annie and Donald noticed the lights in the living room turn off. That was Donald's signal to head back across the street. He got up and they said good night at the front door. Annie watched as Donald walked inside her soon to be new home. She closed and locked the door. Annie was in deep thought as she walked through the dark house to her bedroom.

CHAPTER 9

Thursday Early Morning

The following morning, Annie was up at 5:00 AM, sitting in the kitchen, drinking coffee, and staring out over the ocean. This meditative time really helped Annie figure things out. She was thankful to Donald for taking charge of the remodeling. She was thankful to Marie for letting her apartment go to Donald. She never realized how lonely Marie felt. Annie hoped that Donald would want to stay longer. She was thankful to her mother for helping out in the shop.

Annie's thoughts drifted to the murder of Helen and the burglary the next day. Why did this old truck keep appearing in her life? Could the burglary and murder be related? Annie's first thought was to go through Helen's office. She needed to figure out the utility bills anyway.

With her three o'clock class all set up while she was at the shop last night, Annie decided to spend the time this morning going through Helen's office. She also needed to contact various businesses to open accounts in her name and remove Helen's. She would need to visit with Charles Conklin on Friday to finalize everything. He was going to be a big help to her, she thought.

Annie showered, dressed, and decided to call Donald to let him know she was coming over to work on the office. It was 6:30 AM, and Donald answered his cell phone in a cheery voice.

"Hello?"

"Hi, Donald," Annie said, trying to return the cheery greeting. That was not easy for her these days. "I was going to come over and start working on Helen's office."

"Sure," Donald said, "Come on over. I can make breakfast if you want."

"That would be lovely. See you shortly."

Annie scratched out a quick note for Stella and Marie, grabbed her jacket, and made her way to the door. As she stood on the front porch, she nervously glanced up and down the street. No old pickup. Good, she thought. She quickly crossed the street to her very own home. Okay, that thought really made her stomach turn. She now owned a home, property taxes, upkeep, utility bills, the whole package. She even owned a building downtown! Annie decided that when she sees Mr. Conklin tomorrow, she will work it all out. She made yet another mental note to ask her mother to come to the meeting with Mr. Conklin.

The previous afternoon, Donald had called a locksmith and had all the locks, including Marie's apartment, changed. He had the locksmith open the lock on the cottage door and then had that lock changed too. He labeled all the keys with tags.

As Annie approached the house, Donald opened the front door to greet her. She walked inside where she noticed the kitchen table covered in paperwork, pads of paper with notations and sketches. A kitchen trash can next to the table was filled with wadded-up paper.

"Donald, were you up all night working on remodeling ideas?" Annie asked as she hung her purse on a kitchen chair.

"No, not really," Donald said obviously excited to tell her about his progress so far. "I actually began once you left for the shop."

Annie sat down in a kitchen chair. Donald began to report on his progress of changing the locks on all the doors. He handed Annie a handful of keys with various tags. The tags identified whom the keys belonged to and which lock they opened. Annie was impressed. He then showed Annie some ideas he had about remodeling the apartment and redecorating the cottage. He even had some ideas for the master bedroom, which Annie would eventually move to, and Marie's bedroom, which he wanted to be a surprise for Marie.

Noticing the look of apprehension on Annie's face, Donald added that he was paying for the entire project. He said that if he were allowed to stay in the studio apartment above the garage and use the cottage as an office, he would want to pay for the expense of remodeling and redecorating. With a sigh of relief, Annie agreed. She was hoping he would want to stay longer if he had a nice place to stay. She was beginning to feel the excitement he felt about fixing the place up to make it less Helen's and her sad ending, and more Annie's and her new beginning.

Annie told Donald about her phone call with Dan, and that Dan suggested security cameras around the entire house and out-buildings. Donald agreed and said he would find a low-voltage installer from the Portland area to install cameras. He wanted to make sure local contractors were not aware of the camera installation or locations of the cameras. The burglar seemed to be someone local, and news travels fast in small towns.

♦ ♦ ♦

Annie stood up and announced she was off to sort through Helen's papers in her office. She was about to ask Donald if he wanted to help, when his cell phone rang and he picked it up to answer. Annie found herself wandering through the living room to a closed door, which she knew was Helen's office. She put her hand on the doorknob and found it locked. That's strange, Annie told herself. Why would Helen have locked this door? She tried again. Maybe the door was stuck. No luck.

Annie turned to see Donald pacing the floor in the kitchen while he spoke on the phone. Annie walked to the kitchen cabinet where she saw other keys hanging and tried to find a key that might be marked as an office door key. Having no luck, Annie walked back to the living room to wait for Donald to end his phone call. She would ask him if he noticed the door being locked.

While waiting for Donald, Annie slowly walked through the living room, looking on shelves, tables, looking into drawers, and basically searching for something, but not knowing what. There was a reason someone ransacked the living room. What was it the burglar was after? Annie remembered the photo album. She looked at the bookcase. It was still there.

Annie reached down and pulled the photo album out to look at the photos inside. It seemed like an ordinary photo album. She perused the photos of Helen, Helen and Robert, Marie in various stages of her life with her mother, Stella and Helen, and other people she was not familiar with. Annie wanted to create a beautiful memory album of Marie and her mother for Marie. Another mental note of something to do, Annie thought, she might want to begin a paper list! Her mental "to do" list was growing out of bounds.

Donald ended his phone call and eyed Annie looking through the photo album. He walked over and said, "I thought you were going to check out the office?"

"I was, but the door is locked." Annie said, putting the photo album back on the bookshelf. She walked over to the office door to show Donald that the door was indeed locked.

"The door has been closed the entire time I have been here. I haven't tried to go inside." Donald said, attempting the doorknob himself.

"Yes, it's locked!" Annie said, head tilting in that 'I told you so' look.

"I can call the locksmith back," Donald said, walking over to the table to pick up his cell phone. He checked his phone for the number, pushed the button to dial, and then began a conversation with the person on the other end.

"He will be here in an hour to an hour and a half," Donald announced. "In the meantime, why don't you and I go upstairs and check out the other rooms. I am afraid I have only been through the guest room and bathroom. It might be time to explore the other rooms."

"I was waiting for mom to come over and help me with Helen's room. I really did not feel comfortable going in there on my own," Annie said.

"Okay. I promised you breakfast," Donald began, "Let me clear off the table and move it all to the dining room. What's a big dining room table for if you can't scatter your stuff all over it?"

Annie laughed and helped Donald move all the paperwork to the dining room table. She then washed down the kitchen table, found a small table cloth, and set the table for breakfast. Donald asked if they should invite Stella and Marie. Annie looked at her watch and decided it might still be too early for them. Annie kind of liked having Donald to herself this morning.

◆ ◆ ◆

After the breakfast dishes were placed in the dishwasher, Donald suggested they walk out to the cottage to find out what was in all the boxes. Annie and Donald just reached the door of the cottage, when the locksmith drove up the driveway to the garage in the back. Donald walked up and greeted him and led him inside to the locked office door. He was thankful the locksmith had not yet left his motel room to head back to Portland. It was good timing for Annie to discover the locked door. Annie followed, as she wanted to see the office as soon as the door was opened.

It was no time at all and the locksmith was able to pick the lock and open the door. Annie walked in first. The room was littered with paper, knocked over furniture, and the signs of someone having ransacked the entire office. It was heartbreaking for Annie.

Donald walked to a window and noticed that it was raised about four inches. He turned to Annie and asked her to call Detective Surely. He walked the locksmith out, paid him, and thanked him for his services. Annie dialed Dan's cell number and reported what she had found. Detective Surely said he would be there in a few minutes.

Donald came back and found Annie in tears. He put his arm around her and escorted her out of the office. The police were going to want to see the room undisturbed.

"I can't deal with this," Annie said sobbing. "A friend has been murdered, I have a business to run and this is my most profitable time of the year, and I have another employee to pay since I hired Marie. This house is going to be a money pit for me, and I don't know if I can do this by myself." Annie began sobbing more loudly, while looking around in circles trying to find a tissue box.

"And someone keeps entering the house and ransacking it looking for who knows what!" Annie went to the kitchen, pulled off a sheet of paper towel, and blew her nose. "I am afraid to look in Helen's bedroom. What if that room is torn apart too?"

"Then we'll clean it up." Donald said reassuringly. "Annie, you are not alone here. Aunt Helen left me a great deal of money, which I really don't know what to do with, and I think half of it should go to you and Marie to make sure the house remains in your care."

"No, Donald," Annie sniffed, "I will not take any of your inheritance. Helen wanted that to go to you. You are very kind, but I will figure this out."

"Then I insist on paying rent while living in the studio apartment above the garage. I won't take no for an answer." Donald said firmly. "I am here at your beck and call to help with anything. That means you can count on me. Then again, another option would be to marry me and split the inheritance." Donald grinned at Annie.

Annie smothered a giggle, blew her nose again and said, "Careful, Donald, you might end up with a wife on your hands."

"I guess for now you can just take the rent money from me," Donald said with a smile.

Annie looked admiringly at Donald and was about to say thank you for his kind offer, when the front door opened and Marie walked inside. Stella was right behind her. Both were carrying loads of empty boxes.

CHAPTER 10

Thursday Afternoon and Evening

The morning had moved along quickly with the appearance of Detective Surely and a police officer investigating what he called a second burglary. It seemed the burglar may have locked the office door so no one could walk in while he searched the room. The burglar left through the window in the office. Fingerprints and DNA were taken. Dan announced to Annie that she had access to the office now.

Annie told Dan that she was not able to find Helen's purse, and the keys to the office. She asked Dan if he may have taken the purse when he was investigating the murder. Dan said he would look through the photos taken at the scene, but he did not take a purse into evidence. He would call her later to give her an update.

After Dan left, the three women chose to tackle Helen's room first, as that was the room that Annie wanted redecorated for her use. Donald went back to the dining room to contact contractors and decorators.

The women entered Helen's bedroom with Stella in the lead, she opened the door and was grateful to find the room immaculate. Nothing was out of place or scattered over the floor.

The room was in a light pale blue with a creamy trim. The cream-colored upholstered headboard of the king-sized bed sat against the far wall, draped in a beautiful handmade quilt with blue and cream colors. Lace was sewn into the quilt blocks, and a light blue satin ribbon was part of three borders extending around the quilt. Cream colored lace curtains dressed the windows, which were covered in heavy wooden white blinds which were currently closed. The floor was hardwood with a large square cream-colored fluffy carpet extending out from under the bed. Helen's furniture was also a light cream color with dainty roses adorning the front panels of the drawers. Annie thought it was very much a simple shabby chic look. More feminine than she would do for herself, but it was strikingly beautiful.

Marie stood at the door and did not move. She had been in this room when Helen was here. She helped Helen clean the house many times. This was one of the rooms that she often helped Helen clean, and the bathroom attached to this room. Stella turned to Marie.

"It's okay. Helen would want us to move on with our lives." Stella said in her motherly way, Annie thought.

"I know." Marie said, "I just thought she might still be alive for a moment."

Annie placed the boxes she carried upstairs on the floor and said, "Where do we start?"

"Let's start with the closet." Stella suggested. "It is always a good place to start."

They decided to place all the clothes on the bed and sort through them all at once. There was a lot of admiration for the clothes that Helen wore. She was definitely a stylish person, who had some expensive clothing. Annie asked her mother to feel free to select any of the clothing that she wanted to keep to remind her of Helen. Stella selected a few nice outfits, but said she really couldn't fit more into her own closet. Marie chose some pink scarves, a pretty jacket with beading, and a hat. It was a daunting task, but they finished the closet in a couple of hours. Since most of the clothes were of high quality, Annie thought about taking them to a consignment shop in town.

As they walked downstairs, Donald was pacing the floor again on the phone. It sounded like he was making appointments for contractors to come and bid on the work he had planned to complete. Annie asked Donald if he wouldn't mind breaking for an early lunch, as she wanted to get to the shop to help Lizzy and set up for a class, which began at three this afternoon. He said he was hungry and could stop anytime.

Stella suggested they all go over to her house and she would make the lunch preparations. Donald locked the doors and made sure the windows were locked, including the office windows. He then went to check on the studio apartment and cottage to make sure they were locked up.

♦ ♦ ♦

The four walked over to Stella's house and Stella began to make sandwiches. Donald, Annie, and Marie all asked to help, but Stella told them to go relax on the patio out back, as it was such a nice day to be outside. Annie made iced tea for everyone and they went outside. Lunch talk was about the remodeling, sorting through Helen's things, and planning how to get it all done. Annie felt reassured that she had great support in this group. She was feeling better now that she had talked it over with Donald earlier. Maybe the stress was lessening a bit by just having a good cry.

After lunch, Donald walked back to Annie's new home. Stella refused help in cleaning up, so Annie and Marie walked to the shop. It was such a beautiful day. Too bad there were more important things to do today. Annie would have loved to walk on the beach while collecting shells and agates.

Once at the shop, Annie went to her office to place her purse in the lower desk drawer, hang her light jacket up on the antique hook, and take a quick look at the mail. She perused her email, answered anything of importance, and logged off. At two-thirty, Annie engaged the help of Marie for the upcoming class at three o'clock.

Out in the shop, Annie noticed it was rather quiet for a summer afternoon. She walked up to the cash register and began reviewing the daily sales. Lizzy approached Annie at the cash register.

"Big class today," Lizzy said mockingly. "Are you all ready for ten thirteen-year-olds?"

"Marie is helping me with the class, and I am thankful for that." Annie said without looking up from the paperwork she was going through.

"Oh, to be thirteen again," Lizzy pondered. "Do you realize those thirteen-year-old girls were born in the 21st Century and we were born in the 20th Century?" Lizzy stared straight ahead, her thoughts far beyond the paper shop.

"Oh, please!" Annie said sarcastically, "I have underwear older than those girls." Lizzy gave Annie a sideways look and grimaced.

As if on cue, ten thirteen year old girls came bounding into Ocean Loads of Paper with enough energy to power the city of Bridgewater Harbor, or so Annie thought. Two moms trailed tiredly behind the girls. Marie directed the girls to the crafting tables, where they filed into the area and quickly found seats.

When Annie joined the class, she welcomed everyone and showed samples of what they were going to create in the next hour and a half. While Annie began the crafting session, Lizzy pulled the two moms aside and directed them to the bakery and coffee shop next door. A brush of wind flew past Lizzy as the moms exited the door of the shop in a rather quick manner.

The next hour and a half flew by as Annie guided the young girls to creating beautiful works of art with decorative papers, metal washers, and decoupage glue. She then instructed them how to add cording to make a necklace or bracelet. The girls added beads and trinkets to their creations as they talked excitedly amongst themselves.

Next, Annie taught the students how to make a gift box to place their newly created jewelry into. After selecting a solid piece of cardstock, the girls were instructed to team up at the cutting stations and cut their papers per the instructions she gave in a handout. Annie always gave handouts to her students to encourage them to work on more projects at home. This simple gesture also helped with sales after the class.

After the girls finished scoring their pieces of paper using scoring boards and a scoring tool to create embossed lines at specific points on the cardstock, Annie showed them how to fold, cut, and finish the base of the box. The top of the box was next.

Using decorative cardstock for the top of the box, the girls repeated the paper cutting and scoring, only this time adding a die-cut oval shape to add a window. Using acetate sheets, each student die-cut a larger oval shape to fit over the window area on the inside of the box. They used a glue to hold the acetate in place. To make the box look even better, they cut another piece of cardstock in the decorative paper design using the smaller oval shape they used earlier to make the window. They placed that paper over the acetate on the inside of the box lid.

The inside of the box needed a platform to display the necklace or bracelet. Annie's instructions explained how to make the platform and suggested adding a butterfly, punched out from a variety of butterfly punches she had in her shop using the same decorative cardstock, gluing the center of the butterfly to the platform, leaving the wings lifted up. This would give the ability to place the washer necklace over the wings resting in the center of the butterfly, and display the jewelry inside the gift box.

As the class was winding down, and the girls were finishing up their projects, the two mothers walked back into the shop. Apparently, the bakery/coffee shop is what they needed to revitalize their moods, as they were talking and laughing as they walked through the door of the shop.

The young students, projects in hand, excitedly displayed their creations and begged for the moms for purchases to make more of the same jewelry. Annie suggested simpler ways to cut, score, and make the projects without spending a great deal of money, but the moms decided that the investment was well worth it if the girls loved crafting so much...and it kept them occupied for a while. They purchased a smaller cutting board, smaller version of the score board, and each girl selected two pieces of card stock from the shop racks of paper. Annie suggested using a punch with a circle or square to create the 'window' design of the box. The acetate sheet could be cut to fit inside the box lid and covered with the decorative card stock. The moms were thrilled and quickly moved the girls along with their purchases.

It was five o'clock before the store was once again quiet. Annie could have sworn her ears were still ringing from all the young teenage chatter. She was used to teaching more sedate people, such as those from her crafting group and the senior center. But it was still nice to teach young people who got really excited about crafting.

Marie seemed to be dragging as she stepped in to clean up the crafting classroom, Annie noticed. It was nearing six o'clock, and Annie would be closing Ocean Loads of Paper soon. Annie began helping Marie, and suggested that they have a nice quiet evening and watch a movie. Marie was happy about that.

Annie walked into her office and took her cell phone out to call Donald. She wanted to ask him to dinner, and see how the remodeling plans were going. Donald was happy to come to dinner, and said he would update everyone then. She called Charles Conklin, hoping he was still in his office. She had forgotten to call him earlier to confirm their appointment tomorrow morning. Fortunately for Annie, Mr. Conklin was still in his office and he confirmed their appointment at 9:00 AM on Friday morning.

♦ ♦ ♦

Donald appeared at the front door of Stella's house at the same time Annie and Marie walked up to the house.

"Am I too early?"

"Not at all," Annie said walking through the front door after Marie. Annie set her purse down and walked into the kitchen followed by Donald.

"Hi, Mom," Annie said to Stella. "I invited Donald over for dinner and a movie. I think we all need some relaxation time tonight."

"Hello, Donald," Stella said smiling. "Please make yourself at home. I was putting together soup and sandwiches with chocolate cake and ice cream for dinner."

"That sounds great, Stella." Donald moved in closer to the kitchen counter and offered to help make the sandwiches. Stella pulled out the ingredients, and they worked together to prepare dinner.

Annie, deciding there were enough cooks in the kitchen, walked into the family room and looked through the DVD's to find a nice mellow movie. Marie, who was already sitting in the comfortable arm chair, suggested the movie with a romantic title. Annie suggested something with action and adventure. She would have agreed with the romantic movie if Donald was not watching the movie with them. Annie pulled out a movie with action and plugged it into the DVD player.

Stella and Donald entered the family room with trays of sandwiches and soup. Marie had already set up the coffee table with a table cloth and napkins. Stella quickly chose the arm chair opposite Marie, which left Donald and Annie the small sofa. Annie was wise to the manipulation of seats by her mother. Donald seemed quite pleased with the arrangement.

By nine-thirty that night, Annie found herself crawling into bed early. Her cat, Callie, was already snuggled into the blankets and fast asleep. Annie lay awake thinking about all that had happened since Monday morning. It seemed like months ago, but it had only been days. So much was happening all at once, and she still had the desire to delve into the circumstances involving Helen's death. What if she uncovered something Dan missed, Annie thought. Tomorrow she was going to begin searching the house for anything out of the ordinary.

Annie's thoughts then jumped to Donald. He seemed so comfortable with her family, as if he had known them all for years. She really liked him and wanted to get to know him better. She thought back to Tuesday when she first met him...where he was wearing nothing but a towel wrapped around his waist. She thought of his broad shoulders and...with comforting thoughts, Annie fell fast asleep.

CHAPTER 11

Friday Morning

U p again at five o'clock in the morning, Annie sauntered out to the kitchen to make a cup of coffee. She was in her fluffy robe and thick socks. She sat down with her coffee and grabbed a small yellow pad and pen. She began making a list of things needing attention. She really needed to get all the paperwork finished for the estate, house, and Marie. That would be taken care of this morning when she met with Charles Conklin, the attorney.

As the sun rose and light spread across the ocean, Annie just stared, lost in her thoughts. She did not notice Stella walking into the kitchen until she heard the coffee maker brewing a cup of coffee.

"Good morning," Stella said, taking a sip of hot coffee. The first sip was always the best in the morning. Yes, that first sip of coffee, if it was good, the rest of the day was good, Annie thought. Stella smiled as she set her coffee cup down on the counter.

"Good morning," Annie replied back. She stood and stretched and then remembered that she had not asked her mom to go with her to the attorney's office.

"Mom, would you be able to go with me to Charles Conklin's office this morning?" Annie continued, "I have an appointment with him at 9:00 AM to sign papers and finalize everything." Annie made another cup of coffee and wrapped her hand around the hot brew.

"Actually, I don't have any plans today." Stella said, "I can help where needed."

"Thanks." Annie then said, "I won't wake Marie until seven. She should go too, since part of this appointment is about her."

Annie talked with her mother for a bit longer, then went off to get showered, dressed, and prepare for her meeting with the attorney.

By seven o'clock, Marie had wandered out of her bedroom on her own. She was dressed and ready for the day ahead of her. As she entered the kitchen, she said good morning to Stella, and Annie who was now sitting at the breakfast bar writing notes on a yellow pad. Stella offered breakfast to the two women, which they gladly accepted. The women sat down to a scrumptious breakfast and talked about their day ahead.

With breakfast dishes in the dishwasher and the kitchen cleaned up, Stella followed Annie and Marie to the garage for the drive to Newport to meet with Charles Conklin. The morning was foggy and typical of mornings on the Oregon coast. As they drove, the fog cleared and Marie watched out the window for whales spouting. She would get excited when she spotted a tail of a whale splashing down in the water. Annie thought it would be nice to take Marie to the Oregon Coast Aquarium for an afternoon of fun. Another thing to add to the mental list of things to do, Annie thought. Then an idea came to her to ask Donald if he would like to join them. Annie smiled.

Charles Conklin greeted and led the women to his office, where he invited them to sit in worn red leather chairs. Although comfortable, the chairs showed their age and years of use. Mr. Conklin sat in his chair at his desk and pulled out a file of papers. He spent the next part of the meeting covering the guardianship papers, asking Marie if she approved, which she did, and having Annie sign the papers in front of a notary public Mr. Conklin had asked to notarize the documents. He said he would file all the necessary paperwork.

Next, Mr. Conklin advised Annie about the transfer of the house deed and business into her name. Afterwards, Annie asked questions and felt more at ease with the whole situation. With everything settled, Annie asked her mother if there was anything she might have not asked Mr. Conklin.

"I do have a question for Mr. Conklin," Stella then said. "In the letter that Helen wrote to me, she mentioned valuable paintings she wanted me to have and said the sale of those paintings would provide me with a comfortable retirement. But when I walked through the house, I was not able to locate any of the paintings. Do you know anything about the paintings or their location?"

Mr. Conklin looked at Annie and asked, "Have you read the letter written to you by Helen?"

Sheepishly Annie replied, "No. I just haven't brought myself to do so."

"Well, I suggest you do so soon, as your letter will answer questions people might have."

Annie nodded. She remembered she had the large envelope from Helen in her business tote bag. Time just seemed to fly by and she felt like she was not accomplishing enough and it seemed so overwhelming.

After meeting with Charles Conklin, Annie, Stella, and Marie arrived back home. Annie parked the car in the garage and the three entered Stella's house through the garage door. It was Friday and Annie decided to not go into work today, but to get to work on her house across the street.

After talking with Lizzy on the phone, Annie called Donald and told him she was on her way over. He said he had all the contractors lined up and all the plans were made. Annie was on the phone talking with Donald as she walked through the front door. Donald was at the dining room table with stacks of paper all about.

"I have asked Mom to help Marie pack up all her things in the apartment over the garage today." Annie told Donald, "That way I can tackle the office."

"That sounds like a good plan. I can help where needed."

Marie and Stella entered through the front door carrying yet more empty boxes. While Donald helped them carry the boxes to the apartment in the backyard, Annie got herself a cup of coffee and walked to the office to begin the arduous task of sorting through the desk.

Helen's office was a light beige color with white trim and tall ceilings. A large dark brown desk stood to the right of the doorway. To the left was a window looking out onto the driveway that entered the back from the street. Behind the desk stood a large dark wood shelving unit with cabinets on the bottom, matching the color of the desk. The shelves were neatly decorated with various knick-knacks from travels and photos in frames. Annie noticed a photo of Helen and Marie. It was charming.

After the burglary and the investigation by the police, Annie noticed that Donald had cleaned up the mess and stacked the papers on the desk. A computer stood on the desk. Annie turned the computer on. She was not sure what she would find there. Once the computer booted, she noticed that she needed a password to log into the system. She would need to locate a password she thought. She looked through the drawers for a book or paper or something that might have the password. She looked under the keyboard, mouse, the leather pad that sat centered on the desk, the phone, and anything she thought might be a good place to hide a password. She found nothing to help her.

Next, she sorted through the papers and pulled out necessary utility bills that might need to be paid. As it was, Annie could see by the notations on the papers, Helen had already paid the current bills, and the papers were not yet filed away. Annie looked through the drawers. One drawer at the bottom seemed to be stuck. Annie stood from the chair, leaned over and grabbed the drawer handle, and gave it a good pull. As she pulled, her hand slipped off the handle, sending her backwards into the shelving unit. She wildly grabbed for support, and then felt the unit move. Fearing the whole shelving unit would fall on top of her, she scrambled under the desk.

Hearing a loud commotion, Donald ran to the office to find Annie hiding under the desk.

"What happened?" He said with concern in his voice. Donald walked over and offered a hand in helping Annie up off the floor.

"I was trying to open this bottom drawer when my hand slipped and I toppled over into the shelves." Annie looked at the shelves and said, "I could have sworn they moved sideways when I tried to grab onto a shelf to keep from falling."

Donald began to inspect the units, and at the end which stood in the corner, he noticed the shelving unit was sitting about six inches away from the wall in the corner. He looked at Annie, and then smiled and placing both hands on the side of the unit, he gave it a tug, moving the entire shelving unit sideways down the wall about a foot. He continued to push the unit down the wall, exposing a very large built-in safe.

Annie walked up to the safe. She and Donald just stared at it for a while before Donald said, "Do you have the combination?"

Annie shook her head no.

"Well, it has to be somewhere." Donald said looking around the room. "We will just keep looking."

Donald pushed the shelving unit further down the wall giving enough room to figure out how to open the safe, when he discovered the unit continued to roll. Slowly, as the shelves were moved down the wall, a doorway appeared. Lights suddenly lit a stairway going down. Donald and Annie looked at each other.

"Did you know Helen had a secret room?" Donald asked Annie.

"No." Annie said. "She never said anything about a secret room. I wonder if Mom knew about it."

"Let's find out where it goes," Donald said, heading down the stairs.

Annie noticed, as she descended the stairs behind Donald, that the stairway was nicely finished in light beige carpeting. A railing was on the left wall. The stairs entered down into a small finished basement with carpeting and furniture. It was decorated as a nice cozy reading area with a lamp and two comfortable large chairs. Annie thought this was an odd place for a reading nook.

At the bottom of the stairs on the left was a large canvas print that hung on the wall. As Annie touched the canvas print, she noticed it was tightly secured on one side. She pulled on the other side to find it opened outward. Behind it was a large safe door inset in the wall. She blew out a sigh.

"We should call this the 'safe' house," Donald laughed.

They looked behind paintings on the wall to see if Helen might have taped a password for the safe in the room. Still not finding any information resembling any passwords, Annie suddenly remembered the large envelope she was given from Helen.

"I need to go across the street for a few minutes," Annie said to Donald. "I think Helen left me the passwords in the packet of information that was given to me."

"Are you telling me you haven't read the letter she wrote to you?"

"Well...no, I haven't." Running up the stairs, Annie said, "I'll be just a moment."

♦ ♦ ♦

Annie ran up the stairs and out the front door. She barely glanced at the street as she ran across to Stella's house. Once unlocking the door and entering inside, she raced to her bedroom closet. Pulling out her business tote from the closet, she grabbed the large yellow colored envelope and opened the sealed flap. Inside she found numerous envelopes, one in particular labeled 'Passwords and keys'. She set the password envelope aside and began placing the other items inside the large envelope when she noticed a letter sized white envelope labeled 'To Annie from Helen'. Annie ran her fingertips over the word 'Helen'. Tears stung her eyes.

Taking a deep breath, Annie quickly put the letter inside the large envelope, and placed it in the business tote. With it back in the closet, she raced out of her bedroom through the living room. She stopped when she thought she saw movement outside the living room window. The hair on the back of her neck stood up. Was she imagining this? Stella and Marie were not home. They were in Marie's apartment packing up her things. She stood, listening for any sounds. The place was quiet.

Annie decided to go through the house and make sure all the doors and windows were secure. She sent a text to Donald, who immediately sent a text stating he was securing the wall unit and coming over. In a matter of a couple of minutes Donald was knocking on the front door. Annie looked out the side window to see Donald and then turned the deadbolt to let him inside.

"I just saw someone walking to a white van down the street and take off," Donald told Annie. "It was too far away to get a license number."

"I should call Dan and let him know that the guy came back in a different car." Annie said as she directed Donald to the living room and pointed out the window where she thought she saw movement outside.

Donald said he would check the outside of the house, but Annie asked him to wait until she made the call to Dan. Dan may want the police to check outside first.

Annie pulled her phone out and called Dan.

"Hello?" Dan answered abruptly.

"Hi, Surely. It's Annie."

"What can I do for you?" Dan asked a bit impatiently.

"I think someone was prowling around mom's house," Annie reported. She could tell Dan was not in a good mood. Something happened, but she was not going to ask right now.

"Tell me about it," Dan ordered.

Annie explained everything that happened, including what Donald told her about the white van down the street. Dan listened, but Annie could hear a loud sigh coming through the phone lines.

"Dan, I think it was the burglar coming after something I have."

"It wasn't the person who burglarized Helen's house," Dan said. "I just finished interviewing him and he is still in the interview room. He has not left. There is someone else out there prowling around Stella's house. Let me send patrol out to check the grounds. Wait inside the house."

"Okay."

"And Annie...?"

"Yes."

"When I say wait inside the house, I mean it." Dan said in a demanding tone.

"Donald is here with me. I don't think he will let me go outside until the police get here."

Dan hung up and in a few minutes a patrol car arrived. Donald went outside to meet the officer and explain what had happened. They both walked around the house. Footprints were seen in the flower bed under the living room window. Photographs and measurements were taken of the footprints. The officer called Dan and reported on his findings. Donald had a short conversation with the officer and then walked back into the house. Annie waited anxiously to find out what they found.

When inside Donald told Annie about the footprints under the living room window and that someone was definitely looking inside. Annie admonished herself for not paying attention while crossing the street. She could have seen the white van and noticed it was out of place in the neighborhood. The man could have gotten into the house and had been there while she was in her bedroom. Annie suddenly shivered. Donald put his arms protectively around her. Annie snuggled into his comforting embrace. He was warm and smelled really good. She could stay like this forever, she thought.

Donald pulled her tight and said, "Annie, in the short time we have known each other, I have come to realize how much I really like you. I was wondering how you might feel about me?" Annie pulled herself away and looked up at Donald.

"I really like you too." Annie said softly. "You are the most kind, generous, patient, intelligent man I have met. How can anyone not like you, especially after seeing you for the first time naked with only a small towel wrapped around your waist," Annie laughed.

Donald was just about to lean in and kiss Annie, when the front door opened and Stella and Marie walked in carrying boxes filled with Marie's belongings. Donald and Annie quickly separated as if they were caught doing something they should not have been doing. Stella stopped, eyed them both suspiciously, smirked, and then motioned for Donald to help with the box she was carrying. Donald quickly grabbed the box and asked where she wanted it to go. As Stella led the way, Donald turned to Annie and whispered, "Let's pick up where we left off later." Annie smiled and nodded yes. Marie stopped and gave Annie a long look before she followed Donald with her box in hand.

"Get a room!" Marie then brushed passed Annie.

It was dinner time when all of Marie's belongings were moved to her bedroom. Donald made the job easier by using a furniture dolly to move multiple boxes in one trip. In several hours, the four were able to move an entire apartment of belongings and empty the apartment above the garage. Tomorrow, they would start on the cottage and Helen's bedroom. Everything had to be cleared out before Monday, as the contractors were beginning their job.

♦ ♦ ♦

Since the group was exhausted, Donald offered to go get pizza and beer...soda pop for Marie. They all agreed and gave their pizza preferences. Donald decided to pick up two pizzas and called the order in to the local pizza shop. He then grabbed his jacket, keys to Helen's SUV, and left out the kitchen door. Meanwhile, Annie and Marie went to Stella's house to get some parmesan cheese to grate for the pizza, and makings for a salad. Marie was excited to have a family night, so she suggested a fun movie. She ran to the bookcase where the movies were kept and selected several movies. While Annie was in the kitchen, she thought she heard Marie giggling.

Marie came into the kitchen with the movies under her sweatshirt. Annie wondered what that was all about. They walked to the front door. Annie locked the front door, leaving lights on inside, as she and Marie exited Stella's house and went back across the street. This time Annie looked up and down the street. It seemed like all was well in the neighborhood.

While Annie and Marie were across the street, Stella pulled out napkins, plates, and set up the living room coffee table with a small table cloth. She set out forks for the salad. Annie and Marie came through the front door, locked it, and set their items on the kitchen counter.

With all the preparations made, the three women waited for Donald to arrive with the pizza. It was moments later and they heard a car pull up and into the garage in the back. Within a few more minutes, Donald came in carrying two boxes of pizza. He placed the boxes on the coffee table, as directed by Stella, and presented ice cream for dessert. Dinner was ready.

Annie asked Marie what movie they were going to watch and Marie showed them the four movies she had selected. All of the movies were romantic in nature. Now Annie knew why Marie was giggling in the living room across the street. Annie suggested to the group that Marie be the one to select a movie. They all agreed.

Three quarters of the way into the movie, Annie turned to look at Donald, who was sitting next to her, and noticed that his head was back and he was fast asleep. She chuckled to herself. It was an exhausting day. Tomorrow she would find a way to get back down in the basement alone with him. He might even try to kiss her there, where it is quiet and secluded.

After the movie, everyone helped clean up, the women said good night to Donald and went across the street to go to bed.

"Would you and Marie mind looking-after the shop tomorrow?" Annie asked her mother. "Lizzy has the day off and I was hoping to get some work done around the house before the contractors arrive on Monday."

"I would be happy to help out at the shop instead of moving boxes," Stella answered.

"Open at ten, but don't stay any longer than four," Annie instructed. "Those are the busiest hours."

Stella agreed and went to bed. Marie also went to bed. She seemed happier today. Annie really wanted Marie to be happy. The sooner the house gets remodeled, the sooner they can move on with their lives.

CHAPTER 12

Saturday

Saturday morning came quickly, and Annie was up later than usual. It was almost six o'clock, the sun was up, and Annie wasn't. She yawned, stretched and slowly forced herself to get up and out of bed. Callie, her lazy, sleepy cat decided to once again sleep in longer.

With no time to spare to look at the ocean over a cup of coffee, Annie quickly showered, dressed, and headed to the kitchen to grab a cup of coffee before going over to her house to sort through the office and to find out what was in all the safes she had found so far. She was secretly hoping to find something that would explain Helen's murder. Just a single piece of evidence that would help Dan with the case is all she needed.

Annie pulled her cell phone out of her pocket and called Donald.

"Good morning," Annie said when Donald answered. "Are you ready to tackle the office and secret room today?"

"I'm all yours today."

"I like the sound of that," Annie flirted boldly. "I will certainly keep you occupied.

"Although I love flirting with you over the phone, I would rather you come over here and flirt in person. I have coffee!"

"Oh, you said the magic words," Annie said with laughter in her voice.

"Come over here and flirt in person?"

"I have coffee!" Annie said jokingly, walking through the front door of her "new" home.

By 7:30 AM, Annie and Donald had a plan of what to accomplish today and began by checking out the safe in the secret room. That might prove to be more interesting than the safe in the wall in the office.

As they entered the office, Donald closed the curtains, locked the door, and slid the shelving unit sideways exposing the lit stairway. Annie and Donald descended the stairs once again and stood at the bottom of the steps taking in the room and its possible purpose.

Annie pulled the envelope from her pocket and tore open the flap. She found a folded piece of paper and several keys with labels. She kept the keys in the envelope, took out the folded paper, stuffed the envelope back into her pocket, and began reading the paper.

"This is a listing of safes in the house." Annie continued, "They are labeled with letters."

Donald opened the large canvas painting which concealed a large safe door. On the safe was the letter "B" next to the push button keypad. Annie approached the keypad and punched in a group of numbers. They heard a click. Donald turned the wheel and pulled open the door.

Annie was the first to see a light flash on, illuminating a large room filled with paintings and various items of value. Donald peered around the door over Annie's shoulder and gave a low whistle. Both Annie and Donald were dumbstruck. Annie had no idea what Helen was keeping secret all these years.

Securing the vault door open, Donald and Annie slowly walked into the room taking in the scene before them. It was like a dream. Was Annie dreaming this? She walked up to the center of the room where paintings were displayed on standing panels. Annie realized these were the paintings Helen left for her mother. At least that mystery was solved, Annie mused.

Donald walked over to a panel which appeared to control an automatic de-humidifier unit and heating system. He inspected both systems, which appeared to be very expensive and high quality.

At the end of the wall on the left as they walked through the vault door, housed two large safes inset into the wall. One safe was labeled "R" and the second safe was labeled "H".

"His and her safes," Donald announced. "Do you have the passwords for these safes?"

"Yes," Annie said locating the codes on her piece of paper. She walked up to the safe labeled "R" and punched in the code. Donald turned the wheel and pulled the door open. Inside were stacks of currency on the bottom shelf. The upper shelves contained what appeared to be papers of some kind.

"Is that real money?" Annie questioned.

"I am assuming yes," Donald replied, reaching down to pick up a stack of bills and inspecting them. "My parents keep a large amount of cash in their safe. It is not uncommon."

"The only safe I have is at the office, and it keeps enough for the cash register, and maybe a little bit of petty cash." Annie offered. "I have never seen so much currency in my life!" Annie took a step back feeling a bit overwhelmed.

Donald pulled out a few of the stacks and examined them. He was about to place them back when something caught his eye. He reached in, removed more stacks of currency, setting them on the floor, and then pulled out a very heavy tray of coins.

"Is that gold?" Annie asked, feeling a bit light-headed.

"Yes, and it lives with friends...lots of friends. They look like Krugerrands." Donald pulled out his cell phone. He attempted to get out to the Internet to do a bit of research, but found his phone could not get service in the basement.

"Let's count the coins. I will research their worth as soon as we go back upstairs," Donald instructed Annie. Donald ran upstairs to the office to get a yellow pad and pens. He quietly closed the sliding unit and came back downstairs. Annie was pulling out stacks of currency and making neat and tidy piles of money. Donald looked at her with a smile of amusement. The look on Annie's face was of total shock as she continued to neatly stack the paper money.

Donald pulled out tray after tray of coins. He counted one hundred coins in each tray. Some of the coins dated into the late seventies and early eighties. Annie recorded each tray and count of coins. Donald thought she was so busy inventorying the safe that she may not have realized what she discovered.

"Donald," Annie suddenly sat up straight and looked at Donald with an expression of enlightenment. "This must be what Helen left you in her Will."

"I'm afraid not, Annie." Donald said, "My inheritance is in the bank. Helen left the contents of the house to you."

"What?" Annie said, attempting to stand up, but instead toppled over on top of the coin trays, scattering coins and currency everywhere.

Donald sighed, shook his head side to side, looked down at Annie, who was lying on top of all the money, and said, "Now that's what I call rolling in the dough."

Annie groaned and tried to get up gracefully. Donald offered her a hand. He pulled her up to him. They stared into each other's eyes for what seemed like a very long time to Annie. It was then that they finally kissed. The kiss sent wonderful tingly sensations through Annie's body. She wrapped her arms around him tighter, wanting more.

Donald pulled away. He looked down at the mess on the floor, and suggested they clean it all up before they went any further. Annie took it as 'slow down lady, I'm not that kind of guy'. Disappointed, she slowly turned and began picking up coins and placing them in the coin trays. She felt embarrassed for pushing herself on him. What was wrong with her anyway? She might have been a bit rusty in the dating world, but she certainly had not forgotten how to kiss. Did she suddenly repulse him? Was he in a relationship and not mention it to her? Was he feeling guilty for kissing her? Annie told herself to stop thinking the worse.

Silently, they picked up all the coins and currency and closed the safe. Annie looked at her watch. It was just after three o'clock in the afternoon. Her mother and Marie would be closing the store at four.

"Should we tell anyone about this room?" Annie asked Donald.

"Let's keep this to ourselves for now." Donald responded. "I think we should research the coins and see if we can find out how Robert and Helen came to own them and why."

After taking a look around the room at other items, Annie and Donald then exited the vault room. Then making sure Annie had the paperwork with the passwords for the safe, Donald closed the vault door and covered it up with the canvas painting.

Annie started to head upstairs when Donald grabbed her arm and pulled her close to him. He leaned down and kissed her passionately. She pulled away this time with a look of confusion on her face.

"Why did you pull away from me a few minutes ago?" Annie questioned Donald.

"Did it ever occur to you that there might be cameras set up in the room for surveillance?"

"Oh, my goodness no," Annie said with a startled expression. "Wait...who would be watching the room? Both Helen and Robert are dead."

"Just a thought, cameras may be linked to recorders," Donald said with a smile. "Do you want someone watching us making out?" It was then that Donald pulled Annie closer and leaned in to kiss her. His lips were soft and slightly moist.

Annie again felt the tingly sensation surge through her body. Their mutual passion for each other rose to where Donald ran his hand under her shirt and cupped her breasts. Annie gasped, and reached out to unbutton his shirt. She ran her hands over his taut chest and stomach. Donald pulled Annie's shirt off. He removed her bra. She, in turn, pulled his shirt off. They continued to kiss more and more passionately until Annie felt she could not breathe anymore. She pulled back and inhaled deeply. Donald gently lowered her to the floor. He placed his lips upon hers, sending feelings of pure desire and want through her body. Their bare skin touched and the warmth of his body gave her indescribable pleasure she hadn't felt in years.

Suddenly, the shelving unit began moving. Donald and Annie looked up in surprise. Donald reached over and grabbed a throw blanket that was draped over one of the chairs. He placed the blanket over Annie and himself just in time to see Marie walking down the stairs.

"Marie? What are you doing down here?" Annie said pulling the blanket over her tightly.

"I was looking for you. What are you doing? Are you kissing?" Marie asked innocently.

Stella came down the stairs and stopped suddenly at the compromising position of Annie and Donald.

"Oh, my goodness," Stella said. "Marie, go upstairs right now and leave these two alone."

"Get a room," Marie said giggling, as she turned to walk upstairs as slowly as she could. Stella walked up the stairs behind her, prodding Marie to go faster.

"We have a room," Donald shouted. "It just happens to be Grand Central Station right now."

Annie was mortified. She quickly grabbed her bra and shirt and stood to get dressed. Donald grabbed her wrist.

"Are you kidding me?" Annie said, pulling away. "My mother just caught me naked with a man."

"Annie, she likes me." Donald said as if that made it all okay.

Annie finished dressing and handed Donald his shirt. Donald sighed and stood up to put his shirt on.

"Annie, we are both adults," Donald said, trying to comfort Annie from an embarrassing situation.

Annie looked up the stairs. She suddenly realized that Marie and Stella knew about the secret room. But they may not know about the vault behind the canvas painting, because her mother told the attorney she did not know where the valuable paintings were that Helen had left for her. Annie turned to Donald.

"They don't know about the secret room behind the vault door." Annie said in a whisper. "If they did, Mom would have known where Helen kept the paintings she left for Mom."

"Let's keep this to ourselves for now." Donald advised. "We need to figure out what it is you have."

"Thank you, Donald." Annie said lightly, "I am sorry I got angry with you. You are right. We are adults. I just felt embarrassed when Marie found us in a compromising position."

"Actually, we were interrupted before we got to the compromising position." Donald smiled devilishly at Annie.

Annie kissed Donald and turned to head up the stairs. Donald followed, and closed the wall unit to hide the stairway to the basement. As he approached the open office door, Donald remembered that he purposely locked the door. How did Marie get into the office? Running his hand through his hair, he realized he had left his set of keys on the kitchen table. Next time he would make a point of taking the keys.

CHAPTER 13

Saturday Evening

When Annie walked out of the office and into the living room, she realized that her mother and Marie had left the house and walked across the street. It was at that time Annie's cell phone rang. She pulled the phone from her pocket and noticed it was her mother. She answered the phone.

"Annie," Stella said, "Marie and I came over to tell you that Chinese food is being delivered for dinner. When Donald and you are ready, come on over."

"Mom," Annie began, "I am really sorry you saw what you saw."

"Annie, I am really sorry I wasn't able to stop Marie from going downstairs. I just wasn't paying attention to where she was going in the house."

"How long have you known about the secret room?" Annie asked.

"Since Robert died," Stella replied. "Helen said she used the room as a safe room in case of trouble. She was always afraid of living alone for some reason."

"Does she have any other secret rooms in the house?" Annie asked, wanting to find out if her mother knew about the vault room.

"Not that Helen ever mentioned." Stella stated.

Annie's cell phone began beeping in her ear indicating she had another call coming in. She told her mother she and Donald would be over in a few minutes and ended the call. She recognized the number as being from Dan.

"Hello, Surely!" Annie answered the call in a cheerful voice.

"It's Dan Surely to you, miss." Dan replied. "I apologize for being a bit abrupt the last time you called. I wanted to update you on the case."

"Mom is ordering Chinese dinner." Annie told Dan. "Come over and have dinner with us. We can talk then."

"Actually, that really sounds much better than the burger I was going to pick up." Dan said. "I'll be there in a few minutes."

Annie hung up the phone and was in deep thought when Donald came up behind her and wrapped his arms around her waist. He then turned her around and gave her a long, slow kiss. Annie's thoughts slipped back downstairs to the secret room and what might have happened if they weren't interrupted. Annie took a deep breath and placed her hand on Donald's chest.

"I need to make a quick call," Annie said, selecting a number on her cell phone and making the call. She raised the phone to her ear and looked at Donald, giving him the 'just a minute' signal with her index finger pointed up in the air. Donald shook his head and smiled, then walked to the kitchen to check the back door.

"Hello?" Annie said into the phone. "Lizzy, it's Annie. Can you come over for Chinese dinner right now? Mom is having dinner delivered and she ordered lots of food." Annie was silent for a few moments, and then said, "Great! We'll see you at Mom's house soon."

Annie was grinning when Donald walked back after securing the house. Annie told him about the Chinese dinner being delivered, the call from Dan, and inviting Lizzy to dinner. Donald looked at Annie suspiciously.

"Are you trying to set up Lizzy and Dan?" Donald asked, grabbing jackets for the two of them.

"I haven't said anything to either one of them. If they have an attraction, then I can take full credit. If not, no harm in friends having dinner together."

"I thought match-makers were old spinster women." Donald laughed.

Annie gave him a grimace and put her jacket on to head out into the cool summer evening.

♦ ♦ ♦

Annie introduced Dan to Lizzy and the group sat down at the dining room table. There was much conversation and laughter as the group talked. Dan and Lizzy chatted animatedly about various topics. Annie knew Lizzy was attracted to Dan, but she wasn't sure if Dan would be attracted to Lizzy. As it was, Dan seemed smitten with Lizzy.

Annie was thinking about all the good that had come since Helen's passing.

Donald squeezed her thigh and smiled at Annie. She knew that he was thinking about the match-making she was doing. It was his way of saying he thought it might work out for Dan and Lizzy. She sensed that as well.

Everyone lingered at the dinner table for over two hours. Annie got up and offered more coffee or tea to the people at the table. Dan said he would need to leave, as he still had paperwork to finish. Lizzy mentioned that she too should leave and walk home before it got too dark. Dan offered her a ride home. Annie was thrilled to see the spark between the two.

Dan pulled Annie aside and said he would call tomorrow, Sunday, and catch her up on the case. Annie suggested that Dan come help go through Helen's office with her. Maybe there was something he could see that she hadn't been able to find. She also suggested he may stay to help clear out the cottage, as they could really use the help. She said she would talk to Donald about having a barbecue to feed everyone afterwards. Dan said he would not pass up a barbecue and agreed to be there at 9:00 AM. Time was running out for getting the rooms ready for the remodeling on Monday, Annie thought.

While Dan was saying good-bye to Stella, Marie, and Donald, Annie pulled Lizzy aside and asked if she would be available to help clear out the cottage tomorrow, knowing that Lizzy was always willing to help out a friend. Lizzy agreed to be there at 9:00 AM. Again, Annie was making sure Dan and Lizzy would run into each other in a normal setting. No pressure, Annie conspired to herself.

After Dan and Lizzy left, Donald was saying his good-byes to Stella and Marie. Annie walked him to the door. He leaned in to kiss Annie on the cheek, and whispered, "I would really like to finish what we started earlier, but tonight might not be a good time."

Annie agreed and reached up to give Donald a proper kiss good-bye. They heard giggling and pulled apart to see Marie watching them while peering out of the kitchen. Stella walked out to the hallway, and gently pushed Marie into the kitchen. After one more passionate kiss, Donald opened the front door and headed across the street. Annie watched until he walked through the front door of the house. He turned and waved to Annie. She waved back, closed and locked the door, and then headed to the kitchen.

"I'm listening." Stella said to Annie, not waiting for Annie to make the first comment. Marie was clearing the table for Stella, while Stella loaded the dishwasher.

"I think he likes me, Mom."

"Helen and I always tried to figure out a way to get the two of you together." Stella continued, "She asked him to come visit her on many occasions, but he never seemed to get away from work. She thought that if he met you, he would be instantly smitten. It seems as though she was right after all. I just wished she was alive to see it."

"I don't know if he intends to stay, Mom." Annie said. "He does plan to go back to California in another week."

"Not if he is remodeling the apartment above the garage for his own use." Stella said. Marie brought more dishes to be washed to Stella. Stella pointed to the counter, and Marie set the dishes down.

"Marie, when you've finished, go ahead and take your shower tonight. We have lots to do tomorrow and we should get an early start." Stella told Marie.

"Okay." Marie said and walked down the hall toward her bedroom to get ready to take a shower. She stopped and called back, "I really like Donald. Make him stay."

"I will try, Marie." Annie said chuckling.

"I am really enjoying our little family dynamic, Annie." Stella said turning back to loading the dishwasher. "It has given me lots to think about and a purpose going into each day."

"I never realized how lonely you might be, Mom."

"Oh, I have my clubs and you, and now Marie, but sometimes I feel like I just rattle around in this house by myself, especially when you go to work early and stay late. Lately, the house has been full of life and people."

Annie was thinking about the time she and Marie would move across the street to her new home. Stella would be all alone when they moved out. Annie never realized how lonely that would make her mother.

"We are just across the street, and I am hoping we continue to all eat dinner together every day." Annie said. She removed the table cloth from the dining room table and set it on the kitchen counter. She walked over to her mother and gave her a hug.

Annie then said, "I am thinking of hiring more help at the shop to relieve Lizzy and me from being there all the time. We have lives to live too. It is time to focus on the future."

"I guess Helen's death is affecting all of us." Stella closed the dishwasher door. "It is making us think about our lives and what is missing. I hope you and Donald find a life together."

"I really like him, Mom. He is kind and generous. He makes me laugh." Annie said smiling, "He loves our little family and seems to fit in perfectly."

Annie and her mother sat at the breakfast bar and continued to talk for another hour. Annie said she was tired and wanted to get an early start tomorrow. She told her mother that Dan was coming at 9:00 AM to go through Helen's office with her. They said good night and went to their bedrooms.

CHAPTER 14

Sunday Early Morning

At five o'clock, Annie was up, showered, and dressed. She headed to the kitchen for that first cup of coffee to get her going. Even though she had a very busy day ahead of her, she decided she was going to spend an hour by herself at her usual window waiting for the sun to rise and shine over the ocean. The house was quiet, except for the sound of rain. So much for seeing the sun shine on the ocean this morning, Annie thought.

Holding her coffee in both hands, Annie closed her eyes and let her mind drift to the events of the last few days. She thought about the visit with the attorney, the office, the basement secret room, and the vault room. Since Annie and Donald decided to keep the vault room to themselves a little bit longer, Annie thought it might be a good idea to see what was in the safe behind the wall unit in the office. Whatever was in that safe could be brought out. That way Dan could go through the papers, and Annie could keep the room in the basement a secret.

At six o'clock Annie called Donald to see if he was up. He was still in bed, but told her she was welcome to come over as he was just about to get up and take a shower.

"You can come over and join me," Donald added.

"What a shame," Annie flirtatiously, "I just showered and dressed an hour ago. I'll be over in half an hour."

Annie hung up and made another cup of coffee. She got out a pad of paper and began making a list of things to do today. She had just begun when she heard Marie walk into the kitchen.

"Good morning, Marie," Annie said cheerily. "You are up early."

"Good morning." Marie answered back sleepily. "I like to get up early."

"I was just about to make a list of things to get done today. Want to help?"

"Yes." Marie said, taking a seat at the breakfast bar.

Annie and Marie discussed how to begin getting the cottage cleared out. Marie suggested Annie store the boxes in the garage workshop. She said that the workshop was all cleaned up since Robert had passed away. She told Annie that there was a large work table where they could store all the boxes and not have to set them on the floor.

Remembering work on the remodeling would begin tomorrow, Annie asked Marie if she and Donald had figured out a design for her room. Marie said that Donald showed her pictures on the computer of really pretty rooms and she told him what she liked about the rooms.

"Donald told me that I was not allowed upstairs until the rooms are finished." Marie told Annie. "He said you are not allowed upstairs either. He will take us up there when the rooms are finished."

Annie smiled and told Marie, "I like surprises. Our new rooms will be fun surprises."

"Me too, I like fun surprises." Marie said.

It was six-thirty in the morning when Annie's mother entered the kitchen. She went directly to the cupboard to pull out a coffee mug. She then put the mug on the coffee maker and pulled a coffee pod from a glass jar with a lid. She placed the pod in the slot on the coffee maker and pressed a button. Soon the fresh brewed coffee was finished and Stella retrieved the mug and sat down.

Taking a sip, she said, "How about breakfast?"

"I can help," said Marie.

"Not for me, Mom." Annie said, "I have something very important to do before Dan arrives to help me go through Helen's office."

"Oh?" Stella said with raised eyebrows.

"Mother, really?" Annie said, "I want to sort through and organize papers for Dan to review."

Annie stood up to leave. She gathered her notepad and headed for the front door. Stella said she and Marie would be over in about an hour to begin helping out where they were needed.

"I am closing the shop today, so no worries there." Annie told Stella and Marie.

Annie walked across the threshold of the front door of her new home and announced to Donald that she had arrived. He said he would be downstairs shortly. Annie then walked to the office and began going through the desk. A drawer contained office supplies. There was nothing to indicate why Helen was murdered. She leaned over and again tugged at the stuck drawer, this time being careful not to lose her grip. The drawer still would not budge.

Donald entered the room and said good morning. He walked up to Annie and pulled her up for a kiss. He smelled fresh from a shower and shave. That tingly feeling was coming back. She kissed him back slowly. They pulled apart and Annie sighed deeply.

"I would love to spend the day with you curled up on the sofa under a blanket watching old movies, with no worries in our world." Annie said, staring into Donald's eyes.

"Would we be naked?" Donald asked with a smile.

"No!" Annie added snapping out of her dreamy state of mind, "We could only do that in a newly remodeled bedroom, which is not happening until we get the rooms cleared and ready for the contractors to arrive tomorrow. But first, we need to get started on the office before Dan gets here at nine o'clock. Mom and Marie will be here in another hour.

"Let's get these rooms cleared!" Donald said jokingly.

Annie told Donald about the drawer being stuck. He pulled out the flashlight function on his cell phone and got up close to the drawer to look it over.

"There seems to be a clever locking system on the side of the drawer. Is there a metal nail file or something similar looking in the drawers?" Donald said while continuing to look over the drawer.

Annie searched the drawers again and discovered a metal nail file with a strange notch. She handed it to Donald, who attempted to fit it between the drawer and the framing on the drawer. When they heard a click, Donald turned to Annie with a smile.

Pulling the drawer open, Annie and Donald discovered files of household utility bills, vehicle and personal insurance policies, medical records of Helen's visits to the doctor, files of receipts of major purchases, major stock statements, as well as miscellaneous papers. Annie located a small three-ring binder with business cards in plastic sleeves, and a section of an address book.

Annie thought it would be appropriate to send a card to the people in the address book advising them of the passing of Helen. She would create a beautiful card design and make up as many as it took to send the notices. It was something she felt she needed to do personally for Helen.

After inspecting the locking system, Donald pulled out the file folder containing copies of insurance policies and set it down on the desk. He and Annie looked over each policy, which showed Donald as the beneficiary. Annie was amazed at the total amount of the insurance policies. Donald suspected, due to Annie's silence, that she was realizing how much money Donald had inherited from Helen.

"The policies have already paid out and I have received them." Donald said, closing the file. "I set up accounts at a bank locally. The money is sitting there. I really don't know what to do with it, other than to help remodel the house."

"Is there anything in the drawer that might suggest why someone would want to kill Helen?" Annie asked, wanting to move on. She felt sort of guilty inheriting a house that should belong to Donald.

Both Annie and Donald dug in and looked at each file folder seeking anything that might look suspicious. After a thorough search, Donald suggested they open up the safe before anyone arrived. Annie pulled the envelope with the passwords from her pocket while Donald locked the office door and pulled the drapes. Donald then opened the shelving unit just enough to expose the safe embedded into the wall. Annie punched in the safe code and Donald turned the handle and pulled open the door.

Inside the safe, on shelves, were binders of photos, family mementos, a jewelry box, binders of family history, birth certificates, passports, and three-ring binders of home remodeling projects. Annie pulled out a remodeling binder labeled "Office". Inside it showed drawings of the entrance to the secret room and the vault room directly below them. There was a tabbed section showing all of the contractors involved in the project. Donald and Annie both agreed to not mention this particular binder. Donald wanted to take a closer look later, and decided to carry it up to his bedroom to keep it out of view from others.

The other binders showed labels of various remodeling projects such as the cottage, the apartment over the garage, the garage, and just the house in general. Annie made a mental note to look through those binders later.

The jewelry box contained rings, necklaces, brooches, and earrings, all which appeared to be of great value. Annie pulled the jewelry box out and discovered a small hand-written message. The message stated, "In the event of my death, please give this jewelry to Stella Weston, my dear friend and confidante." It was signed Helen Harper and dated just six months ago.

Annie went to the desk drawer and pulled out the medical file. She was just about to go through it when she heard voices in the living room. She gathered everything up and stuffed it in the safe. Donald quickly closed the safe and slid the shelving unit back in place. Annie closed the medical file and handed it to Donald, who was tucking the binder under his sweatshirt. He unlocked and opened the office door. Annie opened the curtains and followed Donald out of the office.

"I thought I heard voices!" Annie said as she approached the kitchen where Stella and Marie were standing.

Donald said hello as he walked upstairs to his bedroom to drop off the binder and medical folder. He decided to hide it under the mattress, just in case someone came into his room. There the material was out of sight, but easy for him to retrieve later.

CHAPTER 15

Sunday Afternoon and Evening

I n the kitchen, Annie showed Stella and Marie the plan for the day. It was eight o'clock in the morning. Annie realized she had not had anything to eat and only one cup of coffee this morning. She made for herself a cup of coffee and one for Donald, who was coming down the stairs to join the group in the kitchen.

At 9:00 AM, the doorbell rang. Annie answered the door to find both Dan and Lizzy standing there dressed for a day of work. Annie asked them inside and showed them the plan for the day. Dan told the group that he asked a few friends from the police department and fire department to help out as well. Donald said there was plenty for the barbecue later this afternoon.

While Dan and Annie went to look through the office, Donald, with Lizzy's help, took charge of the cottage and upstairs rooms. Stella and Marie prepped the food for the barbecue and then lent a hand moving boxes and clearing the rooms. Marie was helpful in cleaning the shelves and floors. It was not long before Annie and Dan joined the group. Dan looked through the files and did not find anything that would help him with the case. He had already subpoenaed the utility and phone files going back six months. He would continue going through those records.

Annie felt guilty not telling Dan about the secret room, but she kept quiet. Until she could find anything that would connect a murderer to Helen, she would just keep it to herself and Donald. Telling Dan would mean a report would be written, the room searched and inventoried, and since the records were public after the investigation was completed, the entire town would be aware of the secret vault room. She did not want to risk that happening.

With such a large group, the cottage, Helen's bedroom, and the guest room were cleared out in no time at all. Stacks were set aside for donation, trash, and give away. Annie was giving away as much as she could to all of the helpers. One of the police officers said she would be happy to take Helen's bed and dresser set. The guest room set went to one of the firemen. Annie was excited about clearing out all of the things she did not want to keep, and decided to take a look at the kitchen and living room and see what she could clear out now. She really wanted to make this a home for her and Marie with new things they picked out together. She wanted Marie to find comfort here.

While Annie was finishing the last of the kitchen cupboard sorting, Stella was taking platters of chicken and beef to the barbecue for Donald to begin cooking. Marie and Lizzy were busy setting up the tables for everyone to sit down and enjoy a meal. One table was set up for the food, plates, cold drinks, and utensils. Donald was joined at the barbecue by Dan. They struck up a friendly conversation about their careers and were having a good time.

Annie stood in the doorway of the kitchen and watched all of the busy activity on the patio. She loved that everyone got along so well, and she truly enjoyed the "family" feeling. Nothing else mattered right now. Annie stepped onto the patio and asked her mother what she could do to help.

"I think we have it all handled. Go get a cold drink and sit down for a while."

Annie did as her mother suggested. In a moment, Lizzy joined Annie at a table. They watched the guys laughing while Donald turned the meat on the grill.

Annie leaned toward Lizzy and they quietly talked about their schedules next week. There were classes to host and supplies to be ordered. Annie talked to Lizzy about hiring another person to help out part-time to take the pressure off both of them. Lizzy was surprised by Annie wanting to hire another person. Annie was just talking about making ends meet a week ago.

"I came into a bit of money, Lizzy," Annie said softly. "I also have the money coming in from the leases on the building downtown when I inherited R&H Enterprises. I was thinking you and I should form a partnership to keep that business running. We need to find time to sit down and talk about it. What do you think?"

"Annie!" Lizzy stated loudly, "I would be very interested in being a part of R&H Enterprises." Conversations stopped and everyone looked at Lizzy and Annie.

"Sorry!" Lizzy, looking a bit sheepishly, took a sip from her glass of iced tea. People turned back to their conversations as if nothing had happened.

Lizzy and Annie talked about how well they work together and Lizzy loved that Annie trusted her to make decisions on her own. Annie knew Lizzy would be excited to get started right away. Annie was not so sure she was as excited. It was a lot of work to run a building management company. She would leave that discussion for another time.

Annie then cleverly moved on to discussing Lizzy and the relationship forming with Dan. Lizzy said it was too early to say, but she hoped Dan would ask her out on a date. She said she would keep Annie up to date on what happened.

"If it works out, I will take full credit for setting you two up," Annie said, "but if it doesn't work out, I had nothing to do with it."

"You did not set us up," laughed Lizzy.

"I happened to arrange for the two of you to be together without either of you realizing it," Annie stated.

"Well, aren't you the clever match-maker!"

Lunch was served and everyone dished up their favorite side dishes to go with the barbecued meat. Stella and Marie had made a potato salad, a coleslaw salad, and brought out chips, and fresh vegetables. It was certainly a feast for a hungry crowd.

Annie and Lizzy were engaged in conversation when Dan got up and cleared his dishes. Donald followed and the two began talking to the other helpers. Stella and Marie were clearing the table and putting leftovers into the refrigerator. Annie and Lizzy were unaware that people were getting up to leave. They wanted to talk a bit more, but were interrupted when Dan walked up and asked Lizzy if she was ready to leave. Annie thanked everyone for coming to help and walked them to the door. Stella wanted to give Annie and Donald some time to themselves, so she and Marie left to go home at the same time Dan and Lizzy left. Dan kept an eye on Stella and Marie to make sure they got into the house without incident.

When they were alone, Donald asked Annie to go upstairs with him.

"Donald, I am really tired tonight. It's been a long day."

"Annie, I wanted to go through the files and binder we found." Donald then said, "You can take the medical file home and read it alone if you are tired."

Feeling a bit embarrassed by jumping to the wrong conclusion, Annie followed Donald upstairs to his bedroom. This was the first time Annie had been in his bedroom. It was neat and tidy. It appeared he was still living out of his suitcase. The bed was made and a laptop was on a small desk in the corner of the room.

"Donald," Annie began, "Are you planning to go back to California soon?"

Donald moved in close to Annie, put his arms around her, and gave her a soft, gentle kiss.

"It all depends on you." He said pulling her in even closer. "I am thinking if you want me to stay, I will move into the apartment above the garage."

"I hope you would not want to stay in the apartment on a 'permanent' basis." Annie said coyly.

"We should sit down and talk about our relationship and where it is leading." Donald began.

Annie sat on the bed, dreading to hear from Donald that he did not want a long term relationship. She visualized in her mind he was about to say he 'was a free spirit and not the marrying kind'. She had heard this before. Her one long-time relationship and six-month marriage with a college boyfriend had ended when she found him and his free spirit cheating on her. That was it. She thought she was done with men...until Donald came along. She would be heartbroken if he left and did not want to return. But she hoped she saw something different in Donald. He seemed to genuinely like her. Her mind was all over the place when she heard...

"Annie?" Donald said, "Did you hear what I said?"

"Oh, I am sorry, Donald." Annie said realizing she was drifting away to that place in her mind where she constantly battled with her thoughts.

"I said I needed to go back to California in a week."

"Of course," Annie said close to tears.

"Will you go with me?" Donald asked.

"Donald, you want me to go with you?" Annie asked surprised he was asking her to move to California knowing she just inherited a house and was now guardian of Marie.

"Yes." Donald said repeating what he had just told her, "I would like you to meet my parents and my dog, Laddie. I thought you might be able to help me pack up my stuff and decide what to move up here. By the way, I have a dog. I hope that won't be a problem. I know we have not talked about it, but he's a great dog."

As Annie sat open mouthed, Donald explained that Laddie, a black Labrador, was about three years old. He pulled out his wallet and showed Annie a photo of Laddie.

Annie was still attempting to process what Donald was telling her, when she just blurted out, "Donald, are you saying you love me?"

Donald stopped talking and looked at Annie. He walked to the bed and sat down next to her. He looked deeply into her eyes and said, "Annie, I fell in love with you the moment I met you, even though I was dripping wet with only a towel wrapped around my waist."

Annie inhaled and tears welled in her eyes as she exhaled slowly. He loves me, she thought. This was the happiest moment in her life. She never thought she would ever find love in her life.

"Oh, Donald," Annie said, hugging him tightly. "Yes, I will go to California with you. Wait...I have to talk to Lizzy first. I don't know if I can get away from the shop. Lizzy and I will need to hire extra help right away. I guess I could close the shop and risk losing sales...."

Donald put his mouth to Annie's and kissed her to stop her from talking any further.

"We will get this figured out." Donald said, "In the meantime, I think we should let our relationship grow naturally. That means, I will live in the apartment above the garage and work in the cottage office until we both agree it is time to move forward."

Annie wiggled closer to Donald and flirtatiously said, "I suppose you will want to visit my bedroom every now and then?"

"Actually, I think we should meet in the secret room and finish what we started," Donald said in a whisper into Annie's ear. He then began kissing her neck, which in turn began the tingly sensation in her body again.

Coming back to reality, Annie jumped up and announced, "I should head back over to my mother's house and take the medical file with me to read." She knew she needed something to distract her from her current lustful thoughts. If she did not stop now, she would be here until morning. She had only known Donald for less than a week. She really must have more control of herself. What was it about him that made her lose her senses?

Donald smiled at her, stood and reached under the mattress for the binder and file folder. He handed the folder to Annie, who grabbed it with both hands. She headed for the door to the hallway.

"Annie, this is the last chance to be upstairs until the remodeling is completed." Donald said in a suggestive tone of voice, "The remodel is a surprise."

"You won't find me up here until then," Annie said stopping and turning her head in his direction.

Donald laughed and followed her out the door and down the stairs. He walked Annie to the front door, and before opening the door, held her close and kissed her good-night.

Annie walked across the street, trying not to skip all the way. At the front door of her mother's house, she turned and waved. She smiled all the way inside the front door.

After taking a shower and putting on pajamas, Annie picked up the medical file and began to read. She reviewed the office visits, medications Helen was taking, diagnosis, brief notes left by doctors, which all led to an indication of heart disease. Annie set the file down and stared into space, thinking about Helen and trying to recall Helen ever mentioning a heart condition. Annie realized she did not have a close relationship with Helen. That was her mother, Stella, who was friends with her. She picked the file back up and continued to read.

Buried deep down into the records was a brief mention of Helen having once had a baby. That surprised Annie, she would have remembered if Helen had ever talked about a baby. Annie decided she needed to ask her mother about the heart disease and the baby. There was definitely a story behind this. Not that it was a reason to kill her, but just out of curiosity she wanted to know. What happened to the baby?

It was getting late, so Annie put the file in her nightstand drawer and got up to brush her teeth before going to bed. She walked out of her bedroom and noticed that the house was dark and quiet. Her mother and Marie had turned in for the night. Too bad, Annie thought, it would have been nice to ask her mother about the baby tonight. She would keep it for another time. It was not important enough at this point to wake her mother.

After brushing her teeth, Annie walked around the house and made sure all the doors and windows were locked. She peered out the living room window to her house across the street. It was completely dark. Donald had gone to bed too. She thought how nice it would be to lay next to Donald in bed. She imagined his warm embrace and the sweet smell of his lingering aftershave. Annie could not imagine being with anyone else ever again. She smiled and walked back to her bedroom.

Callie, her cat, was snuggled into the blankets. Annie attempted to maneuver her legs around her cat, but gave up and decided to sleep in a bit of an uncomfortable position as long as she could. A few minutes later she gave up and moved the cat. A loud growl of disapproval came from Callie.

"It is a queen-sized bed," Annie said while moving Callie over to the other side. "You don't need the entire bed." Callie got up and hopped off the bed to go eat. For the next ten minutes, Annie heard crunching of the nibbles in Callie's food bowl. Callie then went into the bathroom to use the kitty box. Annie could have sworn that Callie was scratching much longer and louder than usual. Annie rolled over and was fast asleep in minutes.

CHAPTER 16

Monday morning

Monday morning was bright and sunny with a cool breeze coming off the ocean. Annie was just about to unlock the door to Ocean Loads of Paper when she smelled the aroma of the freshly baked goods next door. She went straight to Ione's Bakery and Coffee Shop to get her usual coffee and chocolate croissant.

Once inside the crowded shop, Annie moved her way to the back of the line. As she walked forward, searching her bag for her wallet, she bumped into the tall man ahead of her, pushing him into the woman in front of him, causing her to knock over items on a display to her side.

"Oh! I am sorry," Annie exclaimed. As she looked up, she stared into the exasperated face of Dan Surely. Dan turned and apologized to the woman ahead of him and helped to pick up items knocked onto the floor. He then offered to buy her coffee to further apologize.

Turning back, Dan said to Annie, "I should have known it was you."

"Oh, good morning, Surely," Annie said with a big smile on her face as she pulled her wallet out of her bag.

"It's Dan Surely to you." Dan moved forward as the line moved up to the order counter. Dan signaled to the cashier that he was paying for the purchases of the lady in front of him. The lady looked at him wryly, thanked him, and turned to order a large coffee cake 'to go' with her small brewed coffee. Dan turned to Annie and shook his head at her.

"I will reimburse you for that, Dan," Annie said, looking in her wallet and noticing she had very little cash.

"Don't worry about it," Dan said. "I need to talk to you about something. I was on my way to your shop when I stopped for coffee."

"How did you know I would be in the shop so early?" Annie said surprised that Dan would think she was already at work.

"Everyone knows you are always in the shop early on Monday mornings." Dan said, "I find you very predictable."

Annie thought for a moment, was she really predictable? Does the murderer know how predictable she is in her daily life? This sent chills down her spine. Annie thought she should be more alert to her surroundings from now on.

Dan purchased his coffee, paid for the lady who was in front of him, and then asked Annie what she wanted, as he offered to pay for that too. The young girl at the counter pulled out a chocolate croissant and poured a small cup of black coffee. Annie then realized how predictable she really was to people in town.

"Instead of a chocolate croissant, I would like a bear claw," Annie said, hoping to change her ways. Then added in a moment of anxiety, "But since you pulled the chocolate croissant out of the case, just add it to the bag." Okay, she will work on being less predictable tomorrow. Dan shook his head and paid the cashier.

They exited Ione's Bakery and Coffee Shop and walked to Ocean Loads of Paper. Annie stuffed the pastry bag in her tote bag and handed her coffee to Dan to hold. She then fumbled in her bag for the keys to the shop. She pulled out the set of keys and proceeded to unlock the door. They walked inside and Annie locked the door behind her, as her shop did not open until 10:00 AM.

Dan handed Annie her coffee and they walked up to the counter. Annie removed her pastry bag, walked around the counter and into her office, where she placed her tote bag into the bottom drawer of her desk. As she walked back into the shop area, she noticed that Dan had helped himself to the bear claw pastry.

"What did you need to talk to me about?" Annie asked Dan, as she opened the pastry bag and pulled out the croissant.

At that moment, Dan's cell phone rang. He pulled it out of his pocket and answered. It was a few seconds before Dan indicated to Annie that he needed to take the call and walked to the door. Annie came up behind him, unlocked the door, and let him out, locking the door behind him. Dan turned and mouthed through the glass shop door that he would be back later. Annie nodded that she understood.

Grateful for the time alone, Annie checked her schedule on her cell phone and compared it to the calendar on her desk. She had nothing pressing to accomplish today, so she set out to unpack last week's deliveries. This was something she usually did in the evenings after the shop closed as it seemed busy during opened hours. A couple of hours into unpacking, inventory, and pricing the items, and Annie finished with the work. The shop would be opening in a half an hour. She decided to begin creating ideas for cards at the demonstration table. She pulled out some paper card stock, stamps, stamp pads, glue, and glitter.

"Good morning," Lizzy said as she walked through the door with her usual coffee and pastries for the two of them. "The sun is out and people will be all over the boardwalk watching the whales, drinking coffee, and shopping."

"Good morning, Lizzy," Annie said continuing to set up paper to stamp out images with her clear stamps. "How was your evening last night?"

"We talked in his car in front of my house for an hour." Lizzy continued excitedly, "And he asked me out on a real date!" Lizzy walked over to the street side door and unlocked it.

"That is wonderful, Lizzy," Annie said, not really surprised that Dan would have asked Lizzy out on a date.

"Where is Marie?" Lizzy asked Annie, as she hung up her lightweight jacket in the office.

"She said she was not feeling well. Her stomach hurt. She wanted to stay home." Annie informed Lizzy, adding, "Construction is beginning on the house this morning and she is really excited to find out what will happen in her new bedroom. Marie is probably driving Mom crazy wanting to go over to the house to watch the workmen paint her bedroom."

♦ ♦ ♦

Annie was fidgeting with a bottle of purple glitter. The lid seemed to be stuck. She pulled with all her strength to open the lid, when it suddenly gave way and popped open, rocketing glitter up into the air, then reversing direction and cascading down upon Annie's head and the counter area.

The street side shop door chime sounded and Donald walked into the shop. He walked up to Annie and Lizzy at the demonstration table and stood there staring at Annie.

"Don't say a word. Not a single word," Annie told Donald. Annie stood, and shook her head, attempting to shake out the majority of the glitter on the table in her shop. Her head and shoulders were sparkling in the shop lights.

Lizzy, who was laughing, excused herself announcing she needed to get the deposits ready for the bank, walked into the office, and closed the door.

Donald walked up to Annie and gave her a hug and kiss. "You certainly sparkle when I enter the room," Donald said grinning. He then pulled her close and whispered into her ear, "If you want, I can help you get rid of that glitter in the shower."

Annie's body began to tingle again. A shower would be nice, she thought to herself with a smile. A shower with Donald would be even better. Annie was leaning in to give Donald a kiss when Dan walked through the door. Donald and Annie turned to look at Dan.

Dan in turn, stared at the two and said, "Donald, I see you got caught up in one of Annie's mishaps," noticing the glitter everywhere.

"Caught in the aftermath," Donald replied back.

Lizzy walked out of the office carrying a bank bag, a bit more composed than when she walked in and, seeing Dan, lit up like a Christmas tree. She led Dan to the other side of the shop and they talked for a few minutes.

"You little match-maker, you," Donald said to Annie quietly.

"Donald, why are you here?" Annie said, realizing that construction should have begun two hours ago at the house.

"Your mother and Marie are in the house keeping tabs on the workers." Donald said, "I haven't been to the shop, so I told them I was going to visit you. All of the construction people are there with instructions. They have my cell phone number if they have questions."

"You left Mom and Marie alone with the construction workers?" Annie asked skeptically.

In an attempt to be funny, Donald said, "Don't worry. Those are big, strong construction workers. They can protect themselves against your mother and Marie."

Donald's cell phone rang. He answered and listened for a moment. He sighed deeply and said, "I'll be there in five minutes. DO NOT change the plan of the kitchen in the apartment."

Donald looked at Annie and said, "Your mother wants to change the layout of the kitchen in my apartment. I need to go."

"I will see you at home tonight," Annie said smiling, leaning up to kiss Donald.

"I like the sound of that...'see you at home tonight'." Donald kissed Annie and left the shop.

Lizzy walked back to where Annie was and announced she was going to stick around for a few more minutes so Annie and Dan could talk privately. Lizzy went to the office and placed the bank bag back into the safe. She then came back out and went to help a customer who had just entered the shop.

♦ ♦ ♦

Dan asked Annie if they could talk in her office. She led him to the small room and Annie closed the door. They sat down and Dan pulled out a small plastic envelope with jewelry inside.

"The coroner's office took this off of Helen's body," Dan said in a quiet tone to Annie. "Since you inherited her estate, this belongs to you."

Annie took the bag and looked at a diamond necklace and diamond ring with a gold band. It was Helen's wedding set and the necklace Robert had given to her many years ago. Annie remembered she wore the necklace all the time.

"Actually," Annie began, "It belongs to Mom. She inherited Helen's jewelry. I will see that she gets this."

Dan handed Annie a form to release the jewelry to her. She placed the jewelry in her purse, inside the tote bag. It was strange receiving Helen's jewelry. She had no relatives, except Donald, to give her possessions to in the event of her death. Even though Marie referred to Helen as "Aunt Helen", Helen was not related to Marie. Helen was the neighbor of Marie's mother when Marie was younger. When Marie's mother passed away, Helen became her guardian.

Annie found herself drifting away in her mind again. She took a deep breath and signed the form for Dan and handed it to him. Dan took the form and placed it in his leather-bound notebook.

"Annie, I interviewed the person driving the pickup truck with the license plate on the tailgate. He swears up and down he was not in the house, but outside looking for a dog he thought he hit with his truck. The truck actually belongs to his brother-in-law, who is a contractor. The brother-in-law is conveniently out of town on a cruise and cannot be reached," Donald reported.

"He did walk from the back of the house to the truck." Annie said, "I suppose he could have been telling the truth about looking for an injured dog, but then who was inside the house? Both Marie and I saw someone with a flashlight inside the house!"

"I am not sure I believe this guy's story." Dan continued, "I talked with all the neighbors the morning following the burglary, and after I interviewed this guy. No one saw his truck that night. No one has a dog that was injured or even left out that night."

"I saw the truck, Donald." Annie said, "I saw someone in dark clothes with a hood on his head quickly walk to the truck and take off with no lights on. He did not brake to turn the corner."

"At this point, I don't have any evidence to connect him with Helen's death or the burglary. I just wanted to let you know. I have not given up. I am still waiting for the autopsy report. I should hear from the medical examiner soon. The Crime Lab is still processing evidence."

"I'll keep looking through the house and see if I can find anything that may have connected her to someone wanting to kill her." Annie thought to tell Dan about the secret room discovery, but chose to keep quiet for now.

"Let me know if you find anything unusual."

"Dan," Annie began, "Have you found out anything about Helen in your investigation?"

"She was a very wealthy lady with a lot of social activity." Dan said, "She was on many boards for charitable organizations."

"Should I be notifying people?"

"That is up to you." Dan continued, "If you have her address book, it would be a nice gesture to send out a notice."

"What about her purse? Her purse is nowhere to be found." Annie remembered. "Don't you find it strange that her purse is missing? Can you search that pickup truck to see if it is inside?"

"Annie, I must have probable cause to search the truck." Dan said, explaining that he cannot just stop the man and search his vehicle. "Besides, if he took the purse, he could have gotten rid of it by now."

Feeling defeated, Annie talked with Dan about Helen for a few more minutes. As Dan rose from his chair and opened the office door to leave, he turned to Annie and said, "Something will come up. Don't give up hope."

Annie thanked Dan and stayed seated in her desk chair. After a few minutes, Lizzy entered the office. She took the bank bag from the safe and told Annie that Dan was going to drive her to the bank to make the deposits.

"You need an escort to drive to you two blocks to the bank?" We must have a pile of money in that bag!" Annie said.

"Shhh...he's out there waiting for me." Lizzy said grabbing her purse.

It was quiet so far day today. Annie was standing by the cash register, looking out at the ocean beyond the boardwalk when her cell phone rang. It was Donald.

"Hello, Donald," Annie said, "I could use a warm friendly voice right now."

"Is everything okay at the shop?"

"Oh, yes. It is just slow." Annie reported sullenly.

"Would you like me to come down to the shop and keep you company?"

"No, Donald, I am okay." Annie said cheered up that he offered. "Lizzy went to the bank. She will be back soon...I hope. Dan drove her the two blocks to the bank."

"I sense a budding romance."

"Like ours?" Annie questioned. "Do we have a budding romance?"

"More like hot and passionate." Donald said in a deep whisper.

Annie smiled, thinking about the hot passion in the secret room. She was longing for another chance to get Donald in the secret room, but she still wanted to get to know him better before falling madly in love. She had better get to know Donald soon, as she was definitely on the verge of falling madly in love with him.

Donald told Annie that Stella was making dinner tonight, and that Annie should be home no later than 6:15 PM. Annie said she would close the shop by five and be home shortly after. Lizzy walked through the door of the shop as Annie was saying good-bye to Donald.

A few customers entered after Lizzy and began shopping. Annie greeted them and announced she would be happy to answer any questions they might have.

"Annie," Lizzy said walking up to the counter after putting the bank bag away in the office. "I have been thinking about the partnership in R&H Enterprises. If you are serious, we really should get the partnership formed and talk to the store owners currently leasing stores in the building."

"Of course, I am serious." Annie said. "I should contact Mr. Conklin and see if this is something he can handle for us. Lizzy, you can research the business papers looking for ways to keep the lease payments as low as possible? Of course, you should make a decent salary for your work. If you take charge of paying the taxes and insurance on the building, it would be a huge burden off my plate."

"I was thinking the same, as these are our friends as well as shop neighbors," Lizzy said. "Then I would use the salary from the business in lieu of finding a part-time job in the winter months when the shop hours are shorter. I am not asking for much in the way of a salary."

"It should be a fair salary for your work."

"We can work the salary details out later."

Annie and Lizzy continued to talk excitedly about R&H Enterprises. Annie took notes on what they planned to do with the business. She realized she needed to find the place where Helen kept the records. She thought she might try the secret vault first. She did see file cabinets down there and they were locked. She supposed she had the keys in the envelope. And it would be a good opportunity to get Donald downstairs again...

CHAPTER 17

Monday afternoon/dinner

The afternoon proved to be very busy with customers, as predicted by Lizzy earlier that morning. The sun brought out many whale watchers and shoppers. Annie closed the shop at 5:30 PM, when the last of the shoppers left. As she was locking the door, she noticed Donald walking up. She quickly unlocked the door and opened it for him.

"I thought I would walk you home tonight," Donald said giving Annie a kiss on the cheek.

"Well, that was very thoughtful of you." Annie said, "Let me get my purse and jacket and we can be on our way."

Since Lizzy left at five, Annie made sure all the closing chores were finished and followed Donald out the door. She locked up and they began the short walk home.

"After dinner, would you mind helping me downstairs?" Annie asked Donald.

"You want me to help you with something downstairs?" Donald asked suggestively. "Does this involve removing something?"

"Why yes, it does, Donald," Annie said. "It involves removing a lot."

"Are you toying with me?" Donald reached for Annie's hand as they walked.

Annie told Donald about forming a partnership with Lizzy for R&H Enterprises and the need to find the business papers. Annie surmised that the papers were probably in the secret vault with all the other important things of Helen's. She also wanted to get the jewelry box out of the safe and the paintings up to the office, and give it all to her mother. The jewelry and paintings belonged to her mother. There was no reason for Annie to keep them. Donald agreed and said that they should begin right after dinner.

Annie asked how the remodeling was going. Donald told her that the kitchen in his apartment would be completed by tomorrow. He paid extra to have a rush put on the job, and the crew was working hard. He also put them up in a nice resort hotel so they were comfortable and rested for the next day's work. The hotel was not far away, and that meant they could begin work early and on time.

Donald told Annie that the painters were finished with Marie's room and would begin her bedroom tomorrow. The decorator would finish with Marie's room, and he was hoping the paint would be dry enough to keep the project moving along quickly.

As they reached the front door of Stella's home, Donald pulled Annie close and gave her a long, passionate kiss. She melted into his arms and returned his kiss.

The door opened suddenly and Marie stood there looking at the two. "Get a room!" she said.

Annie rolled her eyes and moved Marie through the door.

"We tried, but we keep getting interrupted," Donald said, as he followed the two women inside the house.

♦ ♦ ♦

Donald finished his last bite of meatloaf and exclaimed to Stella that it was the best he had ever had. Stella had outdone herself with meatloaf, mashed potatoes, brown gravy, and a vegetable medley.

Annie thought the bottle of wine was a great compliment, but after her second glass she was getting a bit buzzed. She poured herself a glass of water, and tried to switch between both during dinner. She feared the wine might contribute to enhancing her lust for Donald. After all, she was going to be alone with him in a few minutes in the secret room. Donald added more wine to her glass as if he could read her thoughts.

After dinner, Annie and Donald walked hand-in-hand across the street to Annie's house. Donald unlocked the door and opened it for Annie to walk through. He turned on the lights in the house and locked the front door.

It was nearing eight o'clock in the evening when Donald suggested they get the papers she was looking for and search a bit further for clues to why someone would want to murder Helen. They opened the vault door and entered the room. It was just as they left it. Annie realized there was so much more to the room than she realized the first time they were there. Two bookcases and two credenzas were on the back wall of the room.

Annie walked up to one of the bookcases and pulled out a large cloth bound book. She opened the book and happily discovered it was the journal, handwritten by Helen. She placed the book back on the shelf and looked for the most current journal book. She pulled the book from the shelf and looked at the last page. It was dated the day of her death.

"Donald!" Annie said, "Look what I found."

Annie showed the journal to Donald. She opened the book up to the last page, which showed the date of her death. Donald looked at the journal and paged through the half-filled book. He then looked at the bookcase.

"There are quite a few journals here."

"Donald, I think I will begin with the last one and read them in the reverse order that they were written. Maybe there is something in the journals about why someone would want to murder her." Annie said as she turned to face Donald, "Did you happen to find any business papers for R&H Enterprises?"

"Not yet, but I did find a closet with shipping crates for the paintings, which now belong to your mother."

"That reminds me. Let's get the jewelry case out of the upstairs safe before we leave tonight." Annie grabbed two of the journals to read. She opened the drawers of the credenzas, but found nothing to indicate business records. She looked at Donald perplexed.

With a sudden look of inspiration, Annie said, "Do you think the business was set up in the cottage?"

"I think you may have something there." Donald said, "I had the helpers clear out what was in the file drawers and pack all the records in boxes. The boxes are now in the garage workshop. It is getting late. We can go through the garage boxes in the morning before the construction people get here."

Annie agreed and they left the vault, locked up, and went upstairs. Annie opened the upstairs safe and retrieved the jewelry box for her mother. She added the wedding set given to her by Dan earlier today.

It was after eleven when Donald walked Annie across the street, kissed her goodnight, and waited until she was inside the house and had locked the front door.

Annie set the journals on the nightstand and crawled into bed. She set her alarm for five in the morning. It was going to be tough to get up, but with enough coffee, she should be able to get through the next day.

CHAPTER 18

Tuesday

By five-thirty in the morning on Tuesday, Annie was up, showered, and dressed. She made a cup of coffee and opened the journal she had carried into the kitchen with her. It began in January of this year, but Annie turned to the last day of writing and read each day in reverse order. It was strange knowing the person she was reading about in the journal. Helen spoke fondly of people, wrote about the charities she was involved with, and now and then a little kind gossip of the townspeople.

Barely starting into the end of the March portion of the journal, Annie decided she needed to get over to the garage and sort through the boxes as it was six-thirty already. Lizzy really needed the files to get a handle on R&H Enterprises. Annie made another mental note to contact Charles Conklin, the attorney, after Lizzy reviewed the records.

Sending a text to Donald, Annie asked if it was a good time to come over. He sent a text back saying he was up and looking forward to seeing her. She smiled and grabbed her tote with her wallet and the journal book and walked across the street to the front door of her new home.

Donald had a cup of coffee freshly brewed when she walked through the front door. He handed the cup to her, after giving her a kiss good-morning, and they walked out the kitchen door to the garage. Donald unlocked the shop door and found the room stacked with boxes. Annie and Donald looked at each other exhausted with the thought of searching through all these boxes. With a sigh they dug into the stack.

"This is it!" announced Annie moments later, looking inside a box holding file folders. "Here are all the business records. Let's carry these four boxes to the house."

Donald suggested they put the boxes into the SUV and he would drive her to work and unload the boxes for her. Minutes later they were sitting in the kitchen finishing up a second of cup coffee. Annie then grabbed her tote and Donald picked up the keys to the SUV and they were off to her shop. Donald parked in front of the shop on the street side of the building, and Annie hopped out to unlock the door and turn on the lights. Donald pulled out a small hand cart which held two boxes and wheeled them inside the building.

Once inside the doorway, Annie directed Donald to put the boxes in the office. She watched the vehicle since Donald left it unlocked. Donald came back and loaded the last two boxes and locked up the SUV. After he had delivered the boxes, he gave Annie a kiss and was off to meet the construction workers at the house.

Annie's cell phone rang and she noticed that it was her mother.

"Good morning, Mom," Annie said with a cheerful voice.

"Good morning. I did not hear you come in last night."

"It was after eleven and I was up at five this morning." Annie was about to clarify that she slept in her own bed, but decided she was old enough to not have to answer to her mother.

"We missed you at breakfast." Annie's mother stated.

"I got up early to go over to the house and garage to find the records for R&H Enterprises." Annie continued, "Lizzy is going to partnership with me on the business. This is right up her alley. She is excited and so am I. I needed to find the business records so she can review them."

"Oh? I thought that was what you were doing last night."

"While Donald and I were searching the files in the office, we found some journals of Helen's and the jewelry that she left for you." Annie told her mother. "I have a class today, so I need to set up at the shop. I will be home early today for dinner." Annie did not want to explain what she was doing the night before.

Annie and her mother talked for a minute more and then ended their call. Annie looked around the shop. She realized she forgot to ask if Marie was coming to work today. She decided to let her stay home again.

◆ ◆ ◆

A senior center bus pulled up in front of the store and ten ladies sauntered into the shop using canes, walkers, and one with a wheelchair. Annie greeted them all while they found their usual places at the tables.

"How are you doing, Annie?" said Elsie sympathetically as she began pulling her chair out to sit. She put her bag on the floor and sat down. Elsie was a small, but wiry lady of about 84 years old. One of the oldest of the group, she was a more mothering type of person than the rest. She always seemed to be watching out for her friends.

"We heard about poor Helen." LaVerne said, "I understand her nephew is staying in Helen's house." Laverne was of medium height, thin, and quite outspoken for a lady of her age. She seemed to follow her own rules and had no desire to let people tell her what to do. This gave her the appearance of being humorous by those who did not know her well.

Lorraine moved to a seat next to LaVerne. "It's not Helen's house anymore, Helen left the house to Annie." Lorraine and LaVerne were the closest of friends. She was tall and thin, and was what LaVerne called a "fashion horse". Lorriane loved the newest fashions for women and had the over-stuffed closets to prove it. Lorraine and LaVerne were known to be the instigators mischief. If the seniors were getting into trouble, Lorraine and LaVerne were in the center of it all.

"How do you know that?" Annie stopped what she was doing and stared at the group. She just found out less than a week ago that she had inherited Helen's house.

"Word gets around, dear. It's a small town after all." Lorraine picked up the birdhouse in front of her and exchanged it with a birdhouse across from where she was sitting.

"Oh, I can't sit here," said Millie, "It is much too bright." She got up from sitting in a sun beam and began to look for another place to sit.

Elsie patted the chair next to her, "Sit next to me, Millie." Millie moved next to Elsie and sat down. Millie loved to be with these particular ladies, because they made her laugh. She got wrapped up in their schemes and lived for the adventures. Millie was also the biggest gossip of the group. She seemed to always know who, what, where, when, how, and why.

Annie was walking around the tables and pouring glue into the small bowls next to each occupied seat.

LaVerne picked up a paint brush and was dipping it into the glue and said, "Let's get back to the hunk of a nephew. Annie, are you doing him?"

Annie stood startled and open mouthed at the question, glue pouring over the sides of one of the bowls. Were there cameras in the secret vault? Did someone have access to those cameras? Was someone spying on them? Annie was horrified at the thought.

"LaVerne! That's not a nice thing to say," Elsie scolded.

Annie grabbed a paper towel and began mopping up the spilled glue. She cleaned up the mess and continued filling the rest of the bowls around the table.

"So, Annie, are you having your way with him?" Millie questioned. "I saw you two holding hands, and the late-night visits."

"Oh, my!" was heard around the room. "Tsk, Tsk," was also heard.

Annie then remembered that Millie lived next door to Stella and could see everything when she sat in her chair in the living room. Wait! Did she happen to see the murderer?

"Millie, did you see anyone at Helen's house the night she was murdered?" Annie walked closer to Millie. There was a moment of silence in the room as all eyes and ears were on Millie and Annie at the moment.

"No. I was at my daughter's house in Portland until a few days ago." Millie continued, "I missed the whole thing. What a time to visit my daughter!"

Lorraine chimed into the conversation, "Just imagine if you had been home. You could have seen the murderer!"

"I know!"

Elsie, being the detective of the group, asked, "Was anything taken? I heard there was a burglary the very next day."

Annie was not sure how much information she should be sharing, but realized that these ladies probably knew far more than Dan at this moment. "We cannot find Helen's purse."

"You know who likes to steal purses?" LaVerne asked.

"Yes, Ronnie, Eddie's brother-in-law," Millie spoke up.

"That's right," everyone said in unison.

"He is a terrible person, Annie." Lorraine commented, "He sneaks into people's houses after they've died and steals their valuables before the relatives can make it into town."

"Oh, he's a terrible person."

"Does he drive an old pick-up truck?" Annie asked the group.

"That's not his truck." Lorraine said matter-of-factly while applying glue to the side of her wooden birdhouse, "That truck belongs to his brother-in-law, Eddie Harris. In fact, Eddie would be mad as a rooster if he caught Ronnie in that truck. I've seen him yelling at Ronnie for taking the truck without permission."

"How does he get the keys?" Annie asked.

"He hot wires it," Lorraine answered in a very loud whisper.

"He does what?" asked a lady at another table.

"I said, he hot wires the truck. He has NO keys." Lorraine yelled across the room.

Customers in the shop looked in the direction of the classroom area. Some walked closer to listen as they appeared to be very interested in a display of buttons on a turnstile.

"Where are we on the hot sex with the nephew?" yelled another lady at the table across the room.

"We don't know that the sex was hot. He could have been a dud." yelled back Lorraine.

"Oh, I've had one of those in my time." LaVerne quipped. Everyone spoke in low tones with an acknowledging agreement.

Could this conversation get any worse, Annie thought feeling her cheeks heat up. "Ladies, continue tearing up the paper in small pieces and gluing it to the birdhouse. I will be right back with the coffee. I have donuts too!"

Excited chatter was heard throughout the room as Annie left to get her purse and go to the coffee shop next door. She signaled Lizzy that she was going next door. Maybe by the time she got back they will have forgotten all about the "hot sex" with the "hunk nephew".

Annie stood in line for what seemed like an eternity, but still glad to have a break from the nosey questions from the ladies who loved to gossip. As she made it to the order counter, she ordered a carafe of coffee and a small dark chocolate brownie for herself, which she stuffed into her mouth before she left the bakery.

As Annie stepped into the paper shop, she heard honking emanating from the street side of the shop. She walked to the classroom area to set the coffee down, and realized half her group was missing. She turned to look outside and was shocked to see the ladies across the street at the side of the old pickup truck in question, which reportedly belonged to Eddie and was stolen by Ronnie, Eddie's brother-in-law.

Lizzy walked up behind Annie, who at this time was exiting the shop to find out what in the world the ladies were doing. From what Annie could see, it seemed they were all gathered together at the passenger side door of the truck. People were watching the ladies causing a commotion about something, but she could not figure out what it was.

Suddenly, the ladies stopped arguing and began to walk back across the street, with LaVerne in the lead. She was clutching her side as she walked quickly, as quickly as an older lady with a cane could walk. A car screeched to a halt on the street in front of LaVerne and the man inside laid on his horn.

"Hey, you old crow, watch where you are going or you'll get hit," screamed the man behind the wheel of the automobile.

"Hit me and watch my feathers fly, buddy!" said LaVerne in a threatening tone, raising her cane in the air at the man.

Annie ran to LaVerne and the other ladies and safely guided them across the street to the shop. She mouthed an "I'm sorry" to the man in the car. He roared off down the street after the ladies had crossed safely. The ladies entered the shop and walked to their table. As they were sitting down, the ladies looked at LaVerne.

"Did you get it?" asked Millie.

LaVerne pulled out a medium sized black leather purse from under her blazer. "Of course, I did."

"I knew it was him. He is a terrible person." Millie sat down in her chair, and the ladies followed suit. They went back to their projects, leaving Lizzy and Annie standing there totally stunned by what they had just witnessed.

Annie turned to look out the window in time to see Ronnie get into the truck. He leaned over the seat as if looking for something. He turned, looking straight at Annie watching him in the window. Chills ran through her entire body. Had she just imagined a cold, dark, menacing peer from a murderer? Did he know the ladies took a purse from the truck? His stare toward her ended as he started the truck and quickly left the area.

LaVerne handed the purse to Annie. "It is Helen's, alright. I would know it anywhere."

"She never was without it," Millie reported.

"Look inside the purse and see if her wallet is there," the ladies encouraged Annie.

Annie opened the purse and peered inside. A wallet lay among items within Helen's purse. She pulled the wallet out and looked inside. No money or credit cards were found, but her driver's license and insurance cards were still in their slots.

Lizzy walked up to Annie, holding her cell phone out to signify Annie had a call to take. "It's Dan on the phone. He wants to talk to you."

Annie sighed, "He called you to talk to me?"

"Your cell phone is in the office." Lizzy handed the phone to Annie.

"What the hell happened in town with your senior group?" Dan shouted loud enough that Lizzy could hear him even though the phone was to Annie's ear. "Have you any idea how many calls I've been getting?" Lizzy winced at hearing Dan yelling at Annie.

"They walked outside, because they saw something," Annie said quietly. "I was in the bakery getting coffee for the group and when I came back they were crossing the street, horns were honking, and there was a lot of commotion."

"Keep those trouble makers contained. Do you understand me?"

"I have no control over what they do!"

"Don't make me come down there, Annie."

"Dan, they found the purse."

"What?" Dan quieted down.

"The purse, Helen's purse, they found it." Annie thought it best to give the purse to Dan as soon as possible. It might help calm Dan down. What she did not think about was how the ladies obtained the purse and whether she should be telling Dan. She was going to let the ladies tell Dan that story.

"Now I have to come down there." Dan hung up.

Annie handed the phone back to Lizzy. "I think your boyfriend is mad at me."

"Boyfriend? We haven't even gone on a date yet." Lizzy was thinking about how turned-on with Dan she was at the moment. She liked his authoritative side, even if he was yelling at her best friend. She turned and walked back to the counter when she heard a customer asking for help.

The senior ladies were busily working on their projects when Annie, with a look of determination, walked up to the women and stood, deciding whether she should be mad, concerned, or happy with them.

"What were you ladies thinking?" Annie chose the mad, but concerned approach. "You could have been caught by Ronnie, hurt, or worse...arrested for breaking into the truck!"

"You mean breaking into a stolen truck to retrieve a stolen purse?" said LaVerne, without looking up from her project.

"Yes...I think...YES!" Annie said trying to make sense of the entire situation.

"We saw Ronnie pull up in the truck and go into the hardware store up the block. We decided to grab the opportunity while it was in front of us." LaVerne said matter-of-factly.

"We are little old ladies older than dirt. Who's going to arrest us?" Lorraine looked up at Annie, "Besides, we retrieved the purse, didn't we? We told you it was Ronnie. He steals from dead people."

Annie sat down at the table with the senior ladies, "Do you think he's capable of murder?"

"Who? Ronnie?" Millie said, "He's a terrible person, Annie. Be real careful around him."

Dan arrived and parked in front of the store. He exited his car, paused as he eyed the senior ladies in the classroom through the windows, and drew in a deep breath. He entered the shop, grabbed Annie by the arm and walked her to a quiet spot so they could talk.

"Where is it?"

"I put it in my office and closed the door. I will get it for you."

"While you do that, I can question these innocent little old ladies." Dan was warned about this group of ladies, and he'd had a run-in with them late last week, so he was going to stand firm and not let them take control of the situation.

"I wouldn't tempt fate if I were you, Dan." With that Annie turned and walked quickly to the office to retrieve the purse. She had to think of a way to get Dan out of there before he asked how the ladies found the purse.

Too late! Annie thought to herself as she approached behind Dan. He was questioning the group.

"Tell me again how you found the purse?" Dan asked the group of four who were identified as being outside earlier.

"We found it on the sidewalk," Elsie said meekly.

"I thought you said you found it on the street?"

"The sidewalk is part of the street," Lorraine interjected.

"You did not find the purse, Elsie. I found it," LaVerne announced to Detective Surely, "And I found it in the rickety old truck that Eddie owns. It was unlocked, so I grabbed Helen's stolen purse."

Annie really did not want this to go any further, so as a sure-fire distraction, she stood behind Dan facing the group and pointing to Lizzy, then to Dan, and then curled her middle finger around her index finger indicating with a broad smile she was hoping they would get together. The group apparently did not know about the budding relationship of these two. It was gossip worthy. The group's eyes widened and Dan lost all control from there on.

"You know, Detective Surely," Elsie started, "Lizzy is single. Have you asked her out yet?"

The ladies were huddled together at the table agreeing with Elsie.

"What? This has nothing to do with the investigation," Dan said. "Who really found the purse in the truck belonging to Eddie Harris?

"Wouldn't they make a cute couple?"

"Maybe he's gay!" a lady from another table across the room inserted.

"I am not gay," Dan said turning to the other group of ladies.

"Then why don't you want to go out with Lizzy? She's such a nice girl. She's single, you know."

"And she's not getting any younger either."

Annie held back a giggle.

"I know she's single. That's not the point. I am here to talk about the purse. Can we focus on the purse, please?" Dan getting flustered with the comments turned to Annie.

"I told you not to tempt fate!"

"Give me the purse," Dan said obviously frustrated. "I need to get out of here and go track down Ronnie." Dan reached for the purse and told Annie he would bring a receipt over to her later. He exited the door as the bus began to pull up for the ladies to head back to the senior center.

Having finished with a customer, an embarrassed Lizzy walked up to Annie.

"Now that was enjoyable," Annie said with a smile on her face.

"Annie, you have a mean streak in you."

Annie and Lizzy helped the ladies place their projects on the counter to complete next week. They might have finished if it was a normal class, but today was just not a normal day. When they were finished, the ladies all got onto the bus and they were gone. Annie stood at the window waving good-bye. She was going to need chocolate right now! She walked to her office to dig through her chocolate stash.

♦ ♦ ♦

By five o'clock in the afternoon the shop had quieted down as shoppers would be heading off to dinner. Annie suggested that since they opened an hour early, they should close now. Lizzy was not about to complain with such logic. Lizzy pulled her car up to the door of the shop, and Annie helped her put the boxes in her car. After helping Annie with closing, the two were on their separate ways.

Annie called Donald as she began to walk home. She briefly told Donald about the incident with the ladies and the dark, cold stare from Ronnie. Donald met her half way and they continued home, walking hand-in-hand together. As they approached the house, Annie made it a point to look toward Millie's house. The lights were on even though it was still daylight outside, and Annie could see Millie watching them from the living room window. Annie waved and Millie smiled and waved back.

"What's that all about?" Donald asked Annie.

"That's Millie, one of my senior ladies in my crafting class." Annie squeezed Donald's hand and said, "She and the ladies asked if we were having hot sex or if you were a dud."

Donald stopped, looked at Annie in sheer disbelief, and asked, "You told them that our sex is hot, right?"

"Donald, why would you think I would discuss our sex life with little old ladies when we haven't even had sex yet."

"Rumors run fast in this town. I want to make sure I look good in these rumors."

Annie laughed as they walked into Stella's house for dinner. As Annie was setting her tote bag down, she heard her cell phone ringing. Digging through her bag she pulled out the phone and noticed from the caller ID that it was Dan.

"Hello, Surely," Annie said as she walked into the family room and sat in a chair by the large picture windows overlooking the ocean.

"It's Dan. Call me Dan," Detective Dan Surely stated, sounding a bit less agitated than earlier today. "Patrol found the old truck, but no sign of Ronnie Carter."

"What does that mean?" Annie suddenly got nervous. She remembered the cold, dark stare Ronnie gave her only hours ago.

"It means that Donald and I are going to make sure to secure Stella's house and your house tonight. By the way, what is Stella making for dinner?"

"How do you know I am at Mom's house for dinner?"

"I am parked outside Stella's house. I saw you and Donald enter the house when I pulled up. And when are you not at your Mom's for dinner?"

"True. Mom is making fried chicken, mashed potatoes with gravy and a vegetable. I am not sure what she has planned for dessert." Annie went to the door and opened it to Dan standing on the front porch. She invited him in and stuck her head out the door looking around the neighborhood to see if she could find anything out of place. Nothing seemed out of order, so she tucked her head back inside and closed the door.

Annie found Dan talking to Donald in the kitchen. Stella and Marie were getting dinner on the table. Stella asked Dan to stay for dinner.

He readily accepted the invitation and excused himself to go wash his hands.

As everyone sat down at the dining table, Donald said, "Annie told me about the little incident at her shop today." Donald smiled as he looked at Annie.

"Those ladies are nothing but trouble," Dan said as he passed the gravy to Marie. "I still cannot believe they took the purse from the truck in broad daylight."

"They do like their fearless adventures." Annie looked at Dan, wanting to change the subject.

"How did they know about the purse missing from the murder scene?"

There it was, Annie thought. She probably should have kept her mouth shut. Now Dan is going to think she blabbed it all to the ladies. She had to think of something to say that would not force her to admit she told the ladies.

"They know everything going on in town." Annie thought quickly. "They even know that Ronnie is a terrible man and tends to steal from dead people." At least she was not lying to Dan.

Dan poured water into a glass from the pitcher on the table. "Ronnie is homeless from what I am told around the station. I checked his brother-in-law's house, but he is not home. The neighbor says that Eddie and his wife went on a cruise. They also noticed Eddie's brother-in-law has been going in and out of the house while Eddie has been gone."

"Are you going to check out the house?" Annie asked lifting a forkful of mashed potatoes to her mouth.

"We tried, but the house was locked up. I even listened for sounds inside, but there were none. Patrol looked for evidence of illegal entry, but Ronnie must have a key."

Annie looked at her mother, who was listening intently through the whole conversation. She realized her mother knew nothing of what had happened today. Annie quickly filled in Stella and Marie on the events of this afternoon. She even told them about the cold stare that Ronnie had given her and that the truck was the very one that was seen by her and Marie the night after the murder.

Marie's eyes opened wide and she looked scared.

"It's going to be okay, Marie." Annie said looking back and forth at Marie and Dan. Annie was thinking it might not have been a good idea to discuss this in front of Marie.

"I am scared. What if he comes back here to kill us?" Marie was looking down at her plate and began to slightly rock back and forth.

Donald, who was sitting next to Marie, took her hand and told her that he would protect her. He would never let anyone hurt her. He said that he installed all new locks on the doors of the house, placed cameras all around the outside, and had an alarm installed in the house. It was really safe now.

"But what about being safe in the shop? There is no alarm in the shop," Marie pointed out to the group.

Donald thought for a moment and turned to Annie. "What about the shop? Should we install an alarm in the shop?"

"I am beginning to warm up to the idea after seeing the look in Ronnie's eyes today." Annie replied to Donald.

"It might be a good idea if Donald could walk you to and from work. At least until we find Ronnie and clear up this murder investigation," Dan said to Annie.

"I agree with that," Donald said.

Marie told Stella she did not want to leave her alone. She would stay home and make sure she would be safe. Stella agreed with Marie and said that they could find things to do, like going to the Newport Aquarium, shopping at the outlet mall, and even working on their baking skills. Marie was feeling a bit better now, Annie thought. She made a mental note to thank her mother later.

While Donald and Dan secured both houses, Marie wandered off to the family room to watch television, and Annie helped her mother clean up the kitchen after dinner.

"Mom," Annie said quietly. "I wanted to thank you for stepping up and helping Marie cope with this situation. It means a lot to me to know you support both of us."

"Both you and Marie have to cope with a very difficult situation." Stella closed the dishwasher door and set the controls to begin the wash cycle. "I am glad I can be here to help out. It makes me feel like I have a purpose and I love you both. Marie is family now, and hopefully Donald will be too!"

Donald walked into the kitchen with Dan at his heels. Both men had completed their task of checking the houses and making sure they were secured.

"Is there anything for dessert?" Donald asked, looking at the kitchen counter.

"I can dish up some ice cream." Stella said in response as she walked to the freezer and pulled out a carton of chocolate ice cream. "Would anyone like sundaes?"

Marie entered the kitchen and announced she would like a sundae. Annie, Donald, and Dan all chimed in agreement. Marie opened the cupboard door and pulled out toppings of various types, and then retrieved the chocolate sauce and whipped cream from the refrigerator. Stella, at Marie's side, grabbed the maraschino cherries. Everyone gathered around the breakfast bar and while Stella dished up the ice cream in small bowls, each person added their favorite toppings and whipped cream.

"Lizzy would love this," Dan exclaimed.

Annie smiled, "You seem to like her."

Dan stopped and looked at Annie. "I would like to see more of her, but right now it is important for me to keep my mind on the case."

"Have you gone out on a date yet?" Annie asked quietly.

"We are going out on Saturday night for dinner and a movie." Dan picked up his sundae and went to the dining table to join the rest of the group.

Stella looked at Annie and said, "When are you and Donald going out on a date?"

Annie suddenly realized she and Donald had never been on a date. Was she so busy she could not fit a date in her schedule? Annie turned and looked at Donald eating his sundae at the dining table. He was talking animatedly with Marie and both were laughing. Dan jumped in with a comment and all three of them laughed out loud. Annie and Stella watched and admired the new family dynamic at work in front of them. Annie chided herself for not inviting Lizzy to dinner.

Dan left after he finished his sundae. Annie gathered the dishes and rinsed them in the sink. She stacked the dishes up for the next load to wash. She then joined the group in the family room.

After a quiet evening watching television with Marie, Stella, and Donald, Annie crawled into bed around 9:00 PM, continuing to read the journal written by Helen. So far just daily happenings, nothing out of the ordinary happened in her life. Only one thing stood out that Helen kept mentioning, and that is about a man who was harassing her about Robert. She did not go into detail, but mentioned the man was continuing to harass her.

CHAPTER 19

Wednesday Morning

Waking up to a meowing cat, Annie realized she had fallen asleep while reading the journal. She looked at her clock and jumped up when she noticed it was seven in the morning. She had made arrangements with Donald to walk her to the shop at seven this morning. Annie took a quick shower and got dressed. How could she have overslept? This was not like her at all. Was the pressure getting to her? Her mind was reeling with questions as she put on her socks and shoes. She left her room a mess and ran out to the kitchen.

Stella, Marie, and Donald were sitting at the kitchen table eating breakfast. They all looked up at her when she ran into the kitchen.

"Was anyone going to wake me up?" Annie said grabbing her favorite Disney mug from the cabinet above the coffee machine.

"I offered, but your mother said you should sleep for another hour," Donald said. He took a bite of the crispy bacon in his hand. "I think she was afraid I would crawl into bed with you."

"Let's not have that kind of talk in front of Marie," Stella said in a motherly scolding fashion to Donald.

"Get a room," Marie piped into the conversation.

"Enough, all of you," Annie said sitting down at the table. "I haven't had my coffee yet." Annie helped herself to bacon and eggs. As she ate, she thought about the day ahead of her and realized she had no classes on Wednesdays. This was a good day to catch up on anything that needed her attention. She wondered how many applicants Lizzy had lined up for interviews. She looked forward to finding a responsible person to work in the shop.

The group was silent until Annie spoke up, "What is everyone doing today?"

"Marie and I are going to the shop to help Lizzy with shipments while you interview applicants for a new employee," Stella said. She reached for her coffee cup and took a sip.

"I am going to put those supplies on the shelves," Marie said smiling. "That is my job today."

"I am going to ask you out on a date," Donald said. "How does tomorrow night sound? We can go to that fancy restaurant here in town."

Annie eyed Stella suspiciously. Stella tried not to make eye contact with Annie. She took a sip from her coffee cup and then picked up her fork, continuing to eat. Annie thought she detected a slight smile forming on Stella's face.

"I have a class Thursday afternoon, but I can be home and ready by seven."

"Great!" Donald picked up his phone and added their date night to his calendar. He helped himself to more bacon and eggs. Noticing his coffee cup was empty he got up and made another cup of coffee.

"Anyone else need more coffee?"

Both Stella and Annie said they were good. Marie asked if Donald would bring the orange juice bottle to the table. Donald picked up the bottle of orange juice from the refrigerator and his coffee then walked back to the kitchen table.

Stella admired the way Donald felt comfortable with her family. She loved the idea of having a son-in-law like Donald. Hopefully a date with Annie will move the relationship further along. It was only a matter of time.

Donald drove Annie, Marie, and Stella to the shop, as he needed to run errands afterward. He dropped them off and proceeded into Newport. He was picking up the last items for Annie's bedroom. It was to be finished by Friday. Stella was going to help him on Thursday to move just enough of Marie and Annie's belongings to their rooms to get them settled on Friday. He had not yet moved into the apartment over the garage, but planned to do so after his trip to California.

It was after nine o'clock in the morning when Annie, Stella, and Marie entered the shop. Lizzy was already busy with applications, schedules, and setting up to open the shop at ten.

"Good morning!" Lizzy set her paperwork down. "Donald sent me a text message saying you were running late."

"I don't know what's gotten into me," Annie remarked. "I hope the rest of the day goes better."

"The first applicant will be here at ten." Lizzy added, "Get a cup of coffee and whatever chocolate you need to get you ready for the long day of interviewing."

Annie smiled and noticed a box of donuts sitting on the counter. She reached in and pulled out a chocolate croissant. Marie pulled out a maple bar. She asked Stella if she wanted a donut, but Stella passed. Stella said she would go next door to the bakery and pick up coffee for the group. Marie went with her.

"So tell me what the plan is for interviewing these applicants," Annie asked as she sat on a chair and ate her croissant.

"Here is the first applicant," Lizzy said, handing the application to Annie.

Annie skimmed over the paper and noticed that the woman had no experience in retail and had not worked in ten years. Although this was not a deal breaker, what she saw listed next was bit unexpected. She listed her education as having a Master in Business Administration, but she never worked in any business field. There was no explanation or information of what she had been doing since she graduated from school. It was resumes like this that raised red flags with Annie.

Lizzy unlocked the doors at nine-forty-five in the morning, as there was a line forming at the door. Annie was eager to find out if her MBA applicant was one of the people waiting to get inside. That would be a good sign. As it was, her first applicant did not arrive until ten-fifteen, and she was dressed to the nines in corporate office attire, which she did not look comfortable wearing. Being tardy for an interview was not a good sign.

Ms. MBA was stiff and stilted in her answers to questions. She actually wanted to ask more questions about the shop than give answers to the questions asked of her. The interview was ended in fifteen minutes, as the next applicant arrived five minutes early, and Annie was not going to make her wait. She had made the effort to be there on time.

♦ ♦ ♦

By noon, Annie and Lizzy had interviewed four applicants, none of whom were a match for the shop as a full-time employee. Annie was getting discouraged when the fifth applicant failed to show up at all.

"I never thought it would be so difficult to find a person with a little bit of retail experience." Annie shoved the previous applications in the "NO" file and realized they were through with interviews for the day. This was not going well.

Lizzy suggested she get some Chinese food for the group for lunch. Annie grabbed her purse and pulled out money to give to Lizzy. If Lizzy was going to make the food run, Annie was going to pay for the food.

Stella was ringing up a customer sales and Marie was straightening shelves when Annie took a moment in her office. Her cell phone rang, and when she looked at the caller ID she noticed it was from Donald.

"Hi, Donald," Annie said cheerily, hoping that Donald was calling to say the house was finished. "I hope you are calling with good news. We interviewed all morning with no luck."

"That is why I called," Donald said excitedly. "I was hoping you had not hired anyone yet. I have the perfect person for your shop."

"What? What do you mean?"

"The decorator's daughter is 20 years old and looking for a full-time summer job to make money for college tuition. She is very responsible, has retail experience, and crafts with paper as a hobby."

"When can we meet her?" Annie poked her head out of the office to see if Lizzy was there. Disappointed that she was still out, Annie stepped back into her office and closed the door. Annie realized that Lizzy would be a while since she was getting Chinese food. It always took longer during lunch time to pick up food.

"She is on her way over as we speak," Donald said. Annie could hear someone talking in the background. "I need to take care of some last-minute details here. Call and let me know what you think of Daisy."

"Thank you so much, Donald. I will call as soon as Lizzy and I make a decision."

Annie hung up her phone and walked out of the office. It was at that time a young woman with long light brown hair entered the shop and asked Stella if she was Annie. Annie walked up to the counter and introduced herself. Daisy, in turn, introduced herself to Annie. She told Annie that Donald Harper sent her over to fill out an application for a job interview. Annie instantly liked Daisy and handed her an application to fill out. Daisy took a seat in the classroom area and began filling out the application.

Fifteen minutes later Lizzy walked through the door with lunch. She placed the food on the counter and walked to the office to put her purse away. There she found Annie with a big smile on her face.

"You look like you have something you just can't wait to tell me!"

"You know me so well," Annie said standing up and closing the office door. "I think I found our new employee. Actually, Donald found her. She is the daughter of our decorator and is looking for a summer full-time job to pay for college tuition."

"So far it sounds good. Tell me more," Lizzy said in her business tone of voice.

"I have her filling out an application in the classroom area right now. She is 20 years old, has retail experience, and is a crafter!"

As Annie and Lizzy spoke, Stella knocked on the door and entered to say that Daisy was finished filling out the application. Annie smiled and led the way out of the office to introduce Lizzy to Daisy.

As the three were walking outside to sit at a table on the boardwalk to interview Daisy, Annie turned to Stella and Marie and asked them to set up lunch in the classroom and they would be in to eat after the interview. It did not take long to make the decision to hire Daisy. She was going to be a perfect fit in the shop. Annie asked Daisy if she would like to join them for lunch. Daisy readily agreed and they all walked back into the shop.

Lunch time was quiet for the most part in the shop, which gave the group time to get to know Daisy. She told them of her plan to get a Bachelor in Psychology and a Master in Special Education. Even though she had scholarships for tuition, and her parents offered to pay any additional costs, she decided she had to make up the difference herself. As Daisy spoke, Annie realized Daisy was willing to work hard for a future goal.

Daisy talked about being a crafter from a very young age. She would make paper beads, cards, and was now attempting various quilling projects. She pulled out a card with quilling on the front from her purse. Everyone was very impressed with the difficulty of the pattern, especially Annie who thought Daisy would easily fit right in with all of them.

Daisy seemed quite interested in Marie and they talked about many things in general. Annie felt good that Daisy was comfortable with Marie. Not a lot of people were when they met Marie due to Marie having Down Syndrome.

As the group got to learn more about Daisy, Daisy began to feel more at ease with the group. She even told Marie that she had a brother who had Down Syndrome. He was a year older than Marie and was also looking for employment. Marie seemed to perk up with this information. She asked Daisy if her brother had a girlfriend. Annie and Lizzy looked at each other. Stella smiled. Daisy told Marie that he did not. Marie smiled and shyly looked down at her food.

"What is his name?" Marie asked while taking a sip from her bottled water.

"William," Daisy answered. "I hope you will get to meet him soon."

"I would like to meet him."

Annie stood and began clearing the table of food containers. Stella and Lizzy helped and the table soon showed no effects of food having ever been on the crafting table.

Annie asked Daisy to follow her to the office. She and Daisy finished up paperwork for employment and talked about various duties Daisy would be performing.

"When would you be able to start work?" Annie asked of Daisy as she put a label on a file folder for the paperwork she had just completed.

"I am ready to begin anytime," Daisy said with excitement.

"Okay, let's plan for tomorrow morning at ten," Annie said standing up and walking Daisy out of the office. "I look forward to working with you, Daisy."

"Thank you for the impromptu interview and lunch. I think I am really going to like working here." Daisy walked up to Stella, Marie, and Lizzy and expressed that it was a pleasure to meet all of them. She said good-bye to Annie and was out the door.

"Well, Lizzy, I think that this day is turning out much better than I expected a few hours ago," Annie said as she noticed the delivery truck pull up outside the shop. She walked over to the door and opened it for the young man with a utility cart full of boxes for the shop. Lizzy agreed while she was printing papers off the computer for Stella and Marie to check in the supplies that had just arrived.

Annie walked to her office and pulled her cell phone to call Donald. She was so excited to tell him about Daisy being the perfect person to work in her shop.

"Hello," answered a female voice.

"Uh, I am sorry. I may have dialed the wrong number." Annie hung up the phone. Wrong number, she thought to herself. She used the phone number she had listed in her cell phone. She did not dial the number, she just pressed the button. Who was the woman answering Donald's cell phone?

Annie jumped when her cell phone rang. She looked at the caller ID. It was Donald. Annie let it ring for a few rings, not really sure she wanted to answer it. Feeling pressure from the ringing phone, she answered it.

"Hello?" Annie answered coldly.

"Annie? Did you call me just now?"

"Yes, Donald. I called and a woman answered," Annie stated objectionably. "Why is a woman answering your phone?"

"Annie, I was up on a ladder adjusting the camera on the porch outside. My cell phone was on the kitchen table. Ellen just answered it for me."

"Who is Ellen?"

"Ellen is the decorator."

"I thought the decorator was a man named Alan." Annie was suddenly feeling really ashamed and silly getting caught feeling jealous.

"Annie?"

"Yes, Donald?"

"I have never given you any reason to doubt me," Donald said quietly. "What's going on?"

"Oh, Donald, I am really sorry. I was just thrown for a loop, because I was so excited to call and tell you that we hired Daisy, and then a woman answered. It just took me back in time to depressing days."

"I am flattered you were jealous, but I will never give you a legitimate reason to feel that way," Donald said. "Let's forget the whole thing. Daisy called her mother...Ellen, and told her that she was hired. She is very excited to work at, what she told her mother, a really fun place."

"I think Marie is excited to meet William, her brother."

"So, I heard," Donald said. "Annie, I have some errands to run this afternoon, and probably won't be back until dinner. I am going with Dan and he just pulled up in front of the house. I need to go now. Ask Stella to hold dinner for us. Invite Lizzy."

Annie heard the doorbell and said, "Good-bye, Donald." How strange that Dan would ask Donald to help him run errands. Then Annie remembered that Dan was looking to buy a house. He was living with his biological mother since he moved back to Bridgewater Harbor a couple of weeks ago. Annie knew Dan was anxious to have a place of his own.

Annie grabbed a tissue and blew her nose. She really felt stupid now. How in the world could she have thought such a thing about Donald? She waited a few minutes, checking her email on the computer, and then went back out into the shop.

The shop was quiet now and it seemed like a good time for Annie to get her supplies ready for her class tomorrow.

CHAPTER 20

Wednesday afternoon

I t was two o'clock in the afternoon and Annie was all set up for her class the following day. She cleaned the classroom and set up project packets for each registered participant. Annie always made a few more packets in case last minute people arrived or someone brought a friend. She had fifteen people signed up for the class, so everything had to be ready so that the class would go off without a hitch. At least this wasn't a class with the senior ladies. Annie was not sure if she wanted to repeat that day anytime soon.

Stella and Marie were finished with their unpacking project. Lizzy helped break down the cardboard boxes and took them to the recycling bin outside at the end of the building. While Lizzy was outside, Stella announced that she was going home. Marie wanted to stay at the shop and continue to work. Annie had lots of projects for Marie to work on and having Marie in the shop this afternoon would be a great help to Annie.

Lizzy bounded into the shop. Annie, Stella, and Marie turned to see Lizzy bent over trying to catch her breath.

"Lizzy, what in the world is going on?"

"I...just...saw...Ronnie...by the...trash bins," Lizzy said between breaths. "I ran all the way back here to tell you."

"What?" Annie went to the office to get her cell phone. "I'll call Dan," Annie said walking back with her cell phone in hand. She hit the button to call Dan's cell phone. The answering machine came on immediately. She left a message for Dan to call her.

Annie asked Stella to stay at the shop for a few minutes longer while she and Lizzy went back to the dumpsters to see if Ronnie was still there. Stella began to object to Annie and Lizzy going after Ronnie, but it was too late, Annie and Lizzy were out the door and quickly walking down the boardwalk. Marie wanted to go with them, but Stella was adamant that she stay in the shop.

Walking past Ione's Bakery and Coffee shop, Annie and Lizzy could smell the aroma of baked goods in the air. Annie wanted to forget Ronnie and make a bee-line for the bakery. She did not think Lizzy would go for such an idea. They walked past the gift shop, where Bonnie was standing at the door wondering why Lizzy was running to Ocean Loads of Paper a few minutes ago. They walked quickly by Bonnie and continued down the boardwalk.

The girls walked quickly past the Candy and Carmel shop, which was later expanded to include a 1950's style malt shop serving the best burgers in town. As they walked along the boardwalk, Annie noticed a dress in Joyce's Boutique and Natural Fiber Clothing shop. She took a long look at the dress in the window and decided she needed to visit Joyce's shop before the dress was gone.

Next was Spencer's Art Gallery, formerly Wells Art Gallery. Local artists displayed various works of art ranging from paintings, pottery, glass floats, wood art, to paper art. Annie loved to browse through the gallery now and then. She made a mental note to take Donald there someday.

The last two shops on the boardwalk before reaching the dumpster enclosure were the Pet Gift Shop owned by a young man named Travis, and Debbie's Quilt Shop, a popular place for locals to pick up just about anything needed to make a quilt and more.

As Lizzy and Annie reached the fenced off area where the dumpsters for the businesses on the boardwalk were kept, they quietly approached and stopped to listen for any sounds. Not hearing any, they looked at each other and Annie signaled that they should open the doors and check inside.

Lizzy, with Annie at her side, began to open the double doors. Just as she pulled the door toward her, Ronnie came out forcefully pushing the door outward. Lizzy jumped to the side missing Ronnie pushing pass her, but Annie was not so fortunate. The door hit Annie hard in the right shoulder and knocked her to the ground. Lizzy screamed and raced to Annie's side. Ronnie ran off down the street and out of sight.

Lizzy carefully helped Annie up to her feet. Annie brushed off her slacks and shirt. Annie realized she was going to have a bruise and made Lizzy promise not to tell anyone, especially Dan, what happened. Annie really did not want to get a lecture from Dan at this time. Lizzy agreed and they decided to look around the dumpster enclosure to see if Ronnie left anything behind. Lizzy kept watch while Annie checked the area out. Nothing looked out of place so Annie and Lizzy left.

Annie was feeling a lot of pain in her shoulder, but was going to attempt to hide any hint of injury from her mother and Marie. If they knew what happened, Annie's mother would be on the phone to Dan in seconds. Annie told herself that she would be fine if she could get some ice on her shoulder.

The fire department was one block down the street and the paramedic truck would have a disposable ice pack. Annie and Lizzy walked there and the firemen insisted they check her shoulder out. When asked what happened, Annie just said she fell and hit her shoulder. She did not elaborate on how the injury occurred. The ice pack felt wonderful and Annie told the firemen she had to get back to her shop.

Approaching the shop, Annie removed the ice pack and told Lizzy that she wanted to convince Marie to go home with her mother. If Marie found out about Annie's shoulder, she would not keep it a secret from Annie's mother. Lizzy agreed as they walked through the shop door to an anxious mother awaiting details.

After telling the two women about seeing Ronnie run out of the trash enclosure and how they were not able to find out where he went, Stella decided to go home and start making plans for dinner. She asked Marie to walk home with her, and Marie agreed. Stella told Marie that they should stop by the bakery shop first to pick up a dessert for dinner. They were out the door, and Annie was placing the ice bag on her shoulder again.

Lizzy convinced Annie to go to the office and sit down for a while to ice her shoulder. Annie was not about to complain and was so appreciative to have a friend like Lizzy. Annie walked to the office and pulled her purse out of the bottom drawer. She searched her purse for aspirin and finally found a bottle. Taking two pills from the container, she took them with the bottled water sitting on her desk.

Annie sat down in her chair and began lecturing herself on the dangers of chasing murderers. What was she thinking? If Donald or

Dan found out, she would never hear the end of it. What if her mother found out what happened? Annie was torn between admitting the truth and maybe just letting it go. Right now, she was going with letting it go.

After twenty minutes of resting in the office, Annie felt much better and walked back out into the shop area. It was quiet and there were no customers in sight. Lizzy was on the computer working on schedules for the next week.

"How are you feeling?"

"Much better now," Annie smiled and said. "I think I will survive, unless Dan finds out."

"We should really find a way to tell Dan that we saw Ronnie," Lizzy suggested. "I think it is important for Dan to know that he is still around town." Lizzy did not want to keep such secrets from Dan so early in their relationship. Annie understood how dishonesty could cause the relationship to dissolve quickly.

Annie agreed and said she would find a way to tell Dan this evening at dinner. She played the scenario in her head... 'Oh, by the way, Dan, Lizzy and I ran into Ronnie today. Well, actually, he ran into me.' She decided she was not going to lie to Dan. If the subject came up, she would tell him the truth. He needed to know that Ronnie was in the area. It's not like she did anything wrong. She just went to the dumpsters. She did that every day. Yeah, that sounded good, Annie said to herself.

It was nearing five o'clock and the shop was quiet. The weather outside was overcast and cool due to the wind. People were not out on the boardwalk and were probably heading off to dinner somewhere. Annie and Lizzy decided to close a half an hour early and began closing procedures.

The two women were walking to Stella's house when Annie suggested they stop by her house and see if Donald was there. They walked up the front steps and tried the front door. It was locked. Annie pulled out her house key and inserted it into the lock. It unlocked easily as she pushed the door open. They entered to a quiet house. All the lights were off. Donald had not returned home yet. Annie and Lizzy walked through the kitchen to the backyard. All was as it should be. They walked back through the house and to the front door. Annie locked the front door and they walked across the street to Stella's house.

♦ ♦ ♦

The doorbell rang at six forty-five in the evening. Annie walked to the front door and looked out the peep hole. Annie opened the door to Dan standing before her. She greeted him and asked him inside. They stood in the hallway when Dan suddenly reached out and grabbed Annie's right shoulder. Annie cried out and winced in pain. Dan took Annie by the arm and pulled her outside on the front porch.

"I got a call from a friend at the fire department today," Dan stated. "What happened?"

Donald crossed the street and walked up at the same time Lizzy opened the front door and exited to the porch, standing next to Annie.

Annie looked at Donald and then to Lizzy. Lizzy nodded to Annie that she should tell Dan what happened. Annie took a deep breath and told Dan about seeing Ronnie in the dumpster enclosure. She told Dan and Donald about Ronnie pushing the dumpster enclosure gate into her shoulder and knocking her down as he ran away.

Dan realized that Ronnie was homeless and hiding from police. He got on his cell phone and reported the sighting of Ronnie. He asked that a police officer check the local dumpsters during the night in case Ronnie returned. After a few minutes of conversation, Dan ended the call. The group walked into the house, with Lizzy and Dan in the lead.

Donald pulled Annie back and drew her close to his body. He asked if she was truly okay. She said she was a bit shaken, but realized that she would need to be more careful about her surroundings until Ronnie was caught.

"I just found you," Donald said. "I don't want to lose you. Please be careful."

Annie kissed Donald and they entered the house. Lizzy was helping Marie place dinner on the table. Stella was busy getting food in serving dishes. Annie offered to help, but Stella told her to sit down and relax. She had plenty of help. Annie suspected that someone had told her of her injured shoulder.

Dinner talk was of the new employee and how well she was going to work out in the shop. Getting her trained would be the big priority. It would leave Lizzy free to work on R&H Enterprises and Annie to create more classes, and even have Daisy teach some of the classes. That left Marie to learn how to ring up sales for customers. Marie was very happy to be included in all of the excitement over the new girl.

Stella had been quiet during dinner. Dan noticed and asked how she was doing. Stella smiled, took a sip of her wine, and passed the platter of meat to Dan. "You looked thin. You should eat more," Stella said.

"You did not answer my question. Is everything okay?"

"Millie, next door, telephoned me today." Stella picked up her glass of wine and took another sip, then picked up her fork, pushed some food around on her plate while she spoke. "She was in downtown Portland with her daughter today. She saw you and Donald. What were you two doing?"

Donald and Dan both looked at Stella at the same time.

"Running errands, picking up items for the house, you know, stuff like that." Donald said while helping himself to more potatoes. He then passed the potatoes to Dan.

Annie looked up in time to see an exchange of looks between Donald and Dan. She looked at Lizzy, who also noticed the looks between the guys. Something was definitely up between the two of them.

"You both went to Portland today?" Annie looked from Donald to Dan.

"Yes." In an attempt to avoid further questioning, Donald said, "I believe you will be able to move your things into your house on Friday."

"Really? I am looking forward to seeing the rooms." Annie was actually excited to see what the second floor of the house looked like. She had been really good at not taking a peek during construction, but it was not easy. "Is your apartment finished?"

"All completed," Donald said.

"Can we all go over and see it tonight?" Annie asked.

"I want to see my room," Marie exclaimed.

"Friday," Donald emphasized. "I was thinking we might have a pizza party night to celebrate. Dan and Lizzy are invited too!"

"Pizza...I'm there," Dan stated. "What time do you want us?"

"What do you think, Annie? Six o'clock?" Donald asked.

"Sounds good to me," Annie said as she lifted her wine glass in a salute motion. "Marie and I should be home from the shop by then."

"I can't wait. I really want to see my room today," Marie said smiling. She was more excited than Annie.

"Like Annie, you must wait until Friday," Donald said to the young woman sitting next to him.

The group finished dinner and Stella announced she would bring dessert to the family room. She and Marie prepared plates of apple pie with ice cream on top of each slice. Marie sprinkled chopped walnuts on the ice cream. As Marie carried in the plates of pies, Stella carried in a tray with a carafe of coffee and cups. Dan and Donald jumped up from their seats and assisted the ladies with the trays.

There was a lot of exciting chatter about Annie's house remodeling being completed. Once the group quieted down, Annie expressed her concern of moving out of Stella's house. She asked her mother if it was going to be a huge adjustment. Stella said she was keeping busy and would probably not be as lonely as she originally thought. Donald and Stella shared a look. Annie was wondering what secrets were being kept from her.

It was a hour later when Marie yawned and said she was going to bed. She said good-night to everyone and walked to her bedroom. Stella stood and said she was a bit tired and was going to her bedroom to turn in early.

Lizzy and Annie cleaned up the dessert trays and coffee cups and took them to the kitchen. Lizzy said she was going to call it a night and asked Dan to take her home. Annie said she was tired and may just go straight to bed.

Annie walked out of the kitchen and saw Dan talking to Donald at the front door. Dan was waiting for Lizzy. She didn't need to ask him, he was expecting to take her home due to the hour of the evening, and Annie suspected due to the two becoming a couple.

Annie and Donald watched the two leave and walk to Dan's car. As they left, Annie turned to Donald and said, "Are you sure I can't come over and have a little peek before Friday?"

"You can have a peek, but not of the bedrooms upstairs," Donald said teasingly. He leaned in and kissed her then said good-night.

Annie stood in the doorway until Donald reached the house and walked inside.

CHAPTER 21

Thursday Morning

The phone was ringing while Annie stretched her arm across the nightstand to pick up her cell phone. Through sleepy blurred vision, Annie could see the time on her clock read 4:39 AM. Who in the world would be calling at this hour, Annie groaned. Her vision cleared and she could see it was Lizzy.

"Hello? Lizzy, is everything okay?"

"Hi, Annie," Lizzy said apologetically, "I just could not wait to tell you."

"Tell me what? Are you and Dan getting married?"

"Don't be ridiculous." Lizzy said, "We haven't been on more than a few dates. Why would you say that? Have you heard something I haven't? Of course, if Dan had asked me I would have said yes, but I doubt that is going to happen anytime soon."

"Lizzy!"

"Yes?"

"You sound like me having a conversation with myself in my head. Snap out of it. Tell me why you called."

"Oh," Lizzy said excitedly. "I have been going through the R&H Enterprise files. Annie...you don't own a building...you own buildings. I am placing an emphasis on 'buildings', plural!"

"What?" Annie just about dropped the phone. "What are you talking about?"

"I am going through the boxes of records and came upon files of the individual shop owners. Suzette's Bed & Breakfast has a file, as well as the Chinese restaurant and the hardware store down the street from your shop. As I dug further into the files, I found the information of the deeds and ownership of the buildings mentioned being in a safe in the vault. Do you know anything about a vault?"

"Um...I know there is a safe in the house," Annie said without wanting to give too much away. "I will check it out this morning and let you know."

"That would be great. Annie, this changes the whole dynamics of the business. I need to be a full-time manager of the accounts."

"Lizzy, have you been up all night going through those records?"

"What time is it?"

"Four-thirty in the morning," Annie said, looking at her clock, it was actually four forty-five in the morning now.

"Wow!" Lizzy said, not realizing she had called Annie so early.

"Why don't you take the day off and get some sleep. I can handle the shop."

"I will be in this afternoon. I can't wait to tell you about what I have been discovering about this business."

It was too early to feel excited about being a property owner, Annie thought. She needed a shower, coffee, and a chocolate croissant. Annie stayed in bed for another half an hour running through her past week of activities. It was mind boggling. She just wanted her life to get to a normal state. So much was happening recently. She threw the blankets off and sat up.

Callie was not about to get up from her cozy warm blanket, and only opened one eye slightly to watch Annie crawl out of bed and head to the bathroom.

A long hot shower was not helping much to revive Annie this morning. She had a fitful night dreaming of her new bedroom. It was a large open space and she kept trying to find Donald, but could only hear his voice. She kept telling him that the bedroom was much too big. He assured her that it was the perfect size.

Annie thought about the dream in the shower and was wondering if she might be suppressing thoughts that Donald wanted to keep his distance from her by living in the apartment over the garage. It is just a silly dream she thought and turned the water off.

Just as Annie finished dressing, she noticed a text message on her cell phone. It was from Donald.

"I thought you might be up early. Would you like to come over for breakfast?"

Annie sent a text that she would be over shortly after she put nibbles in Callie's food dish. She filled the kitty dish and wrote a note to her mother as to her whereabouts. She said she would be back before nine o'clock to pick up Marie and walk to work. It was six o'clock already.

Annie grabbed her purse and jacket and walked out the front door, locking it behind her. She peered up and down the street for anything unusual or out of place. Everything seemed normal for her street. She walked across the street and let herself in the house.

Donald walked down the stairs and greeted her with a kiss. He pointed to the kitchen table where two cups of coffee and a plate of chocolate donuts and chocolate croissants lay. Annie sat down and pulled a croissant off the platter and onto her plate in front her. Donald had read her mind, or was she being predictable again?

Donald began the conversation with small talk. He seemed a bit nervous, which was strange behavior for him. Annie listened to him ramble on about something unimportant. Enough, she thought.

"Donald, what is going on with you?" Annie put her croissant down and looked straight at him. "Dan and you are acting peculiar. Mom and you are giving each other strange looks. I am beginning to think something's up and no one is willing to let me in on the secret."

"I can't tell you right now. Will you just trust me and wait until tonight?"

"Now I am really curious." Annie picked up her croissant and began pulling it apart and eating it in small bites. "Can you give me a hint?"

"No."

"It's about my new bedroom?"

"No hints."

"You are leaving me and going back to California?"

"Yes, but only to pack and move up here. That's not it."

"Can you give me a small hint?"

"No."

"Dan is going to ask Lizzy to marry him?"

"How would I know about that? Let's not talk about marriage."

My dream was right, Annie thought. Donald wants to keep a bit of a distance between them. He was not interested in marriage right now. How could that be, he said he loved her. What if he left for California and never came back? It would be an easy way to end their relationship. Annie was feeling depressed now.

"...and you will have to wait until then." Donald said finishing a sentence that Annie only heard the end of, because she was off in her thoughts again.

Annie decided not to ask Donald to repeat what he said. She was making a big deal out of nothing. Donald did say it was a surprise. He was not a mean person. He loved her. Good grief, she thought, stop thinking the worse. Donald reached over the table and took Annie's hand in his. He sensed that she was anxious about his surprise.

"I made reservations at the nice restaurant in town for seven o'clock tonight. I will pick you up at Stella's." Donald's hand was warm. He continued, "This will be our first official date."

"If things go well on this date, will you show me my new bedroom?"

"I might be persuaded!" Donald said.

Annie decided to leave well enough alone. She turned their attention to the pizza party on Friday night. Donald said he would pick up the pizza if she wanted to make dessert. Annie thought ice cream cookie bars would be fun. She and Marie could make chocolate chip cookies before everyone arrived. Donald liked the idea. He already had soft drinks and other refreshments. He even got beer for anyone who liked beer with their pizza. The party was set.

Annie looked around the kitchen. The house was hers. She and Marie would be living in this house in a matter of a day. A new chapter in her life was about to begin. Annie expressed her thoughts to Donald. He, too, was beginning a new chapter in his life. In a matter of less than two weeks they both had major changes in their lives. Their changes affected those around them...Marie, Stella, Lizzy, and Dan. We must be prepared for what life brings us, Annie thought.

It was then that Annie remembered Lizzy's early morning phone call. Annie told Donald about the "buildings...plural" comment that Lizzy made. She also told him about the deeds being in the vault room. Annie wanted to go back to the vault room and locate any information that Lizzy might need.

Donald, now intrigued by this information, offered to help Annie go through the vault room and search for the R&H Enterprises files. He suggested that if they were not able to find information related to the company, then they should again search the boxes left in the garage. Annie agreed and then remembered that the passwords to the vault door and safes were in her bedroom at her mother's house.

Annie left Donald to put away the remainder of the donuts and quietly entered her mother's house. Not hearing sounds in the house, she sneaked into her bedroom. Callie was still asleep on her bed. Annie went to the closet and retrieved the tote bag containing the large envelope from Helen. She located the envelope with the passwords and quickly crammed the other envelopes into the tote bag. She hid it once again in her closet and closed the closet door.

Callie yawned and stretched, turned around and plopped back down on the bed. Annie walked over to Callie and scratched her on the head. Callie meowed loudly. Annie tip-toed out of the bedroom and out through the front door. She looked up and down the street, and then ran across to her house.

"Okay, let's do it!"

Donald put the cleaned coffee cup in the cupboard, and closed the door. "Thought you would never ask," Donald said teasingly.

The two entered the office, closed the curtains, and locked the door. Donald then slid the bookcase to expose the staircase. They descended down the stairs with Annie in the lead. Annie stopped for a moment remembering the time she and Donald were naked on the floor. Her stomach was getting all tingly again. Donald was directly behind her. Annie took a deep breath and continued down the stairs.

Donald opened the canvas painting which revealed the vault door just as before. Annie entered the password and the vault door produced a clicking sound. Donald pulled on the door and it opened. Again, lights flooded the large vault room.

Annie walked through the vault door and entered the room. She was noticing so much more now that it all made sense. A lot of valuable items were on display in this room. The paintings, sculptures, collectibles, books, and some things that were just there as sentimental value stood out in the open on display. Annie walked up to a shadow box display of blue and white baby clothes. She wondered why Helen had an attachment to this particular framed set.

Donald called Annie over to the two safes embedded into the wall. They had already been through the safe labeled with an "R", but had not had time to open the safe labeled "H". Annie pulled out her passwords and entered the code onto the keypad. They heard a whirling sound and Donald turned the wheel handle. The safe door opened.

Annie walked up to the safe. The safe consisted of several shelves of brown accordion style folders. Annie pulled a folder out and looked at the label.

"This might be it," Annie said. "It says *'Leases of the Boardwalk Building'*." She slid off the elastic band holding the file together. As she thumbed through the file, she pulled out her own lease agreement. A note was attached to the file. 'My favorite tenant...keep rent low'. The note never mentioned why. Why would she be Helen's favorite tenant when she never spoke to Helen about leasing the shop space? Annie did not even know Helen owned the building.

Donald grabbed the file that Annie was now handing to him. He searched through the file as Annie pulled another brown accordion file out of the safe. They spent the next hour reading through the files in the safe, gathering insight into Annie's newly acquired business.

Sitting on the carpeted floor with files spread all around her in neat stacks, Annie announced she was done and needed a break. Donald put down his stack of papers and claimed there was nothing out of the ordinary as far as the business went. He and Annie talked about how everything seemed on the level.

Annie gathered up the files that she felt needed reviewing by Lizzy for business purposes. She stood, stretched, and put away the remaining files into the safe.

On the top shelf was a pretty paper covered box with a matching lid. Annie pulled the box from the shelf and opened the lid. Inside was a photo of a baby boy wrapped in a blanket who appeared to have just been born. Only the baby and the mother's arm and hand were in the pictures. No face of the mother. The left hand in the photo showed a beautiful wedding ring.

"It is almost nine o'clock, Annie," Donald announced.

Annie put the photo back into the box and covered the box with the lid. She slid the box back on the top shelf and stepped back to survey the room, making sure nothing was left out. Donald closed and locked the safe.

They left the vault room with the files, locked the door, closed the canvas painting, and headed upstairs. After securing the office, they opened the curtains and left the office. Annie was getting used to the routine of entering the vault now. It seemed natural to her. She wondered how long she and Donald would be able to keep the vault room a secret.

♦ ♦ ♦

It was nine-thirty in the morning on Thursday when Annie and Marie walked through the shop door. The shop opened at ten o'clock, so Annie asked Marie if she would be willing to go next door and get a coffee and chocolate croissant for her and anything Marie wanted. Annie handed Marie money, and Marie was out the door.

Marie found Daisy in line inside the bakery. Daisy's mother and brother, William, had dropped Daisy off at her new job, as her mother was going to the bakery to get coffee and pastries anyway. Since she was early, Daisy went into the bakery with her mother and brother.

Daisy introduced Marie to William, Daisy's brother. The two, although shy at first, seemed to hit it off and talked until Daisy insisted they get to the shop. She did not want to be late on her first day.

An afternoon class was being held that today and Annie was checking the classroom to make sure she had not forgotten anything when she set up the class yesterday. This session was only an hour long. The students, of varying ages, were making a no-glue box with floral decorations and other embellishments on the outside. To Annie it was quick and easy, but to the students who had not created such a project an hour was barely enough time. Annie usually kept her students going so they would all finish on time.

Daisy entered the shop with Marie following through the door behind her. Daisy had a tray with drinks, while Marie carried a paper bag with pastries. Annie was grateful for the coffee right now. The chocolate croissant was an added pleasure.

It was noon by the time Annie had Daisy up to speed on the shop and its operations. Since Daisy had retail experience, training her was so much easier than Annie had expected. Annie showed Daisy and Marie what she was teaching in today's class. Marie came up with embellishments for sample/display boxes, while Daisy created several no-glue boxes as examples for the class. Annie thought that Daisy would be an asset in the shop and would give her and Lizzy more time to spend in other duties, such as R&H Enterprises.

Annie just happened to look out the window on the street side of the shop. She was now looking at the building with new eyes. This was her building. She noticed bits of wear that needed attending to immediately, and then thought about asking Lizzy to help host a meeting to discuss the needs of the tenants. 'I hope we know what we are doing,' Annie thought to herself and shivered. Owning a small paper shop was one thing, but owning buildings with multiple businesses was another. Annie kept her eyes on the building across the street and was in deep thought.

The building Annie was looking at was built in the 1950's. It was long like the one her shop was located in, but it had a second story which housed Suzette Meyer's 'Bridgewater Inn', a Bed & Breakfast business.

The entrance into the Bridgewater Inn was located in the center of the building on the street. Two stained glass doors invited guests inside. An elevator stood behind the stairs, which were located in the center of the lobby ascending to a hallway and the guest rooms. An office stood behind the elevator and the stairs. There were comfortable chairs in the lobby for guests to linger or wait out the rain. A coffee station was set up in the lobby area near the electric fireplace which was against the wall on the left of the entrance. The gift shop was at the far left side of the back next to the office. A modern-vintage theme was created throughout the Inn. Suzette loved yellows and spring colors. It showed in her decorating style.

The Inn consisted of eight bedrooms, each with a full bathroom. The bedrooms had fantastic views of the ocean. Eight additional rooms across the hall were not yet remodeled, but had potential to be guest rooms in the future. On the first floor, there was an office and check-in counter, and next to it a gift shop of local items for sale. A dining room for breakfast and evening wine tasting events rounded out the main floor.

Suzette Meyers was a forty-year-old divorcee from Washington with two cats. She combined her money from the divorce along with stocks and began the bed and breakfast business on the Central Coast of Oregon. With the help of her sister, she remodeled, cleaned, and decorated the once 1950's hotel to its current state. She ran a very successful inn. It was written up in magazines and always booked even in the winter when business slowed down and tourism practically disappeared. The winter storms usually brought in overnight guests from the Willamette Valley.

Looking at the building, to the far north of the structure was a parking lot for the guests of the inn and some parking for local business owners in the back. Annie noticed on the north side of the building was an empty shop. She wondered how long that shop had been empty. It was not something she noticed before. Annie made a mental note to ask Lizzy if she knew the answer from reading through the material in the boxes.

The stores in the second building were much larger than the building where her shop was currently located, but they were stores that needed much more space. They tended to be less boutique shops and more common businesses; such as restaurant, hardware store, and realty office.

Jerry's Leatherworks was next to the empty shop. Jerry Robinson opened his shop only a year ago. He had a large supply of leather, tools, leather dyes, books on leatherworking, a large section of leather stamps, belt buckles, snaps, glues, whole leather craft kits, sewing machines, light tables, thread, patterns and anything a person would need to work on leather projects. In the back of the shop was a classroom. Next to the classroom was a rest room and office.

The classroom had benches which were rented to people who wanted to work on their hobbies, but did not have the money or space to invest in the equipment to make leather projects. Classes were taught in the evening, so the classroom was open to hobbyists during the day at a small fee. The fee included a work space and use of the equipment.

Jerry had a large following of leather workers up and down the coast. Between his classes and day time work in the shop, he was a busy person. Jerry was in his late thirties and came to the Oregon Coast from California. His parents were born in the mid-sixties and were a bit into the hippy generation, as he referred to them. He was a clean-cut guy who expressed an interest in Annie.

Annie remembered once going into Jerry's shop to purchase a small anvil for using when she punched letters into metal tags as embellishments on her cards and boxes. She recalled the earthy aroma of leather. It was a nice smell, but not something she would want to work in daily.

Jerry would often find a reason to run into Annie at the bakery, the town meetings, and sometimes just come into her store under the pretense of purchasing colored cardstock for a use in his shop. Although Annie never saw a romance forming between them, Jerry stopped his visits once Donald came to town. Where she used to see him at least once or twice a week, she had not crossed paths with him in two weeks now.

Next to Jerry's Leatherworks store stood the city realty business. It had four employees who were full time realtors along the coast. They were in and out of the business daily. Annie never really spent time getting to know any of them, as they did not stay in their office for long periods of time.

Next to the realty office was the famous China Sea Chinese Restaurant owned and operated by Jose Javier Angel Garcia and his wife Kim. Kim was not Chinese as one would think, seeing that she co-owned a Chinese Restaurant. Kim was blond as blond can get with a small curvy voluptuous body who often wore quite snug fitting clothing. She was the reason young men came to eat at the restaurant frequently. She never flirted with these men, but she was the friendliest person you would ever meet. Jose worked in the kitchen, but he kept his eyes on Kim.

The China Sea Chinese Restaurant was the best Chinese food on the coast, at least that is what Annie and her family and friends thought. Annie's favorite was the fried shrimp, lemon chicken, and the pork chop suey combination. The portions were large and the price was right. Many people were seen filling the restaurant from lunch through dinner. The restaurant closed at 8:00 in the evening and was closed on Sunday and Monday. Jose and Kim did not overwork themselves and their customers were happy with the hours the restaurant was open.

Looking toward the south end of the building, Harrington's Hardware Store took up two shop spaces. Fred Harrington was a third-generation shop owner of this hardware store. His grandfather opened the shop in the 1950's, when the building was first built. Back then Fred's grandfather had the only hardware store for miles up and down the coast. He did a great business and it continued today with Fred.

Annie is friends with Diane, Fred's wife, who is a hobby crafter and sells handmade cards in the hardware shop. A strange place to sell cards Annie once thought, but the cards are popular and Diane has a successful sideline business. Diane Harrington often attends Annie's classes and is a very good customer.

♦ ♦ ♦

Annie was interrupted from her deep thoughts as Lizzy came bounding through the shop door.

"I am sorry I am late." Lizzy stopped and looked at Annie with a tone of exasperation. "Did you not see me standing out there waving my arms at you?"

"No. Sorry." Annie moved from the window and said, "I was thinking about the building across the street."

"Oh yeah, we have to talk about that." Lizzy rushed off to the office and over her shoulder said, "Did you find any other paperwork regarding the business?" Lizzy was dressed in a short dark leather skirt with a blue silky long-sleeved blouse and black pumps. She looked very stylish for an average day in the shop.

"Yes, in the office, the brown accordion folders on my desk. Help yourself." Annie followed Lizzy to the office to make sure she found the folders. Lizzy was hanging her jacket up and getting money out of her wallet to run next door and get coffee.

"Do you have a hot date with Dan tonight, Lizzy?" Annie asked.

"As a matter of fact, I do."

"I will be right back," Lizzy stated. "Would anyone like something from the bakery?"

"I need chocolate," Annie called back to Lizzy.

"Daisy, Marie, would you like anything from the bakery? It is my treat!" Lizzy said walking to the boardwalk side door of the shop. Daisy and Marie stopped what they were doing and signaled to Lizzy that they were okay for now. Lizzy exited the door and walked to the bakery shop.

While Lizzy was at the bakery, Annie took the time to review the list of students for her next class. Fifteen people were on the list. She noticed that Diane was not attending today. She would catch up with her later and see if Diane wanted a quick lesson on making the box or just the instructions. Annie had good instructions for the students so they could go home and make additional boxes with supplies they bought from her shop.

Lizzy walked back into the shop with a chocolate covered iced donut for Annie and coffee. They went to the counter and sat down to discuss R&H Enterprises, but were interrupted when students began entering the shop for the class. Annie asked Marie and Daisy to assist with the class and help with customers as needed. Lizzy stayed at the check-out counter and continued to review the files in the brown accordion folders.

Once Marie showed the students into the classroom and checked off their names from the paid list, she joined Annie at the front of the room. Marie handed out instructions for the class. Annie introduced herself and Marie. Daisy had left to help customers by this point. When she came back, Annie introduced her between instructions.

Scoring boards were placed on the tables in a way that two students could share one tool. Each person scored their already cut paper according to the directions Annie was giving. Marie helped those who were struggling with the scoring technique by demonstrating how to hold the scoring tool at an angle to keep it in the groove of the board. If the tool was at the wrong angle, it skipped into the next groove, and the score line would not be straight. Accuracy is important when making boxes.

After the class put together their boxes, Annie asked Marie to demonstrate some of the embellishments that they could add to their boxes and the different looks each one added. Marie passed around the different boxes with added touches that she and Daisy had made earlier. People commented on how difficult it looked to make some of the pieces, but Marie said she would demonstrate how to make them.

Annie helped on one side of the classroom and Marie helped on the other. Together they assisted their students in creating lovely boxes to take home. There was a lot of chatter and laughter as the class was nearing an end. Annie thanked everyone for coming and asked them to look at the schedule for the next class they wanted to take. Classes were filling up, so Annie asked them to sign up soon.

Donald walked through the door just as the last student left the classroom area to shop for supplies. He walked up to Annie and kissed her on the cheek. He said hello to Marie, who giggled at the sight of Donald kissing Annie.

"Is she going to giggle every time I kiss you?"

"I don't know. Keep kissing me and we will find out." Annie moved out of the classroom and to her office. Donald followed and took a chair next to her desk.

CHAPTER 22

Thursday Late Afternoon

I t was late afternoon, when Annie was just about to sit down in her desk chair. She heard her cell phone ring. She opened the bottom drawer of her desk and pulled out her purse to retrieve her phone. Annie did not recognize the number on the caller ID, but decided to answer it anyway.

"Hello", Annie said into the cell phone.

"Annie, dear, this is LaVerne." LaVerne sounded a bit frantic Annie thought.

"LaVerne, is everything okay?" Annie gave Donald a concerned look.

"Annie, we need your help! We did not know who to call, but I told Lorraine that you would help us." LaVerne was almost whispering at this point.

"LaVerne? What is the problem?"

"We are stuck in a bit of a situation," Lorraine spoke into the phone. "Can you come help us out?"

Annie looked at her watch. It was three in the afternoon. She needed to get home by five to get ready for her first date with Donald. She figured she could go to the retirement home and help the ladies with whatever needed doing. That would only take about a hour, right?

"Sure. Where are you?" Annie figured they were in one or the other's apartment. The senior retirement home was only a few blocks away. It was not going to take too long to help them out.

"We are at Eddie's house on the north side of town. We are hiding in the garage, but got stuck," LaVerne told Annie in whispered tones.

"What?" Annie shouted into her phone. "How in the world did you end up in Eddie's garage? Why are you in Eddie's garage? Where is Eddie?" Annie was on the verge of panicking now. What were these ladies thinking? Were they breaking into Eddie's house, and most importantly, why?

Donald stood, trying to get Annie's attention to find out what was wrong. She signaled him to wait a minute. Annie got a local phone book out and asked Donald to look up Eddie's home address.

"Tell me what happened? How did you get in this situation?" Annie listened while LaVerne told her the events that led up to the two getting stuck in the garage. She scribbled Eddie's full name on a piece of paper and handed it to Donald.

LaVerne told Annie that the ladies saw Ronnie in the truck earlier in the morning on the street near their retirement home. Eddie drove up and starting yelling at Ronnie. Ronnie looked scared according to LaVerne. Eddie pushed Ronnie to the ground and they saw him pointing to his truck while continuing to yell at Ronnie. The ladies thought that the truck must be very important to Eddie. They wanted to find out why.

Lorraine got on the phone and said that she and LaVerne convinced Millie to drive them to the street where Eddie lived. They saw Ronnie leaving with the truck and figured he was taking it to Eddie's house. They wanted sit in the car and spy on Eddie and Ronnie. As it was, Millie had a doctor's appointment and could not stay long. The ladies decided to get out of the car and pretend to be out on a walk. Ronnie left the truck in the garage at Eddie's house and walked away.

The ladies did not see Eddie at home, so they decided to break into the garage and see what was so important about the truck. Lorraine said she picked the lock, a skill she learned from her husband who was a locksmith. She said she's usually packing a gun, but her son took it away after the last incident where she almost got in trouble. Annie rolled her eyes while listening to the conversation.

"Well," Lorraine said, "Just as I get the lock opened on the side door, we hear Eddie come home!"

"Oh no," Annie gasped into the phone. "Are you hiding in the garage now?"

"Yes, and we need help getting out. Eddie is in the house right now, but he will probably come out to make sure the truck is in the garage."

"Can you sneak out?"

"No, there is a large wooden crate that has fallen against the door." Lorraine told Annie that she needed someone stronger than they were to push from the outside and move the crate away from the door.

"I am on my way," Annie told Lorraine. "Keep down and do not let Eddie catch you in the garage. Hide if you have to. Eddie would have no problem in having you arrested for breaking into his garage."

Annie hung up the phone and quickly told Donald about the situation. Donald said the SUV was parked outside in front of the shop. He began to walk out of the office with Annie, stopped and asked, "Should we call Dan?"

"Oh, let's not bother Dan with this," Annie said to Donald as she walked passed him out of the office. "He has enough to worry about right now. Not to mention that he is not really the person to be rescuing these two at the moment."

♦ ♦ ♦

Donald raced up the side street toward Eddie's house. He was following the GPS in the SUV when it showed they were near the street on which Eddie lived.

"Let's not get too close. Eddie is home and we really don't want him to see us." Annie announced, looking for a good place to park out of the view of Eddie's house.

Donald parked in front of the neighboring house, behind a truck. The shrubs bordering the neighbor's yard and Eddie's yard were about four feet in height, and a good cover for Annie to run along to get to the detached garage near the back of Eddie's property.

"Please do not call Dan," Annie pleaded to Donald.

"I promise not to call Dan," Donald said looking straight ahead. "Dan just passed us and is parking in front of the house as we speak."

"Oh, no!" Annie said groaning, quietly opening the passenger door and exiting. She poked her head inside the car and said, "Text me if either one of them heads back to the garage. I will try and get the ladies out as fast as I can. Be ready to get out of here as soon as we get back. I really do not want Dan to catch me here."

Annie quietly closed the door of the car and walked through the neighbor's side of the yard and down to the backyard, behind Eddie's garage. She knew she was asking a lot of Donald to not call Dan. She would really try to make it up to him later. Right now, this would be their little secret.

Annie cautiously walked around the back of the garage to its side door. She could hear Dan talking with Eddie. It sounded like Dan was asking Eddie questions about Ronnie's whereabouts. Annie stopped to listen a bit. Ronnie was not anywhere to be found and Eddie was claiming he had not seen Ronnie or the truck. Dan asked about Eddie being on a cruise with his wife. Eddie told Dan that he only took his wife to Seattle to meet up with her sister, as they were the ones going on the cruise. Eddie said he had business to take care of in town, and wanted to get back as soon as possible.

A quiet tapping sound was heard and Annie turned her attention to LaVerne in the garage side door window. As Annie walked up to the door, she saw Lorraine walk forward from the shadows of the garage. LaVerne pointed down to the large wooden crate that was wedged up against the door. Annie sighed, and then turned the knob on the door and pushed with all her might. The wooden crate began to move inward and Annie opened the door to let the ladies out.

As Annie signaled the ladies to remain quiet, she motioned for them to go around to the back of the garage and through the neighbor's hedge. Then Annie whispered to Lorraine, as she passed through the door, "Donald is parked in front of the neighbor's house. Get in the car quietly. Lorraine gave Annie the "OK" sign and followed LaVerne out the door and around to the back of the garage.

As Annie was about to walk out, she realized that the truck was in the garage. She also noticed that the truck had left front end damage and silver paint scratches on the bumper. Annie quickly pulled out her phone and took a picture of the truck and bumper damage. She then, for some reason, decided she should put the wooden crate back up against the wall where she assumed it was before the ladies came into the garage and knocked it over.

Annie picked up the heavy crate, realizing that she was not as strong as she thought. Fortunately, she was able to lean the crate up against the wall. It looked like it was going to stay so she decided to get out of there quickly. She opened the garage and door just as the wooden crate started sliding down the wall to the door. Annie stopped to look at the crate falling, and in a split second the crate was wedged up against the door with Annie caught between the door and the door frame. She let out a 'oof!' and hoped that neither Dan nor Eddie heard her. As Annie struggled to get free from the doorway, she realized she was stuck. In a panic she sent a quick text to Donald to come and rescue her.

The ladies were just getting to the car when Donald exited and told the ladies that he needed to help Annie. He told them that she got stuck in the door. Donald ran behind the hedge to the backyard of the neighbor, crossing into Eddie's backyard and to the back of the garage. As he came around the back of the garage, he stopped and nearly burst out laughing. Half way in and half way out of the door way was a very unhappy young woman. Annie signaled him to not make a sound.

Donald and Annie's attention were instantly diverted when they saw LaVerne and Lorraine walking up the street to Eddie's front walk. Donald quickly pushed the door open and pulled Annie all the way out. They ran behind the garage as the wooden crate made a thud on the garage floor. Fortunately for Annie and Donald, the senior ladies could be heard loudly greeting Dan and Eddie, who were standing in the front yard. They were out of the view of the garage, and the ladies were keeping them busy while Annie and Donald ran to the car.

Annie stopped and grabbed Donald's arm. She peered through the hedge and was able to get a good view of the group on the front yard walkway. The ladies were cleverly maneuvering Eddie and Dan with their backs to the neighbor's yard where Annie and Donald were watching. Dan then moved to the side and then closer to the ladies. He was able to see the surroundings. This was a move that Annie's father had taught her. Be aware of her surroundings.

"It is so good to see you Eddie," Lorraine spoke in a very loud voice. "Is Doris home? We came to see her about a quilt project."

"No," Eddie replied back in a raised voice, matching that of Lorraine's. "She is on a cruise."

"Oh goodness." LaVerne commented, "Please have her call us when she returns."

"Yeah," Eddie said in a much quieter tone.

Dan eyed the ladies suspiciously and then looked over toward the neighbor's house and around the yard. It was at this time that Donald grabbed Annie's arm and began to run, which startled her causing her to trip over a root in the ground. She went down with a loud thud and high-pitched noise came from her opened mouth. Donald ducked down next to Annie. Both Annie and Donald lay still, listening for any reaction to the fall. Annie had her hand over her mouth. She began breathing heavily. Her heart was thumping wildly.

"Oh, deary me!" Lorraine looked at LaVerne and said loudly. "Was that you? What did you eat for lunch?"

LaVerne, realizing Lorraine was covering up for the sudden noise in the neighbor's yard, answered, "Oh, I am so sorry. You know how it is with us older folks." LaVerne started waving her hand around as if to fan an imaginary odor in the air.

Eddie, who was standing directly across from LaVerne, turned his attention to her and wrinkled his nose. It appeared he was holding his breath. He took a step backwards and revealed a disgusted look on his face. The only thing Dan could smell was a cover up from the noise he heard in the neighbor's yard. As he looked past Eddie's grimaced face, he noticed Annie and Donald racing out of the neighbor's yard. He rolled his eyes, his jaw muscles tightened, he took in a deep breath, and then turned his attention to the ladies.

"Well, ladies, if you don't mind leaving us to continue our discussion...", Dan stated, guiding the ladies down the yard sidewalk to the street sidewalk. He then said to the ladies in a quiet tone, "Your ride awaits. Go home!"

While tripping over the hedge root, Annie realized she had sprained her ankle. Donald had to half carry her back to the SUV. Once safely in the vehicle, Annie began rubbing her ankle. Donald asked if there was a first aid kit in the car with an ice pack. She said she did not think so, but that would be something to add to the car later. Annie could tell Donald was thinking the same thing, and with all her mishaps, a first aid kit would not be a bad idea at all. Maybe she should have a change of clothing, water, and food as well. Another item for her mental note list.

The senior ladies quickly walked to the car and got in the backseat. Donald started the engine and backed down the street until he could make a U-turn and drive away from Eddie's house. Everyone was silent until they got back in town.

"Well, that was a hoot!" Lorraine said with a smile on her face. "We almost got caught."

"So, what's with this business of me letting one go? You could have easily been the one who farted," LaVerne stated to Lorraine.

"You were closest to Eddie. It made more sense to keep him distracted if the fart came from you." Lorraine stated while looking through her purse. "Besides, one of us had to make a big deal out of it. You were not going to admit you made a stink."

"True." LaVerne said, "But next time you be the stink culprit."

"No next time, ladies," Annie said from the front seat of the vehicle as it drove through town and headed toward the senior living apartments. "Please promise me you will stay out of trouble. If Dan had caught you, he would have had you arrested."

"Oh phi-sh! We know Dan's mother. She would have gotten mad at him." LaVerne said, "She comes to the senior center on Tuesdays and Thursdays for exercise class."

Lorraine, changing the subject, then said, "Did you know that she is seeing that man who moved into Apartment 157 just recently. They have been quite the couple. All the single ladies are jealous. A new man in the building and she comes from outside and grabs on to him."

"I wonder if Dan knows about the new man in his mother's life?" Both of the ladies then looked at Annie. She was still turned around in her seat listening to their conversation. She stared at them for a moment, and then turned around in her seat to face forward.

Did Dan know about this man in his mother's life. Annie thought to herself. He must know. Although, his mother had been quite busy lately. Dan's mother turned down a luncheon meeting with Annie's mother recently. They always liked to go to lunch together. Stella even met Dan's mother at the senior center for exercise classes. Come to think of it, Annie told herself, they had not seen each other since last week. At least Annie's mother had not mentioned seeing Dan's mother. Usually Annie knew when they had met and Stella would catch up on the happenings in Dan's mother's life.

Annie was in deep thought when Donald pulled up to the sidewalk of the senior living apartments. He got out of the SUV and opened the door for LaVerne, and then went around to the other side and opened the door for Lorraine.

"You are such a nice boy. I hope you and Annie invite us to the wedding," Lorraine said, patting Donald on the arm.

LaVerne whispered, "That's a nice ring you got for Annie. Are you going to give it to her tonight at dinner?"

"How do you...? Never mind." Donald walked up to the driver's side door and with a half-smile he said, "Good-bye ladies!"

The seniors walked arm-in-arm up the sidewalk to the apartment building in deep conversation. As they reached the front door, they turned and waved good-bye to Donald and Annie. Donald started the SUV, put it in gear, and drove away.

"Penny for your thoughts," Donald said to Annie who was still in deep thoughts over Dan's mother's new man.

"Only a penny?" Annie responded.

CHAPTER 23

Thursday Night

No more was said until Donald pulled to the curb in front of Annie's shop. Lizzy was straightening up the shelves and watched the SUV pull up. She stood at the door watching and waiting for Annie to walk inside. Donald walked to Annie's side and opened the passenger door. Annie stepped out and reached up to give Donald a kiss. Donald moved his hand from the car door to Annie's shoulder. A sudden gust of wind blew the door into Annie's hip with such force that it bumped her into Donald, who then fell sideway into the car.

"Ouch!" Annie cried out. She stumbled on her ankle causing even more pain.

"I think I should help you to the shop," Donald said recovering from the push into the car.

"I am a disaster!"

"Yes, you are my Disaster Girl." Donald helped Annie to the front door as Lizzy opened the door.

Annie turned to Donald, "Next time you see me I will be wearing a cape."

"If that is all you are going to wear, we might have to change our plans to dinner at home."

"You are not getting out of this dinner date," Annie said walking through the shop door. Lizzy closed the door and Donald walked back to the car. He started the engine and drove off.

Lizzy asked Marie to go next door to Ione's bakery and get some ice in a plastic bag. Marie quickly walked through the door to get the ice. Lizzy helped Annie to the office and into a chair. She retrieved an empty box from the storage room and put a sweatshirt of Annie's, which was on one of the hooks, under Annie's injured ankle.

Marie, with Ione at her heels, hurried into the shop. Ione peered into the office and saw Annie with her leg up on the box. She asked Marie to get some paper towels to wrap around the ice bag. Marie went to the counter where the paper towels were kept and grabbed a handful. She handed them to Ione. Ione placed the wrapped bag of ice on top of Annie's ankle. Annie winced, but the coolness felt wonderful on her injury.

"Anyone care to tell me what happened, or do I need to hear it through the grapevine?" Ione pulled up a chair and sat down in the office.

Annie realized that she needed to give Ione a logical explanation without telling her the whole story. As it was, Ione was part of the grapevine in town. Anything Annie told her would eventually get back to Dan, and probably within the hour.

Annie began to slowly explain what happened, when it dawned on her that she could explain it all away by telling about the car door hitting her in the hip and causing her to turn her ankle. Yes, that was the story, Annie assured herself. She told such a story to the group huddled around her. They listened with pure signs of pity as she told the story. Sadly, it was all the truth. Apparently, she really was Disaster Girl.

♦ ♦ ♦

Marie and Daisy had completed cleaning up after the class earlier. They made sure that everything was put away and that tools were cleaned and put back where they lived. Marie liked to say that tools lived in a certain place. Annie began using the term, because she liked the way Marie thought about life. It was simple and innocent. Everything had a place to 'live'.

While Annie stayed in the office and checked emails, opened mail, and pampered her ankle, Lizzy brought in the day's receipts and handed them to Annie to review. Lizzy had closed the shop at four o'clock.

"Good day today, despite the part you have not told me about," Lizzy said closing the office door with the two of them inside. "Spill. What happened?"

"Are you going to blab to Dan?" Annie said as she put the receipts down on the desk. She did not need to look at the receipts right now.

If anything was out of the ordinary, Lizzy would have mentioned it as she walked into the office.

"He already knows you were at Eddie's," Lizzy said. "He called me on his cell after he left Eddie's house. He said you and Donald were up to something and he saw you both in the neighbor's yard. What he did not understand was why the 'Silver Snoopers', as he so affectionately calls the ladies, were in the neighborhood. He said they were out of place. He wanted to know what I knew about the situation. I did not know, so it saved me from telling him anything."

"You cannot tell Dan," Annie pleaded. "He would yell at me nonstop if he knew what happened. I would not put it past him to have me arrested for burglary."

"Oh boy," Lizzy drew her chair closer to Annie's. "What in the world happened?"

"Well...LaVerne and Lorraine called me to say they were sneaking around Eddie's garage and got stuck inside," Annie repositioned herself in the chair. She moved the ice pack to a different location on her foot. "Donald was here, so he drove me out to Eddie's house and I got them out of the garage, but then got myself stuck in the door. Long story, don't ask."

Lizzy giggled.

Annie gave her a look and then said, "Donald saw Dan looking our way and panicked. He grabbed my arm to run and I stumbled and turned my ankle. I must have made a sound at that point, as I heard the ladies talking loudly, but we were running to the car. The ladies soon followed and we got out of there. I had no idea Dan saw us. Did he say if Eddie saw us?"

"You will need to ask Dan. I claimed to not know what was happening, remember?"

Daisy knocked on the door of the office and announced that she was checking out and going home for the day. Marie walked up to the group and stated that Donald had pulled up in front of the shop to take them home. Lizzy grabbed her jacket and handed Annie hers. Marie gathered her jacket and canvas bag and headed to the street side shop door, where Donald was standing just outside. Lizzy was the last person out of the door as she locked up and turned to Annie. In a whisper she said, "Have a great time tonight, and try to stay off your ankle."

Annie thanked Lizzy and gave her a hug. Donald opened the car door for Annie as Marie climbed into the backseat. Donald closed both Marie and Annie's doors and walked around to the driver's side. Annie could have sworn she saw Donald smile and wave to Lizzy. What was that all about? She turned to Lizzy who looked a bit guilty and turned away to walk down the street.

Donald got into the car, started the engine, and happily drove away. Annie said nothing all the way home. She kept telling herself to stop over analyzing the wave Donald gave to Lizzy. She knew Donald was in love with her. Annie continued to brood as Donald pulled to the curb at Stella's house. Marie bounded out the door and into the house. Donald opened the door for Annie.

As Annie carefully got out of the car, she said, "Are you planning something?"

"Yes," Donald said happily, "I am planning our first date. This is our first official date!"

"Oh," Annie suddenly relaxed. "You are absolutely right. Our first date. I am excited too!" She chided herself for getting suspicious. This was their first date. They were now dating. They were a couple. Yes, she was happy about that. Wow, she thought, they were finally going on a date. It felt like she already knew Donald so well. This date will be like all the other dinners she has had with him, just in a restaurant instead of home.

Annie limped up to the house with Donald holding her arm. He was such a gentleman. She was so happy to be in love with him. At the door, Annie turned to Donald and kissed him. He opened the door and said, "I will pick you up at seven." He turned and walked away.

Annie limped into the house. Stella and Marie were standing in the hallway. Marie giggled. Annie looked at the two of them.

"What in the world happened to your foot?" Stella asked while helping Annie to the family room.

"I cannot sit down right now or I will never get up," Annie exclaimed as she hobbled to her bedroom. "I really need to get dressed for dinner. I will tell you the whole story after I finish dressing." With that said, Annie opened her bedroom door and walked inside.

Beautiful red roses were on her bedside table. She stepped gingerly to the vase of roses and bent down to smell the flowers. The scent was intoxicating. Annie smiled. This is why everyone was acting strangely. They all knew she was getting roses. Lizzy probably helped get them for Donald. It was a very sweet gesture from Donald. Annie saw a note attached and opened the envelope.

"Let's make this a night to remember! I love you, Disaster Girl. Donald."

Annie laughed. She set the card down and went to her closet to pick out the perfect outfit for tonight. She wanted to ice her ankle before Donald picked her up, so she hurried to take a shower, wash her hair, and put her make-up on while thinking about which earrings she was going to wear. Forty-five minutes later Annie was dressed and ready for her date. She carried her shoes and evening bag to the family room, where Stella and Marie were watching television. Stella got up and handed Annie an ice bag wrapped in a towel.

"I thought you might want to relax for a half an hour with the ice bag." Stella sat back down, "It should help with any pain tonight."

"Thank you, Mom." Annie put the ice pack on her swollen ankle.

"You look beautiful, Annie," Stella said lovingly. "I wish your father were here to see you."

"I wish he were here too, Mom."

Annie told her mother and Marie about what happened at Eddie's house. Stella was mortified that the ladies would even think of going to Eddie's house and breaking into his garage. Annie agreed, and then her mother reminded her that Annie committed the same crime. Annie begged her mother not to tell Dan the entire story. He would be terribly disappointed in her if he heard the whole version.

♦ ♦ ♦

At seven o'clock sharp, Donald rang the doorbell. Annie sat up quickly and grabbed her shoes to slip on her feet. Her ankle was feeling much better with the ice treatment. She even took a couple of aspirin to help with the pain.

Marie ran to the front door. She pulled it open and there stood Donald, dressed in a dark blue suit with a a crisp light blue shirt and dark blue tie. He walked in to the family room. Annie noticed the look of love and approval on his face as he stood staring at her.

"Hello Donald."

"You look incredible tonight." Donald smiled and leaned in to kiss Annie on her cheek.

Annie looked at Marie, "What? No comment from you?"

Stella quickly put her hand over Marie's mouth to prevent her from saying anything. Marie giggled.

"There it is!" Donald said, "The giggle."

Marie continued to giggle.

Stella moved the couple to the front door. "You two have a beautiful time. We won't wait up for you."

Donald escorted Annie to the passenger side of the car. He opened the door and she slipped in without incident. Annie surprised herself. She looked elegant like a royal duchess, and she was able to enter a vehicle without injuring herself in any way. Yep, this was going to be a wonderful evening.

The restaurant Donald took Annie to was on the south side of town. It was one of the fanciest eating establishments on the Oregon Coast. Donald navigated into an empty parking spot near the entrance of the restaurant. He exited the vehicle and quickly moved to the passenger side and opened the door for Annie. She was grateful for his kind manners, as she was prone to a possible fall while exiting herself. Tonight, she cared about her clumsy disposition and wanted to have an injury-free evening.

Once inside the restaurant, they were seated near the window with a breath-taking view of the Pacific Ocean. The sun would be setting in a couple of hours, which caused the water to sparkle like diamonds. It was bright, but the view was worth it.

After ordering, Annie noticed Donald was fidgeting at the table.

"Not used to dressing up for dinner?" Annie said smoothing out her dress, being a bit uncomfortable herself.

"Actually, there is something I want to give you and I was not sure when it would be a good time," Donald said pulling out a dark blue box.

A ring box, Annie thought to herself as she stared at the box. She was definitely ready to say yes to Donald if he asked her to marry him. She was truly in love with this man.

Donald sat the box down in front of her. She picked it up and hoped that Donald would not notice her hands shaking. As she slowly opened the lid, she said, "A diamond..." wait a second, she thought, "A pair of diamond earrings! Oh, Donald, they are lovely." She stared at the earrings. Was there a ring under the platform? She thought it best not to investigate. She took her earrings off and began to put the first diamond earring on her left ear. It was then she realized how large these diamonds were. They were not inexpensive at all. She screwed the earring back on and proceeded to place the other earring on her right ear.

Annie pulled out a mirror from her purse and tried not to make a show of admiring her new earrings in the restaurant full of customers. Donald was beaming with joy. Annie loved the earrings and leaned over to kiss Donald. Donald quickly placed both hands on the water glasses on the table so they would not spill when Annie bumped into them.

So, no proposal, but the earrings were a wonderful beginning. Annie was pleased with their first date so far. They had only known each other for two weeks. What was the rush, Annie thought? She knew what the rush was. She wanted to wake up next to him each morning. He was a major part of her life now. She was not the long engagement kind of girl. Annie was trying to smile and listen to whatever it was that Donald was talking about. What was he talking about? When did he start talking? Annie took a sip of her water.

The wine that Donald had ordered arrived at the table. Once their glasses were filled, Donald raised his glass to make a toast. Annie raised her glass to his. "To happy endings tonight." Donald smiled clinked his glass to Annie's.

"Cheers!" Annie took a sip of the wine. It was a local Pinot Gris from the Willamette Valley of Oregon. "I really should take you on a tour of the Willamette Valley wineries. Oregon has some of the best wines and breweries."

"That sounds like an overnight trip to me," Donald said raising his glass.

Annie took another sip of her wine. She was beginning to relax. So, Donald gave her earrings instead of a diamond ring. This was the beginning of the courtship. Annie took another sip of wine. She was consoling herself. He was not after her for sex, he was truly in love with her. The ring would come...eventually. She took another sip of wine. So would the sex.

Annie was feeling really good by the time dinner arrived. They ate and talked about Donald's work, which he said he needed to get back to sometime next week.

Annie perked up. "You are going back to California?" she asked.

"Yes." Donald said, taking a bite of his fish dinner. "We talked about this."

"Are you coming back?" Annie was a bit shaken now. Was it the wine or was she actually shaking?

"I am going back to California to pack up my things and move them here. I want you to go with me. I want my parents to meet you. You have not said whether you would do that or not."

"Of course, I will go with you. I need to make arrangements with Lizzy to keep the shop open, and Mom to take care of Marie first." Annie took another sip of wine.

"It is all set then. I will make arrangements tonight and call my parents in the morning. We will leave on Saturday." Donald continued eating while they talked about life in California compared to the Oregon Coast.

After the check was paid, Donald walked Annie to the door with his arm around her waist. Apparently, she had more wine than she thought. Donald opened the door of the car and Annie slumped inside. Certainly not as graceful as the first time she got in the car tonight.

As Donald drove the car to the north on the highway, he stopped at a view point overlooking the ocean. It was dark, but the sky was full of stars. The light of the moon was dancing on the water. Annie stared at the moon. Donald put his arm around her and leaned in for a kiss. Their kisses became more and more passionate. Soon the windows were fogging up and Donald turned over the engine to lower the power windows.

"We should probably head home now." Donald started the car and proceeded down the highway. As he pulled into the driveway of Annie's house, Annie noticed he was pulling into the garage.

"Are you going to walk me to my door?" Annie asked.

"Yes. I just wanted to get the car in the garage first."

Donald walked around the car to the passenger side and opened the door for Annie. She attempted to slide out, but was stuck in the seatbelt. Donald leaned down and pushed the button, releasing the belt around Annie's lap.

"You may need to sober up a bit."

"Not until you take me in the house and have your way with me," Annie said as she leaned on Donald for support.

Donald walked Annie to a patio chair and sat her down. He then unlocked the kitchen door and entered the house. He soon returned with a bottle of water and a cup of coffee.

"Here, drink one of these." Donald looked at Annie, then handed both drinks to her. "Maybe drink both of these."

They moved to the patio sofa and talked until Annie was feeling much better. She figured they were probably outside for an hour. Donald asked her if she wanted to take a walk. She told him she was getting a bit tired, and maybe he should walk her home.

Donald got up, offered his hand to help her up from the patio sofa, and guided her to the kitchen door. He picked up Annie's purse from the table on the way.

"I thought you were going to walk me home?"

"I am. This is your home," Donald said opening the door and stepping aside so she could enter.

◆ ◆ ◆

"You wanted a peek at your new bedroom tonight, remember?" Donald said as he took Annie's hand and guided her to the stairway. She climbed the stairs carefully and walked to the door of her new bedroom. There was a red ribbon across the door. On the ribbon were red die-cut hearts. Annie looked down at the carpeted floor. There were little paw prints with hearts die-cut out for toes and a circle cut out as the pad of the foot. They appeared to be walking to the door and possibly inside. Annie mused that Marie must have been busy in the shop.

Donald moved around Annie and with his right hand opened the door of the bedroom. He followed her into the room and closed the door behind them. Annie stood for a moment taking in the scene before them. Scattered throughout the room were battery type candles flickering in a soft glow. Across from Annie was the king-sized bed. The comforter was drawn back half-way down the bed as if turned down for the night. On the comforter were red rose petals tossed with abandon across the bed.

"Meoooow!" Callie woke up from her nap in the middle of the bed. Annie walked up to pet her fluffy kitty and noticed a dark blue ring box under Callie's paw. She turned and looked at Donald. Donald smiled. Annie turned back to Callie. Picking up the box, Annie opened the lid to discover a large diamond solitaire ring set in gold. Annie's eyes filled with tears as she again turned to Donald. This time Donald was on one knee holding a bouquet of red roses tied in a large red bow.

"Annie...will you marry me?"

"Oh Donald, of course, yes," Annie said with tears flowing, "Yes, I will marry you!"

Donald stood and tossed the roses on the bed. Callie let out a loud yowl and jumped off the bed, walking directly to her food dish. Donald took the ring out of the box and placed it on Annie's finger. Annie then kissed and hugged Donald.

"I see you had help getting this all set up," Annie said with a smile. She looked around the room at all the little touches left by her mother and Marie. On the end of the bed was white satin lingerie with a matching robe. Next to it lay white boxer shorts with large red hearts. Donald picked them up and laughed. Annie suspected these particular items might possibly be from Lizzy.

"Yes." Donald looked around the room, "I was not expecting so much romantic display, but I have to admit I like it. Your mom, Marie, and Lizzy out did themselves."

"I suspect Lizzy with the lingerie."

Callie jumped back up on the bed and walked near Annie. Annie instinctively began to pet Callie. "This is your new home, Callie. What do you think?" Callie walked away from Annie, curled up on the comforter, and fell asleep.

"I guess that answers your question," Donald said.

Donald gave Annie the tour of the bedroom. Over by the bay windows, Donald explained that Annie could sit in the cozy sitting area in the morning and watch the sun rise and see the ocean. He showed her the remote control for raising and lowering the curtains. Annie was thrilled and the seating area was so inviting. It was going to be difficult to get moving in the morning.

Next, Donald showed Annie the new bathroom. It was large with a large walk-in shower to the right as she walked inside the room. Adjacent to the shower was a padded bench and towel warming racks on the wall. Across from the shower was a vanity with double sinks and mirrors above the sinks. A water closet was located further down the room, with a walk-in closet at the end of the room. Annie walked to the closet and opened the door. It was huge, Annie thought. Her clothes were hanging on the racks. A large cabinet was sitting in the center of the closet room. Inside the drawers were her clothes all neatly placed by her mother. The room had a small window looking out over the backyard. Annie felt truly blessed by all that was happening to her right now.

Annie turned to Donald who was standing on the other side of the large bathroom. She noticed that the other side mirrored her side with the exception of a large jetted tub instead of a shower. There was a separate water closet and walk-in closet.

"This must be your side of the bathroom?"

"Believe it or not, this was all here before. I just had it updated. Helen and Robert lived quite nicely in their unique house."

Annie walked to Donald's walk-in closet and noticed that the clothes he had brought to Oregon were neatly placed on the racks.

"Your mother put my clothes in here." Donald said apologetically.

"Well, we are getting married. It would seem silly for you to sleep in the apartment above the garage now."

Annie walked back into the bedroom and noticed a tray of chocolate covered strawberries and a bottle of champagne chilling in an ice bucket.

"Donald...I think I want to take a shower before going to bed...care to join me?"

CHAPTER 24

Friday Morning

The morning light woke Annie from a blissful sleep. She opened her eyes and saw Donald's arm draped across her hip, as she was lying on her right side. She looked at her left hand. The ring was still there. It was not just a dream. She was actually engaged to be married to Donald.

Annie slid out of bed quietly and walked to the sitting area at the bay window. She sat on the small white sofa and picked up the remote control to open the curtains. A partial wall between the bedroom and sitting area was designed by Donald to allow Annie to get up early and let Donald sleep in without being disturbed by the light. The sofa backed up against the partial wall. Comfortable chairs flanked the sofa. A large cat tree was setting on one side, next to a kitty feeding station. Round end tables were on each end of the sofa. Fresh flowers sat on the coffee table in front of the sofa. Annie looked around the light teal color on the walls with the white and gray accents in the room. It was the perfect bedroom.

She pushed the button on the remote and the curtains rose to expose the houses across the street, and the Pacific Ocean before her. It was awe inspiring. In the distance was a fog covered ocean, but up close the sun was beginning to appear and splash color on the water. Annie felt Donald enter the seating area and sit down next to her. It was six thirty in the morning. He was wearing his funny heart boxers.

"Good morning!" Annie said admiring the boxers.

"This may be the first and last time I wear these silly things," Donald said.

"I think they are rather sexy," Annie said with a big smile across her face. "At least save them for our anniversary."

Donald leaned over and kissed Annie. "I am going to take a shower and leave you to your morning quiet time. Would you like some coffee?"

"Yes, that would be lovely."

Donald ran downstairs in his boxers to brew two cups of coffee. As he was taking the coffee up the stairs, Stella unlocked and opened the front door.

"Oh my!" Stella said, turning to cover Marie's eyes. Marie giggled.

"What is it with the Weston women and me half-naked on these stairs?" Donald continued up the stairs with the coffee. "I thought you were coming over at seven?"

"We wanted to get an early start," Stella said loudly as she directed Marie to the kitchen. "Lizzy and Dan will be here at seven for breakfast." She turned to take another look at Donald racing up the stairs in his red heart boxer shorts and shook her head laughing.

Donald entered the bedroom and closed the door quickly. He handed Annie a coffee from the tray he was carrying. "Take a couple of sips, put the coffee down and come take a shower with me. We don't have much time."

"Really, Donald?" Annie raised her eyebrows at Donald, and took a sip of her coffee.

"Your mother and Marie are here and they are making a surprise breakfast for us. Dan and Lizzy will be here in half an hour."

Annie jumped up, "Oh my goodness. I should have suspected something like this would happen." Annie turned to Donald with a smile on her face, "But then again I was a bit distracted last night." She leaned in to kiss Donald, took his hand, and quickly headed straight to the bathroom.

Donald lifted Annie's satin nightgown over her head and exposed her naked body. The silky material dropped to the floor in a puddle. He brought her close to his body and she reached her arms around his waist and slid his boxers off his body. They kissed passionately. Donald reached into the shower and started the water running, then he moved to a drawer in the sink vanity and pulled out a package. He returned to embrace Annie in a kiss. In a few moments the two were standing under the water.

♦ ♦ ♦

As Annie was putting away her hair dryer, she heard the front doorbell ring. She cleaned up the bathroom as quickly as she could and walked into the closet to find clothes to wear to work today. Donald was shaved and dressed. Annie heard Callie complaining while Donald made the bed. He was trying to convince her to move. He ended up pulling the comforter over the cat and leaving her alone.

Donald and Annie left the bedroom and headed downstairs. In the kitchen they found Dan and Lizzy already getting themselves coffee. Annie could not help but notice that Lizzy looked happier than she had ever seen her. In fact, so did Dan. He was an absolute gentleman around her. He was even dressing much better than usual. There was a definite romance brewing between the two.

Annie's mom was getting breakfast dished up and Marie was helping to set the food on the table. Marie was dressed in a very cute outfit, obviously with the styling help of Annie's mother. Marie was smiling and happily chatting with Stella. They all stopped at the appearance of Annie and Donald coming down the stairs.

"Well? How was your first date?" Lizzy asked expectantly.

Annie held her left hand out and showed the group her ring. "We are engaged!"

Everyone congratulated the couple with lots of hugs. Stella announced that breakfast was ready and they all entered the dining room to sit down. There was a lot of chatter and excitement about the engagement. Things quieted down when Donald announced that he and Annie were going to California on Saturday to pack up his house and move it all up here.

"Am I going to live here?" asked Marie. "What will happen to me?" Annie saw sudden panic in Marie's eyes.

"Of course, you are going to live here," Annie stated looking at Marie. Annie realized that Marie had not seen her room yet. "After breakfast we will all go see your new bedroom upstairs."

"I am finished. Can I go upstairs now?"

"Let's wait for everyone else to finish, Marie," Stella suggested, knowing how exciting this was for Marie, but seeing that Marie had not eaten much yet.

Marie picked up her fork and began to eat quickly. "Am I going to California too?"

Donald looked at Annie, "There is really no reason why she can't go with us."

"I could go and keep Marie company when you two need to run errands and what-not." Stella raised her eyebrows and tilted her head at the 'what-not'.

"Here is an idea," Donald said to Annie. "We all fly to California. Your mom and Marie can stay in a hotel for a couple of nights and maybe help with the packing. Then I will treat them to Disneyland for a few days while you and I drive my truck and Laddie back home here."

"I get to fly in an airplane?" Marie said excitedly.

"And we are going to Disneyland for a few days!" Stella exclaimed while looking at Marie. "I have not been there in years. Thank you, Donald. I say let's do it!"

"But I want to go to Disneyland too!" Annie said with a pout on her face.

"I will promise to take you soon after we get settled in the house," Donald said as he leaned over and kissed her on the cheek. "It can be our honeymoon."

Everyone talked excitedly about the trip to California. Annie noticed that Dan and Lizzy were talking quietly among themselves. Lizzy was smiling at Dan. Annie could tell they were quickly becoming a couple.

Dan suddenly spoke up, "Lizzy and I have a suggestion." Everyone listened intently. "While you are gone, Lizzy offered to stay in Stella's house and I will camp out in the guest room here. That way both houses will be occupied and kept secure while you are gone."

"Will you take care of Callie?" Annie asked Dan.

"I will make sure she is taken care of, Annie," Lizzy interjected. Lizzy knew how important Callie was to Annie. Lizzy did not want Annie to worry about anything while they were gone.

Donald and Annie looked at each other and agreed. They all looked at Stella who said she would have Annie's old room fixed up today and Lizzy could move in tonight. Stella actually looked like she was enjoying all the arrangements. It was just she and Annie for so long, and now she had this amazing extended family.

Annie suggested that they all meet here tonight for a pizza and movie night and get the details of house-sitting ironed out. Donald agreed, as they would be leaving early on Saturday to catch a flight in Portland to San Jose. Everyone loved the idea and even Dan thought a night of relaxation with friends was what he needed right now. Besides, how could he pass up pizza!

Marie finished the last bite of her breakfast and announced that she was heading upstairs to see her new bedroom. Everyone laughed and stood up from the table to follow Marie. Donald pulled Dan aside and handed him a spare key to the house, apartment above the garage, and the cottage. He told Dan of a special code for the alarm would be entered for Dan's use and showed Dan how to use the code. Lizzy would be given her own code.

They went up to join the women to view Marie's new bedroom. Donald was actually looking forward to seeing Marie's look when she saw her room for the first time. Although he did very little with the room, he did hire the decorator and suggested what style Marie would like. Marie also had input as to what color she liked and what she wanted it to look like.

As the group filed upstairs, Marie waited anxiously by her bedroom door. Donald had previously locked it, because Marie kept sneaking upstairs to peek while the construction people were there. Donald walked up to the door and unlocked it. He slowly opened the door to tease Marie. She pushed it open and walked inside.

CHAPTER 25

Friday Afternoon

When Marie entered the bedroom, she saw a full-sized bed with metal wrought iron head and foot frames containing swirl designs. The frames were creamy white with pink roses adorning the joints of the swirls. The comforter was cotton with gathered areas creating a star pattern throughout the entire area. Large white pillows stood in the far back of the bed, and creamy pinkish/white shams were purposely positioned in front. A wicker breakfast tray, nicely arranged with doilies and a beautiful miniature tea set, sat at an angle at the center of the bed almost near the foot. White long-legged nightstands stood on each side of the bed. On each nightstand was a small lamp with a white shade containing clear beads hanging from the bottom of the shade. White sheer lace curtains covered the windows and a sheer valance was draped over the top of the window frame. A pale pink vintage dresser stood on the wall next to the bed. An oval white wicker mirror was above the dresser. Further above the dresser on the wall was a shelf with vintage feminine articles in whites and pinks. A creamy white linen chair sat near the window overlooking the ocean.

"This is my room!" Marie turned and looked at Donald. She turned to look at the room again. This time she walked inside and pointed to various objects as she again stated, "This is MY room!"

"Yes, this will be your room now," Annie said walking in and putting an arm around Marie.

"No," Marie said pulling away from Annie and gesturing with her arms swinging wide. "This is the room my mom made for me!"

"I don't understand," Annie stated.

"I think I know what Marie is talking about." Donald explained to the group that he took copies of photos from the photo album showing Marie and her mother in a bedroom that Marie had before her mother passed away. He gave the copies to the decorator and asked if the bedroom could be decorated as close as possible to the room in the photos. "Apparently, the decorator did a great job, as Marie seems to like it."

"I love it," Marie said. "I am never leaving this room! It is my perfect room!"

Annie barely knew Marie's mother, as it was a time when Annie spent a great deal of time at her shop trying to make her business profitable. She did remember Marie and her mother living next door to Helen. Helen and Marie's mother often visited with each other. Annie thought this might be why Helen became Marie's guardian after Marie's mother death.

The group was quiet as they looked around the room. Marie was the first to break the silence. Tears were streaming down her face. It was the room that Marie's mother had decorated for her before passing away. Marie turned and hugged Donald tightly. This was her dream room. Annie now recognized the room in photos from the photo album. It was more beautiful in person.

"Donald, you did an outstanding job on the room." Annie was trying to take in the outstanding detail.

"I really cannot take any credit for this room," Donald said. He looked at Marie, putting his arm around her shoulder he said, "Marie showed me photos from the album that Helen kept."

"I love it," Marie exclaimed loudly, jumping up and down. Everyone chimed in and pointed out their favorite areas of the room.

Annie noticed that Dan was not in the room. She walked out into the hallway and saw him standing at the end of the hall talking on his cell phone. Annie walked up to Dan as he finished his call. Donald followed Annie out of the bedroom while the rest of the group continued to look around the room.

"I just got called out." Dan said continuing to look at his text messages.

Lizzy and Stella walked from Marie's bedroom and joined the group. "Is something wrong?" Lizzy asked Dan.

"The truck has been found."

"In the garage of Eddie's house?" Annie asked. Donald moved closer to Annie. He was hoping Annie would not go into details as to why they were at Eddie's house.

"No," Dan said. "Actually, it was found in the ocean on the rocks. It had not quite made it completely into the water." Dan told Lizzy that he would call her and let her know if he was able to meet her later tonight. Lizzy said she understood.

Annie was walking Dan to the front door. As Dan reached for the doorknob, he turned to Annie and said, "You and I need to talk about the garage incident."

Annie winced, but knew he was right. She really did need to tell him the whole story. Now that the truck was found over a cliff, she needed to tell him about the damage on the bumper. "Call me as soon as you can. I will tell you everything."

"If I get a break, I will see you at the shop in town." Dan opened the door and walked out.

◆ ◆ ◆

Marie remained in her room while Annie, Stella, and Lizzy cleaned up the breakfast dishes. Donald pulled out his laptop and went to the office to make reservations for Stella and Marie to accompany them on the plane to California, and to make reservations for the flight and hotel at Disneyland. It was last minute notice and would cost a lot more, but it was all worth it to have the family travel together.

Annie entered the office to tell Donald that she, Marie, and Lizzy were going to walk to the shop this morning. Donald gave her an itinerary for Saturday and a copy for Stella. Annie asked that Donald leave a copy on the counter for Dan and Lizzy, as she briefly looked over the schedule. It looked like a fun trip. She was actually getting excited to go. Then she realized that she was not even packed, nor was Marie. Annie kissed Donald good-bye and headed out of the office to find her mother.

Stella was just finishing up in the kitchen when Annie walked in with the itinerary. Stella offered to help Marie pack this afternoon if Annie would send her home early from the shop. Annie agreed and reminded her mother of the pizza and movie night tonight. Was Annie taking on too much right now? She may be up late packing. Annie decided that it was worth it all to have this time with family and friends.

Lizzy had gone upstairs to get Marie. She and Marie were walking down the stairs when they saw Annie waiting at the front door. They said good-bye to Stella, who was walking out the door to her house across the street. She too had a busy day. She was getting Annie's old room ready for Lizzy to stay while they were away and she had to pack for herself and Marie. Stella decided she should research Disneyland and make sure they were taking proper clothing. She was also having lunch with Dan's mother, Lois Surely, at noon. She hoped that Lois would not cancel again.

Stella really wanted to find out more about this gentleman Lois and other ladies had mentioned. Apparently, a new man moved into the senior apartment building and all the women were talking about him. From what she heard from friends, this gentleman was quite a charmer with the ladies. Most of the men at the senior apartment complex were married, but a few of the single men were single for a good reason, Stella thought. This new man was a breath of fresh air to their small town. Stella was grateful she did not have to live in the retirement community just yet. She thought she was too young, but still enjoyed the activities and classes taught at the senior center. Stella unlocked her front door and went inside.

The morning proved a busy one for Ocean Loads of Paper and the neighboring shops. Annie spent 15 minutes standing in line at the coffee shop to get the usual and something for Lizzy, Marie, and Daisy. When she finally returned, the shop was so busy her coffee got cold. The shop traffic slowed a bit and Annie went to the back room where she kept a kitchenette and a small table for breaks. She put her coffee in the microwave and set the timer. As the coffee was warming, Annie looked around the storage room and began thinking about adding another office area for Lizzy. They should not have to share a tiny office, and most of the time Lizzy was working at the counter computer. Annie made a mental note to ask Lizzy about a future office space.

The chime sounded on the microwave and Annie was forced back to reality. She grabbed her coffee and went back out to the shop area. More customers came streaming in and the women were busy for the next hour, when they were finally given a break from tourist traffic. They were taking a deep breath as the last customer walked out, when in walked a large group of people from the senior residential living community. In the lead was LaVerne, followed by Lorraine, Elsie, and Millie. Behind them entered several gentlemen, one in a walker, and ladies with canes all excited to browse through the shop.

"We're the Silver Sleuths!" said the older gentleman with the walker. "Just call us the SS," he said moving his walker to where Annie and Lizzy were standing. The others joined him.

Annie and Lizzy exchanged looks of concern. Lizzy leaned over to Annie and whispered in her ear, "That's not what Dan calls them." Annie tried not to smile. She knew to what Lizzy was referring.

"We have added a few members to our little group," Millie said quietly. "This is Morty. He has special skills."

"I certainly do, sweetie, but you never take advantage of them," Morty interrupted.

Millie turned a shade of pink and looked at LaVerne.

"She was not referring to sex, Morty," LaVerne stepped in and positioned herself between Morty and Millie. "Annie, we came to have a discussion about the garage incident and what Lorraine and I suspect is going on with Ronnie and Eddie."

"Elsie, take everyone to the classroom where we can all sit around a table and tell Annie what we know," LaVerne commanded. Elsie began directing the seniors to the class area. "Save a spot for me, Annie, and Lizzy. Lizzy, we are inviting you in this meeting since you are the girlfriend of that hunky detective."

Lizzy looked at Annie. Annie shrugged her shoulders and motioned that they join the group. Annie began to walk to the class area and sensed footsteps behind her. She turned to see Marie and Daisy following her. Annie then suggested some things the girls could do on the other end of the shop and attend to customers. The girls gave Annie a defeated look. They turned and walked to the other side of the store.

Annie took a seat in the center side of the table facing out into the store so she could monitor the customer activity. Lizzy sat next to Annie. LaVerne sat across the table from Annie. The rest of the group settled around the table.

LaVerne took a deep breath and looked around the table. She then focused directly at Annie and said, "Remember the wooden crate in the garage that was so heavy it blocked us inside and we had to call you to rescue us?"

"A time that will be forever embedded in my memory," Annie returned.

LaVerne leaned in and everyone else leaned in to listen. With a look of sheer seriousness, she stated, "Here's the catch...we talked to Abby at the grocery store, who heard from her neighbor that her sister-in-law knows someone who is best friends with Eddie's wife. We heard that Eddie has been real upset with his wife over her brother always taking the truck. She was actually letting Ronnie drive the truck! Do you remember when we told you about Eddie knocking Ronnie down on the street in front of our retirement home? Well, Eddie shouted at Ronnie and told him to take the truck back to the garage and get out of town or he was a dead man. That is why Ronnie is hiding around town. He is afraid of Eddie."

"And no one has seen Doris Harris for a while," Millie said in a low whisper.

"I would bet she is a dead woman!" exclaimed Bernie dramatically.

"No!" Annie interrupted, "She is on a cruise with her sister."

LaVerne lowered her voice and stated, "Remember the sister-in-law who knows someone who is friends with Eddie's wife? Well...Doris Harris, Eddie Harris' wife is an only child! She has NO sister."

"He killed his wife!" Morty shouted.

"Ssssh!" several people gestured to Morty to keep his voice down.

"We should not jump to conclusions just yet," Lizzy interjected. "Have any of you talked with Detective Surely yet?"

"No, they have not." Dan stood at the table totally unnoticed by anyone. His towering dark figure appeared a bit scary at the moment. Annie was wondering how long he had been there and what he overheard. "Annie, I need to talk with you in your office...NOW!" Dan turned and walked to Annie's office. Several of the seniors gasped at the presence of Dan.

Annie rose from her seat and took in a deep breath before following Dan. She turned and looked back at Lizzy, who shook her head in a manner to suggest 'you are in trouble now'. Dan was not happy with the seniors butting into his investigation and now it seemed like Annie was in the middle of it also.

CHAPTER 26

Friday Night

Annie approached the office where Dan was standing just outside the door. He motioned her inside. She walked into the room, Dan followed and closed the door. Annie just stood there looking directly at Dan, not knowing what to expect.

Dan sat in Annie's office chair. "Damn-it, Annie, why do these senior snoopers know everything that is going on, sometimes before I do?"

"From what I can gather, they have some sort of network in town," Annie said, relaxing a bit.

"They are right, you know." Dan said soberly.

"What?" How can...wait...right about Doris Harris being dead?"

"Yes."

"You have found her body?"

"Yes."

"Oh no, she was the body in the wooden crate?"

"Yes."

"In the garage?" Annie began to recall the incident in the garage. The large wooden crate that she struggled to lift up on end in the garage...the large wooden crate that slid down and trapped her in the door...the possibility that Eddie could have caught her in the garage and killed her too!

Annie must have lost the color in her face, as Dan quickly jumped up and moved Annie to the office chair. She placed her hands on her head in an effort to make the room stop spinning around her. She instinctively lowered her head to her lap.

LaVerne knocked once on the door and forcefully entered the office. "If you are going to arrest anyone, you had better arrest myself and Lorraine."

"Yes...what?" Lorraine looked at LaVerne perplexed as she followed LaVerne into the office.

"Annie had nothing to do with our being at Eddie's place."

By now Daisy, Marie, Lizzy and a crowd of seniors were all standing at the door of the office trying to listen in on the conversation. Daisy saw Annie leaned over in her chair. Alarmed, she grabbed a handful of paper towels and asked Marie to get some cold water on the towels. Marie quickly went to the sink in the classroom area.

"And what were you ladies doing at Eddie's house?" Dan said as he stepped closer to LaVerne and Lorraine, who were standing inside the office at this point.

"What were we doing at Eddie's?" Lorraine whispered to LaVerne.

"We were looking for a kitten we saw run away from us toward the garage." LaVerne stood tall with her chin pointed straight out.

"Yes, that sounds good...I mean, that is what we were doing. There was a little kitten and we were trying to catch it before it got hit by a speeding car." Lorraine took a step closer to LaVerne in a unification stance and held her chin high.

Dan stared at the two of them. There was a awkward pause and then Dan said, "What color was the kitten?"

"Black," said LaVerne.

"White," said Lorraine.

"Orange," said Millie, who was standing just outside the office.

The ladies looked at each other in confusion.

"Was it...black...white..., or orange?" Dan leaned closer to the ladies and raised his eyebrows.

"It was a Calico!" said Morty loudly, sitting in the seat of his walker on the opposite side of the door from Millie.

"A Calico kitten?" Dan said, looking at Morty, a bit skeptical.

"YES!" All three women chimed in together.

"Oh, boy!" Annie groaned softly. She still had her head in her lap hoping this whole incident would end and end now. Marie ran in with wet paper towels and placed them on Annie's neck as per the instructions from Daisy. Annie felt the comfort of the cold water on her neck. She would have felt so much better if Marie had wrung out the dripping wet towels before bringing them to her. Annie now felt cold water streaming down her back as she sat up.

Dan, who was watching the whole scene before him could not hold back a smile. Typical Annie. Unfortunate events just find her. He turned his attention back to the Senior Snoopers.

"And how did you get into the garage?"

Lorraine piped up, "Oh, I just picked the lock."

"Excuse me? You picked the lock?"

Annie cringed. Did Dan have enough handcuffs to arrest them all and send them to jail right now? She imagined life in jail with the senior ladies. Could Lorraine pick the lock on the cell and get them all out? Annie was brought back to reality when she heard LaVerne talking.

"Oh, don't listen to her. She's a senile old lady. We 'opened' the door and walked in looking for the kitten." LaVerne was feeling pretty proud of her ability to cover the story.

"The kitten entered a locked garage?"

"Well, we saw something move," Lorraine injected.

"It could have been a rat," LaVerne quickly added.

"A rat?" Lorraine shivered. "We were in the garage with a rat?"

LaVerne turned to Lorraine and gestured for her to be quiet.

Dan then advised everyone it was time to leave. He escorted them all out, except Lorraine and LaVerne, who he told to wait for him in the classroom. He wanted to talk to them further, but first he needed to finish his conversation with Annie.

"I think Annie needs chocolate," LaVerne said watching the seniors leaving out the door. "Lorraine and I will go to the candy shop and get her some chocolate."

"I would rather you two stayed in the shop so I don't have to track you down later. I am not going to be nice if I have to spend time tracking you two down." Dan's tall figure loomed over the ladies, but LaVerne was not one to be intimidated.

"Oh, poo! We'll be right back with the chocolate."

"It should be dark chocolate." Lorraine advised as they walked out the door of the shop, "Dark chocolate is so much better for you and tastier too!"

Dan shook his head and re-entered the office where he found Annie sitting up and looking much better. He closed the office door behind him and pulled up a chair across from Annie. The paper towels that Marie had given Annie were no longer cold, so Annie threw them in the trash can.

"As I was saying...Doris Harris was found dead this morning." Dan paused and then continued. "She was apparently thrown from the pick-up truck when it went over the cliff. The sheriff's department reported evidence of broken up pieces of wooden boards all the way down the rocky cliff. It appears she was in the wooden crate in the back of the truck as it went over the cliff. Someone was trying, unsuccessfully, to cover up the murder of Doris Harris."

"Eddie!" Annie stated as she felt her back straighten up. "He even told you that she was on a cruise with her sister, which was not true, because she is an only child. LaVerne and Lorraine told me that." She was feeling a whole lot better now and was ready for that chocolate. Where were those ladies with that chocolate?

Annie remembered the photos she had taken of the damage to the front of Eddie's truck. Digging through her purse in the drawer of her desk, she found her cell phone. She pulled the photos up on her phone and forwarded them to Dan's cell phone. He looked at the close-up photos and praised Annie for the detail in the photos. He said he would get the photos printed and ask around if there was an incident involving the truck earlier.

Dan and Annie discussed the garage incident in detail. Dan stated that he was in the process of writing a search warrant on Eddie's house and garage. He just needed to interview her and the seniors first. Dan told Annie that Ronnie was still wanted for questioning and could not be found at the moment. All Annie could think of was that she felt better and was relieved she was not in trouble with Dan.

LaVerne and Lorraine entered the shop with coffee and chocolate. They walked directly to the office as Dan was opening the door. Lorraine handed the coffee and chocolate to Annie, who graciously accepted the gift. Dan then escorted the ladies to the classroom to talk with them.

Lizzy quickly walked in to check on Annie. "Wow! I really thought you were a goner." Annie held out a small bag, offering chocolate to

Lizzy. She looked at the candies and selected a chocolate covered caramel piece. Annie set the bag of chocolates down on her desk and took a sip of coffee.

While the two were in the office, Annie told Lizzy about Doris' dead body in the wooden crate and how she could not believe she was so close to a dead body and did not know it. Lizzy shuddered. They were quiet for a few moments until a soft tap on the door was heard.

"Come in," Annie said.

It was Daisy announcing that it was five o'clock and time to lock up the shop. Annie and Lizzy quickly got up and walked out into the shop. Dan was still interviewing the seniors in the classroom. Annie thanked Daisy for her quick thinking with the cold compress. Daisy smiled and picked up her personal belongings to exit through the boardwalk side of the door. Annie locked up after her.

Annie walked over to the street side of the shop and locked the door. On her way back to the office, she signaled to Dan to take his time with the interview. He was just winding up with the seniors and offered to drive them back home before returning to the station. They got up and walked to the street side of the shop. Annie followed to let them out. Dan made a quick detour to talk with Lizzy before leaving. Annie saw him kiss Lizzy on the cheek. She smiled and quietly moved her attention to the seniors who were now outside on the sidewalk.

◆ ◆ ◆

Annie, Marie, and Lizzy walked to Annie's house to prepare for their pizza night. As the women walked home, Stella, in her blue sports car, sped pass them and pulled into her garage. Lizzy told Annie that she was going to talk to Stella about care instructions for the house while they were in California. She quickly ran across the street before Stella closed the garage door.

Annie and Marie walked up to the front door and found Donald on the front porch with his laptop and an iced tea sitting on a side table. Annie thought Donald seemed to be really enjoying life at the moment. He appeared comfortable in her house. She wanted to sit on the front porch cuddled up next to him with an iced tea and read, but she knew she had a houseful of company arriving in a few hours and needed to get to work on the cookies.

Marie had already walked into the house and headed directly upstairs to her room. Annie pondered how long it would be before Marie left the secure sanctuary of her room to come downstairs and help with cookie making.

"I am just finalizing some plans for our trip tomorrow and then I will come inside and help with dinner," Donald said not looking up from his computer screen. He continued to type as Annie walked into the house. She too went straight up to her new bedroom. She could not believe how wonderful her master suite turned out. Donald had done what Annie would never have bothered to do, because her shop needed her attention so much more than her limited home life. That is changing now, Annie thought to herself. It was time to make family and friends a priority.

As she entered her bedroom, Annie found Callie asleep on the small sofa in the alcove area. Annie went over and petted Callie on the head. "Mrrph!" Callie said as she lifted her head briefly and then went back to sleep. Annie fluffed a few pillows, looked out over the ocean, and turned to again look around her bedroom...hers and Donald's bedroom. Annie began to think about the night before. Was it all really happening to her?

Glancing at her watch, Annie realized it was nearly six o'clock and people would be arriving soon. She exited her bedroom and knocked on the door of Marie's room, asking her to come downstairs and help her make cookies. Marie bounded out of her room and passed Annie on the stairs. They both laughed when Marie was the first to reach the bottom of the stairs.

Annie considered an apron, but told herself 'what's the use?', she was likely going to make a mess anyway. Marie pulled the cookbook from the shelf near the dining room table. Annie noticed how unsteady the bookshelf looked and made a mental note to ask Donald to secure it to the wall. Looking at the book shelf, Annie noticed that Donald had placed Helen and Robert's copper-pounded entwined whale sculptured urn on the top shelf. She thought it looked too heavy to be up there and considered a different place to display it. Maybe the fireplace mantel. She had to think about this.

Marie opened the cookbook to cookies and asked Annie what cookies they would be making. Annie found the recipe for chocolate chip cookies and read the ingredients to Marie. Marie began retrieving butter, sugar, flour, vanilla extract, salt, and chocolate chips and putting them on the table. Annie looked through the cupboards for the walnuts that she bought earlier.

Donald walked into the house with his glass of iced tea, his laptop, and an empty plastic container of what once was walnuts. The two women in the kitchen stared at Donald. He looked at them wondering what was wrong. Annie walked over and took the empty plastic container from his hand.

"Did I just eat all the walnuts meant for the cookies?"

"'Afraid so, buddy!" Annie threw the container in the kitchen trash bin and pulled out her cell phone to call her mother.

"Mom, do you have any walnuts? I am baking cookies for dessert and ran out of walnuts," she said looking straight at Donald. "Thanks! I will send Marie over to pick them up." Annie hung up the phone and set it down on the kitchen table. Marie was out the door and across the street in quick order.

Donald set his laptop down on the kitchen counter and turned to embrace Annie. His hugs were warm and inviting and sent a tingly sensation throughout her body.

"I missed you today, Disaster Girl." Donald said softly, continuing to wrap his arms around Annie.

"I am looking forward to snuggling up next to you tonight." Annie then lifted her head looking at Donald and said, "Actually, I am really looking forward to meeting your parents and Laddie. Too bad it will be a short trip. I would really like to go back and spend some time there."

"We do have a very important decision to make right now," Donald said kissing Annie on the neck.

"What would that be?"

"When are we getting married?"

Annie was lost in the attention her neck was getting. The kissing moved up her neck and around to her mouth. She was considering foregoing cookies for dessert and taking Donald upstairs to ruffle the sheets on the bed. His muscular body was pressing into her body, as his lips found hers over and over. While they kissed, Donald's hands moved down her back and around her waist, pulling her shirt up slightly. His hands moved up her back again and he began to unhook her bra.

"Donald!" Annie suddenly pulled back. "Marie will be back in just a moment."

Too late, Marie had just walked in the front door. "Get a room!" Marie said and placed the walnuts on the kitchen table with the other ingredients.

"We have a room now," Donald said. Marie giggled.

Annie smoothed her shirt and cleared her throat. "Marie, we need to get the baking utensils out." She walked up to view the recipe and make sure she had all of the items needed for baking cookies. Then she gave Marie a verbal list of supplies they would need for this project. Marie removed a large ceramic bowl from the cupboard, measuring cups, measuring spoons, a mixing spoon, and a liquid measuring cup.

Donald moved in close to Annie and said, "You haven't answered my question."

"You were distracting me," Annie said smiling as she was preparing the equipment to make the cookies. "Let's talk with your parents first. I would like them to be at our ceremony."

Donald admired how Annie included his parents. She was very family oriented and he discovered how much he was enjoying the closeness of his new-found large family.

Marie brought over a cookie sheet she had lined with parchment paper. She had made lots of cookies with Annie's mother and Helen in the past. Chocolate chip cookies were her favorite and Annie was hoping they would be making enough to leave for Dan and Lizzy while they were staying in the houses during the week.

Annie pulled out eggs from the refrigerator and completed the list of ingredients. As she and Marie were mixing the first batch of cookies, Donald took his laptop to the office. Annie turned on the oven and set it for the temperature instructed in the cookbook.

Donald walked into the kitchen as the first tray of cookies were coming out of the oven. He waited a few minutes until the cookies were transferred to a cooling rack before grabbing a couple. Marie took a cookie as well. Annie chided the two for eating up their dessert before dinner.

"I ordered the pizzas while I was in the office," Donald announced while chewing on a cookie. "I should head out and pick them up now."

Donald kissed Annie on the cheek and grabbed his keys for the SUV.

He walked out the kitchen door and Annie heard the car pull out of the driveway moments later.

CHAPTER 27

Disaster Girl Strikes!

Dan waved to Donald as he drove toward the street where he had lived most of his life. As he turned the corner, he spotted a white van sitting directly in front of Annie's house. Recognizing the vehicle, Dan slowly maneuvered his unmarked patrol vehicle to the side of the curb. He instantly called for backup officers as he could see the figure of man walking up to Annie's door. He pulled out his portable radio and plugged the ear piece into his ear. His vehicle was out of view behind a neighbor's boat. Dan quietly opened his car door and with the prowess of a stalking cat he edged his way through the bushes to the side of the house.

Annie and Marie were inside the kitchen sneaking cookies and laughing about funny things that had happened in the past week when there was a knock at the door. Annie wiped her hands on a kitchen towel and walked to the door thinking Donald had forgotten his wallet or her mother and Lizzy forgot the key. She opened the door smiling, but that smile quickly eroded to fear as she stood looking straight into Eddie's dark narrow eyes.

Dan was about to announce himself and draw down on the man at the door, when Annie answered the door and the man forced himself inside. Dan signaled on his radio of a situation and asked the officers to arrive unannounced. He was in stealth mode as he edged toward the front door.

Annie staggered backwards into the house after Eddie had pushed hard on her upper left chest. Her eyes were focused on the gun in Eddie's right hand. She managed to pry her eyes from the gun and looked straight into the glaring dark, angry eyes of the man in front of her. She continued backing to the kitchen table. Marie stepped back from the opposite side of the kitchen table, eyes wide with fear.

"Here's how it's gonna go," Eddie said in a low raspy voice. "You are going to give me lots of cash and I am going leave this town and never return."

"You can take all the cash I have, just put the gun down."

"It's in the safe," Eddie stated as he moved closer to Annie. "Helen kept lots of cash in a safe. I know, because I was blackmailing her and she paid off nicely. The old bat had to go and have a heart-attack the last time I was here. Now, if you want to keep the information quiet from your boyfriend, you'll pay me NOW!"

Annie could see Dan glancing in the room from the front door. He kept hidden around the door frame, but occasionally glanced inside. She could see the gun in Dan's hand. Realizing she was in the line of fire, Annie backed up against the bookcase.

"I don't know anything about a safe or money. I just inherited the house. That's all."

"Don't lie to me, Missy," Eddie shouted in fury. He raised his gun and pointed it at Marie.

"NO!" cried out Annie. "Please, no. Take anything you want, but don't hurt Marie."

Marie spotted Dan at the front door. He was sending her hand signals to be quiet, get down on the floor on his command, and to not look directly at him. Marie was silently obeying his commands. Her eyes were wide and she was frightened.

Dan was not quite sure if Marie understood him completely and needed to come up with a plan quickly. He noticed Annie's cell phone on the kitchen table and knew she kept the volume up full on the ringer so she could hear incoming calls when the phone was in her purse. He needed a distraction. While he ducked behind the front door jam, he quietly pulled out his cell phone and pulled up Annie's phone number. He again glanced into the room to make sure Annie was out of the way. Perfect, she was up against the bookcase. He pushed the button to call Annie's cell phone.

Annie was physically shaking as Eddie held a gun pointed at Marie. Tears were streaming down her face. She stepped forward just as her cell phone blasted a ring tone, which frightened her, causing her to jump back into the bookcase. Annie saw Marie drop to the floor. She did not hear a shot fired. Why did Marie drop to the floor? Did she faint?

It was at this point the entire world suddenly appeared in slow motion. Items from the bookcase were slowly shooting forward and crashing onto the floor. Annie seemed to move in slow motion as she looked up and stepped sideways. Dan was running in slow motion in a low tackle run toward Eddie. Eddie lowered his right arm and turned his head to look up, he then turned his head and shoulders in the direction of the kitchen table as a large pounded-copper sculpted urn with entwined whales came crashing down on his upper back and head.

Dan slowed down and reached for the bookcase, stopping it from completely falling on himself as Eddie made a face plant right into the open ten-pound bag of flour sitting on the kitchen table. The explosion of flour was immediate. A white fog of fine powder filled the kitchen air. Eddie fell to the floor, the undamaged urn lying next to him. Dan quickly handcuffed Eddie.

The gun Eddie once had in his hand dropped to the floor and skidded next to Marie. Annie made a dash for the gun and expertly emptied its contents into her hand. Her father had taught her gun safety in her teenage years, so she was used to guns and did not fear, but respected them. Once Dan had secured Eddie, Annie handed the gun and bullets to Dan.

Dan contacted dispatch using his portable radio to advise that the situation was contained. County deputies and local police officers streamed cautiously into the house confused by the white powder swirling about. Dan was kneeling down next to Eddie and talking on his radio to dispatch. He was calling for an ambulance.

Annie went to Marie's side. Marie was curled up in a fetal position and shaking. Annie sat down next to her and hugged her, telling her it was all over. She was safe now. Annie was shaking herself. She wasn't sure she could stand up, but she needed to get Marie away from this scene. She forced herself to stand and helped Marie stand. She was going to open the back-kitchen door to get some fresh air when she noticed her mother standing just outside the front door.

"Dan?" Stella said with a shocked look in her eyes.

"It's okay, Mom," Dan said walking toward Stella and a wide-eyed Lizzy. "Annie and Marie are fine."

Lizzy had never heard Dan refer to Stella as 'Mom'. So many things to process right now. Lizzy was in a daze as Dan moved Stella and her to the front porch chairs and asked them to sit down and wait for Annie and Marie to come outside. Dan went back inside the house. Lizzy asked Stella why Dan called her 'Mom'. Stella told her that he had always called her 'Mom' and referred to his biological mother as 'Mother'. Stella said Rich and she always considered Dan as a son, as well as respected the wishes of his biological mother and included her in decisions which were made for Dan in his earlier years. He grew up in a very stable, loving home always knowing his mother. Stella told Lizzy that Dan tended to be reserved around people, but loosened up around people he trusted. Dan had always been the over-protective brother of Annie, which often ended up in arguments between the two.

As Donald drove up to the house and into the driveway, he noticed numerous patrol vehicles parked on the street. Without bothering to park the car in the garage, Donald stopped the vehicle in the driveway and got out. Donald was stunned and confused as he carried the two large pizza boxes to the back-kitchen door. He looked inside the window and saw police officers milling about. He then saw Annie and Marie standing with their backs to the opened door.

Donald walked inside the kitchen in total shock. White powder was still floating in the air. A man was lying in handcuffs on the floor. Things that once were displayed on the bookcase were strewn about in broken pieces. Police were everywhere. Annie turned and realized that Donald was standing behind her with pizza boxes in his hands.

"Hey guys, the pizza's here," joked Dan, as he nodded at the dazed and confused Donald.

"What in the world happened?" asked Donald, placing the boxes of pizza on the kitchen counter. Annie threw her arms around Donald for comfort. She grabbed Marie's arm and pulled her close. The three hugged for a long minute before Donald again asked someone to explain what happened.

"I'll let Annie explain." Dan said watching the deputies walk Eddie out to a waiting paramedic unit to be looked over before going to jail.

"Sorry about the mess. Hey, can you save me some pizza? I will be over as soon as I interview this guy. It is going to be late, so if you don't mind waiting up, I would appreciate it."

♦ ♦ ♦

Dan left through the front door, as an officer was snapping photos of the scene. Once the officer left, Dan advised Stella that she could go inside to see Annie and Marie. Lizzy stayed back to talk to him. Just as she began asking a question, an officer walked up to Dan and asked to speak to him. Once Dan left, Lizzy walked through the front door and stopped to view the scene. The kitchen was covered in a light layer of white dust. A powder film covered Annie and Marie's hair and clothes.

"You are my Disaster Girl!" Donald stated, breaking the silence.

Annie began to laugh, which caused everyone else to join in laughing. It was over, Annie thought. She knew what happened to Helen. Eddie was no longer a threat. Now she realized that Ronnie was never a threat to her, just a common thief. Laughter seemed to be the only thing to do now. The place was a total mess. She wondered how she was ever going to clean it up.

"Annie, you and Marie take the pizza and some napkins to the dining room table," ordered Stella. "Lizzy grab a broom and let's get a bit of this mess swept up so we can walk through here."

"Mom," said Annie. "Let's all pitch in and clean up. Then we can relax and eat pizza together." Annie grabbed the cooking utensils from the kitchen table and placed them in the sink. Stella filled the sink with hot water and soap and began washing up. Marie grabbed a towel and was drying the dishes. She was silent. Stella tried to joke with her, but Marie was still silent. Stella put her arms around Marie, and Marie hugged her tightly.

Marie asked if she could go to her bedroom. Annie came over and asked Marie if she would like to take some pizza with her. Marie nodded yes, and Annie went with Marie to the dining room to get some pizza on a plate for Marie.

Dan walked through the open door as Annie and Marie were at the bottom of the stairs. "Is everything okay?" He noticed Marie's demeanor as he walked up to them.

"Marie is wanting to go to her bedroom. I think this whole ordeal has been a bit much for her." Annie said as she started guiding Marie upstairs.

"Wait a second," Dan said placing a hand on Annie's shoulder to stop her. "Marie, would it be okay if you and I take some pizza out onto the front porch and talk this over?"

Marie nodded her head and stepped down the stairs and walked to the front porch. Lizzy handed Dan a slice of pizza and napkins. She carried out bottles of water for them to drink and set them down on the table. Marie motioned for Lizzy to sit down with them and offered Lizzy a slice of pizza from her plate. Lizzy accepted and grabbed a napkin.

Dan, Marie, and Lizzy were out on the front porch for twenty minutes before returning inside the house. It was starting to get chilly. Marie came inside and went back to helping with the clean-up. She seemed in a much better mood now.

"What did you say to her?" Annie asked Dan, as Dan grabbed another piece of pizza.

"We just talked." Dan was heading out the door with Annie following, when he turned around and said, "I might just make a good father after all." Dan closed the front door behind him leaving Annie standing inside the house in awe.

Dan wants to be a father? Is Lizzy aware of this? Annie looked to her mother for answers. "Did you hear what Dan just said?" Annie asked her mother.

"Of course, he wants to be a father, but he feared he would end up like his own father and it kept him from having a relationship long enough to make that happen. I think he has fallen in love with Lizzy." Stella picked up the rest of the dishes to be washed and put them in the sudsy water in the sink.

Lizzy stood still, looking at the front door. Annie could swear she saw tears forming in her eyes. Lizzy quickly recovered and continued to sweep the floor. Annie walked over to Lizzy and playfully nudged her in the shoulder with her shoulder. Annie smiled at Lizzy and went back to cleaning up.

As Annie was walking over to the kitchen table, she bumped into the pounded-copper urn still lying on the floor. She carefully picked it up and inspected it. Miraculously, the waxed seal had not been broken on either whale containing the ashes of Helen and Robert. Annie gingerly wiped the flour from the urn. She decided to place the urn in the office on a sturdier table in front of the window. It actually looked more like a sculpture on that table and less like an urn.

With a final wipe of a speck of dust on the sculpture, Annie said, "Thank you, Helen and Robert, for saving our lives. You will always be in our hearts."

Annie turned to notice Donald standing in the doorway. She walked up to him and put her arms around him. After a moment, they walked back to the kitchen. It all seemed surreal now. Her world was changing, but now it seemed calmer and made sense.

CHAPTER 28

Late Friday Night

With the kitchen cleaned and back in order, Annie and Stella were outside on the patio shaking out their brooms and dust cloths. They took a moment and sat down to talk. Lizzy noticed them on the patio in deep conversation and asked Marie and Donald to let them be alone. She wished she had that type of relationship with her mother and father, but theirs could only be described as civil at best. Lizzy went to the living room and sat with Donald and Marie. Marie yawned and decided to go to bed. She headed upstairs slowly and Lizzy heard her door close. It had certainly been a very long day for all of them. She wondered how long Dan would be at the station. Would he even make it back at all?

When Annie and Stella returned from the patio, Lizzy got up and offered to warm the pizza in the oven if anyone was still hungry. They decided to keep it in the refrigerator and wait for Dan to return. Just as everyone had settled back down in the living room, they heard a key in the lock on the front door. Dan walked in looking exhausted from the days' events. Everyone got back up and Stella went to put the pizza in the oven. The group gathered on the patio in the backyard and soon were eating pizza with grated cheese topping and drinking beer, water, and pop.

"Well, I have information, but everyone has to keep it to themselves for now." Dan said grabbing a slice of pizza and asking for the grated cheese. "Eddie made some confessions before deciding to ask for an attorney. I think he was just getting tired and wanted to return to his cell."

All ears were on Dan as he took a bite of pizza, chewed, and picked up his bottle of beer. He was off duty now, so he decided on beer and pizza to end the night. Annie waited about as patiently as she could and then spoke up, "Well?"

"Well..." Dan said putting down his beer bottle. "Eddie confessed to more than what I would have expected. He actually did not physically kill Helen. She did die of a heart attack, which is what the autopsy report indicates, but he may have caused the attack. He admitted to that at least. He caused Helen such stress over time that her heart gave out."

Dan took a drink of beer and another bite of pizza. "Apparently, those marks you photographed on the pick-up truck, Annie, were paint transfer from Robert's car, as Eddie used the truck to force Robert off the road and over a cliff, killing Robert on impact. That is why Eddie did not want Ronnie driving the truck around town."

"But why? Why would he want to kill Robert?" Annie asked.

"Robert refused to succumb to Eddie's blackmail anymore. It angered Eddie. Robert was Eddie's source of income. Eddie never had a real job."

"Wait a minute. Eddie mentioned something about blackmailing Helen when he was here." Annie put the glass down that she was holding in her hand. "Why would he be blackmailing Helen?"

"I was not able to get to that before he asked for an attorney. I had to end the interview at that point. Eddie did confess to killing his wife, Doris, and dumping her and the truck over the embankment and into the ocean. Only the truck never made it into the ocean and Doris' body was ejected from the truck before the truck was stopped by the rocks below."

Everyone was silent for a moment. They could hear footsteps and talking coming from the driveway and nearing the backyard. Millie, from across the street, appeared first followed by Elsie, LaVerne, and Lorraine. The four ladies greeted everyone as they walked up to the patio.

Stella was the first to greet the group. "Good evening, ladies. Would you like to sit down and join us for pizza?"

"I'd like to sit down," LaVerne announced, "but if I eat pizza I will be up all night with gas." LaVerne sat down followed by the rest of the seniors.

"We came over to find out what all the commotion was earlier this evening," Millie said brushing specks from the table cloth.

Dan stood up and pulled out his ringing phone while walking a distance away from the group. He listened for a moment and then walked back to where Lizzy was sitting and placed a hand on her shoulder. Dan told the group that he needed to leave.

Patrol had picked up a suspect, and he was wanting to talk to Detective Surely. Lizzy took that to mean he was heading back to the station. Good thing he only had a few sips of his beer. Apparently, the case was continuing to evolve and needed his attention. Dan made his apologies and headed for the door. Annie told Dan to come back and stay in the guest room so they could see him in the morning before they left. He said he would try to be quiet when he let himself in the house. Lizzy followed Dan out to the front yard.

"I bet they get married before you two do," Millie said watching Dan and Lizzy walk to the front door through the kitchen windows.

"Don't count on it, ladies." Donald got up and was beginning to clear the boxes the pizza came in. "I plan on marrying this lady as soon as she is willing."

"Oh, I do hope we are invited," Lorraine stated.

"I just love weddings," announced Millie. "The food, the music, the decorations..."

"Not to mention the two young people getting hitched," LaVerne interrupted.

"Well, of course! I was getting to that before you interrupted me." Millie continued. She tilted her head as if in a dream state, "The two young love birds at the altar."

"You should have the wedding right here in this backyard," exclaimed Elsie, looking around. She appeared to be planning the wedding at the moment. "You could use that walkway as an aisle and the minister would be standing on the porch of the cute cottage. Chairs could be situated all around the yard. Oh! It would be so lovely!"

Annie's attention and smile on her face told Donald that they were going to be married in the backyard. She did not even need to discuss it with him, the look on her face when she turned to him was all he needed to shake his head in agreement. Perfect, Donald thought, the wedding venue has been set. Now for an actual date.

As if she read Donald's mind, Millie said, "I think you should get married as soon as you get back from California."

Annie did not even bother to ask how Millie knew they were going to California. She gave up asking them how they got their information. There was obviously some cosmic grapevine that eluded Annie and went straight to the senior ladies. Annie decided to just agree it was quaint and leave it at that.

Lizzy walked back out onto the patio and rejoined the group. This was the happiest Annie had seen Lizzy in a very long time. In fact, Dan was beginning to become more and more human, Annie thought to herself. She smiled. She suddenly realized that Dan was joking more, smiling more, being more involved in her family life...just like he was before her father's death. The real Dan was beginning to show through the past of stress, heartache, and misery he had attempted to cover up all these years. Annie was so pleased that Dan and Lizzy found themselves in a relationship together.

"Annie? Did you hear me?" whispered Lizzy as she nudged Annie's arm.

"Oh! I am sorry, Lizzy." Annie wondered how long she had been daydreaming. She looked around the table and noticed that several conversations were occurring at once. No one seemed to notice that Lizzy had come back to the group. "I was thinking about how wonderful Dan and you look together."

"Yeah...he is wonderful...," Lizzy sighed. "Annie, grab something off the table to take to the kitchen and follow me."

Annie picked up her glass and followed Lizzy to the kitchen. They walked over to the kitchen sink where Lizzy looked around to see if anyone was in the room or listening. Satisfied that they were alone, she said, "Dan told me that Ronnie has been arrested and he is willing to bargain for information that leads to Helen and Robert's death."

"You mean information about Eddie blackmailing the Harpers?"

"Yes, he wants to plea bargain for a lesser charge against him for the burglary he committed at Helen's house...your house...this house." Lizzy then lowered her voice and said, "Please act like you never heard this bit of information when Dan tells you. I really should not have said anything, but I just could not keep it from you. Ronnie was hiding in your yard waiting for Dan to come over, when Eddie pulled up and entered the house."

"He was here!"

"Yes, he was looking for a place to hide, because Eddie threatened to kill him."

"That is exactly what the senior ladies told me."

Donald walked through the kitchen door with a tray of glasses and used napkins. He stopped when he saw Annie and Lizzy at the sink staring back at him. "Did I interrupt girl-talk?" Donald set the tray down on the counter near the sink. "The party is breaking up and everyone wants to turn in for the night."

"Wow!" Lizzy said looking at her watch. "I had no idea it was this late. I have to open the shop tomorrow, so I will say my good-nights and walk over with Stella."

"I am walking the Silver Seniors back to Millie's house. Stella and you can walk with us." Donald turned and walked to the kitchen door to retrieve the group to walk home.

Annie and Lizzy walked to the patio to say good-night to everyone. Annie picked up the last plates from the table and told Donald she would lock the kitchen door. Donald told her he would not be long.

Annie entered the kitchen and finished putting the last of the dishes in the dishwasher and started the load washing. She jumped when she heard the front door knob turn. Donald walked through the door and made sure he locked it up. He started to turn off the front porch light, but then changed his mind and left it on in case Dan used that door when he came home.

Annie wondered if this house was as active as it seemed to be in the last two weeks. There were a lot of people coming and going, a lot of unwanted criminal activity, and she smiled when she thought of the good things that had happened too. She met Donald here in this house...Marie found a permanent home...and Lizzy and Dan were now a couple.

Donald began checking doors and windows and turning lights off. He left a light on in the entryway for Dan. It could be hours before Dan got back to the house.

Annie began walking up the stairs. She was truly exhausted. All she wanted to do was sleep. What a time to remember that she was leaving tomorrow morning for California and she had not packed a thing. She began making a mental list in her head when she felt hands guiding her up the stairs and to the bedroom. She kicked off her shoes, pulled the covers back, and sunk down onto the bed, laying her head on the pillow.

CHAPTER 29

Saturday Morning

It was seven o'clock when Annie awoke to the smell of coffee...and...bacon? Annie opened her eyes for a second time to clear the fog in her head. Donald was looking out the window at the ocean and eating a strip of bacon. Annie looked at her nightstand and realized there was a cup of steaming coffee right in front of her.

Donald turned when he heard Annie stir and sit up. "Good morning!" He walked over to the bed and sat next to her.

"Hmmm...good morning." Annie took a sip of the delicious, dark roasted, heavenly scented coffee. "Boy, did I sleep well."

"You needed it after last night."

"Oh!" Annie groaned. "That wasn't a nightmare?"

"Afraid not." Donald took the cup from Annie and took a sip of coffee to wash down the bacon he ate. "But the worst is behind you. Eddie is in jail. You should get up and change your clothes. You still need to pack and your mother is making breakfast for everyone. You are the last straggler."

"I won't be long." Annie realized she was still in her clothes from yesterday. She quickly got up and hurried to take a shower. The water was warm and relaxing to her tired body. Thoughts of California made her feel revitalized. She needed to spend some time away from this place. She needed to forget what happened last night. How in the world did she get herself into this mess?

As she was dressing in her walk-in closet, she pulled out her suitcase and unzipped the main compartment. There inside were Helen's two journals. She had completely forgotten all about them. She pulled them out and found one of her tote bags that she decided to take with her. She placed the journals in the tote.

Staring at the journals in the tote jogged her memory of the canary colored envelope which contained the letter from Helen as well as other envelopes which she had been procrastinating reading. She started to panic as to the whereabouts of the envelope and searched frantically around the tiny room. Hanging in the back of many tote bags that she had collected over the years, many of which had multiple items still in them, Annie found the tote with the envelope. She pulled the smaller envelopes out of the large package.

The letter to Annie from Helen was on top of the stack. She stared at it for a moment. She set the other envelopes down and sat down on the dressing room bench to finally read the letter. She had put off reading the letter for far too long now. Why did Helen leave her so much? Annie thought she did not deserve any of what Helen had given to her. Were the answers in the letter from Helen. Annie was scared it was all a terrible mistake and her life would come tumbling down.

Taking a deep breath, Annie began hearing what her father always taught her. '*Annie, you should have a plan, and then have a back-up plan.*' She looked up and turned her head side to side, expecting to see her father sitting next to her. What would her back-up plan be if everything fell apart? She and her mother would find another house to live in, but what about Marie? Annie would petition the court to regain guardianship of Marie. Annie then realized that Dan would never take the house from her mother. Deep down inside he really was a great guy. Okay, she told herself. Life would move on. She still had her paper crafting shop. And then there was Donald. He promised his love to her. They would all be okay. She would survive.

Annie turned the envelope over and began to break the seal with her fingers. As she tore the flap carefully open, she realized her hand was shaking. She took a deep breath and pulled the handwritten letter from the paper container.

"*My dearest Annie,*

By now my death has occurred and you have had the Will read to you by Charles Conklin, my attorney. Hopefully, my ashes are with my darling husband, Robert, in the entwined copper whale urn. Be comforted that I am in a happier place now. I do not want anyone crying over me. My life was long and exciting, as you will soon find out.

You may be wondering why I chose you to inherit my house and belongings. Although we never spent much time together, I learned about you and your life through my dear friend, Stella. Stella loves you so much and she is so proud of your accomplishments. I only wished I had a daughter just like you. Since I did not have the opportunity to raise children of my own, I have always thought of you as what my daughter would have been. The closest I have come to a child of my own is my nephew, Donald. He has been well taken care of in my Will.

It was my desire that you meet Donald and the two of you fall in love. If you did, you might have started a life here in Bridgewater Harbor. Donald is a remarkable and talented man. If you get a chance to meet him, I know you will fall in love with him instantly. My wish is that my death will bring you two together.

As for your inheritance from me, this house holds many secrets and treasures. I hope you will find the time to locate my journals and read them. I share many of the secrets in the daily writings. The journals explain my life and how I lived my existence to its fullest. There were a few major disappointments over the years, but for the most part I was happy.

My dear husband, Robert, was a compassionate man and spent many years traveling to foreign countries to offer his medical services at no expense. You can read all about his travels in my journals. Robert often brought back artifacts given to him in payment for services. He always found a way to later return the majority of the tokens of appreciation to the people without hurting their feelings. He really tried to make their corner of the world a better place when he left. I wish you could have known him better.

By now you will discover that I left Robert's business, R&H Enterprises, Inc. to you, instead of Donald. There is a very good reason for that. I wanted the owner of the business to remain in town and continue to work among the tenants of the buildings. Robert loved this town, and when the opportunity came to purchase the buildings, he jumped at the chance. There are secrets to discover as you read my journals. Please seriously consider keeping the business. If it becomes a burden, you may enlist the help of Donald to partnership with you. My only wish is to keep the ownership of the buildings local.

Please watch over Marie and help guide her through life. She is so special to me. You were the only person I felt would understand her and be young enough to take care of her. She really wanted a job to earn her own money, but I was frightened that she would be ridiculed and harassed. I could not allow her to be hurt. Maybe she could help out in your store part-time. It would mean so much to me. Marie has her own money left to her by her mother from an insurance policy and sale of their home. It is located in a safe in the house. You will find the code to this safe in an envelope which I have left with this letter.

Your mother, Stella, is a wonderful woman. She has been my friend through the end. I will always cherish her companionship and advice. The death of your father was so difficult for her. I only fully understood, after Robert passed, how empty a surviving spouse feels. I hope she forgives me for not being a more compassionate friend. I would have liked to have been a better friend. She was right by my side when Robert passed away. I will always be grateful for that.

Any further information will be found within the house. Please take care of yourself and enjoy life. I will be watching over all of you from Heaven.

All my love,

Helen Harper"

Annie lowered the letter to her lap and tried to let it all sink into her brain. Why had she not spent more time getting to know Helen while Helen was alive? Annie suddenly felt a twinge of guilt. Was she doing the same to her mother? Not anymore, she told herself. She was going to make changes and enjoy life. She had so much to be thankful for with Donald, Marie, and her mother being close.

Annie placed the letter back into the envelope and placed it in the larger paper container. She decided to read the information in the other envelopes on the plane to California, or better yet, during the ride back from California in the truck.

The door to Annie's closet slid open and there stood Donald. Annie still had a towel wrapped around her wet body. She quickly stood up and began flinging clothes into her suitcase. Donald walked into the closet, closed the door, and walked up to Annie. As he wrapped his arms around her he began kissing her neck.

"Your mother told me to hurry you up," Donald said kissing her shoulders.

"I think she sent the wrong person to get me to hurry up," Annie said feeling the tingling sensation move powerfully through her body.

Donald's hand moved from her arm to her towel, and in a quick smooth action the towel had dropped to the floor. All thoughts of hurrying up were the furthest from Annie's mind.

◆ ◆ ◆

"It is about time, Annie." Dan said cutting up a slice of ham on his plate. "Some of us have jobs and need to get to work." Lizzy nudged Dan in the shoulder. Dan smiled at Lizzy.

"I am sorry," Annie stated sarcastically to Dan as she walked up to the kitchen table. "Some of us had a gun pointed at them last night!"

"Yeah!" Marie broke in to the conversation.

"Alright you two, enough already." Stella took Annie's coffee cup from her and placed it on the coffee maker and pressed a button. "Annie, sit down and the two of you be nice to each other. And Marie, do not get involve with your brother and sister's bickering."

Dan and Annie looked at each other and laughed. Yes, they were a family getting back to some normalcy. It felt good and it felt even better now that Marie was included as a sibling.

"I have an important announcement to make. It involves you both." Stella said placing the hot coffee in front of Annie's plate.

Annie began dishing out scrambled eggs onto her dish and passed the plate to Donald. She already knew what the announcement was, but was sure no one else did. Stella had talked to Annie the night before and they both came to an agreement that would benefit all in the long run.

"We are all ears, Mom." Dan looked at his watch. "Just let me call the office first. I want to make sure my Captain knows I am coming in late today." Dan got up and walked to the living room to make the call.

"Just how many hours of sleep did Dan get last night?" Donald asked Lizzy.

"He told me that he came in around two in the morning. He sent me a text at six this morning, so I am thinking less than four hours sleep." Lizzy noticed Dan walking back to the table.

"I am good until noon." Dan returned, sat down, and placed his napkin back on his lap. He picked up his fork and began eating.

Stella put her fork down, pushed her plate forward on the table, sat up and placed her folded hands on the table. "Now, I have talked to Annie about all of this and we came to an agreement."

Everyone looked at each other with expressions of curiosity. Donald was the only one who kept eating. Annie eyed him suspiciously until he looked directly at her. He winked and gestured to Annie to pay attention to her mother. Annie turned her gaze toward Stella.

"I realized how lonely I was going to be in that big house, and I feel that in my senior years I do not want to be responsible for a large house anymore. So, I am moving out of my house and into the apartment above the garage."

Dan looked up from eating, "Are you selling the house?" Dan put his fork down. He looked at Lizzy and then back to Stella, "I want to buy the house from you. It was my childhood home after all. I need to find a house and it has always been the perfect home to me."

"I am sorry, Dan," Stella stated. "But I cannot let you do that."

Dan looked at Stella and was speechless. Tears were welling up in Lizzy's eyes. Dan looked at Donald and then at Annie. Annie seemed to be enjoying this. Both Annie and Donald were looking smug for some reason.

"What is going on with you two?" Dan questioned Annie and Donald.

"Now Dan, be nice." Stella advised, "I am GIVING you the house as an early inheritance."

"Me?" Dan asked. He was totally surprised. He looked at Lizzy, whose eyes were welling with happy tears this time. Dan looked around the table and then got up and walked to the front door, opened it, and looked out across the street. He ran his fingers through his hair and turned to ask Stella, "Your house? You are giving me your house?"

"Yes, that is what I said. It is my gift to you. I had lunch with your mother yesterday. I told her what I wanted to do and she gave her blessing."

Dan closed the front door and quickly walked over to Stella to give her a big hug. "Thank you, Mom!" he whispered in her ear.

Stella then told Dan that she needed to downsize and was wondering if he wanted most of the furniture. She was not going to be able to take the majority of the possessions she owned.

"I could always sell the furniture or give it away if you don't want anything."

"No!" Dan said happily. "I will take it all!" Much of the furniture held memories for Dan of growing up in that house. He loved everything about the house.

Annie noticed that Dan looked at Lizzy for her approval. She shook her head in support. Lizzy stood and hugged Dan tightly.

Everyone stood up to congratulate Dan. When Annie went to give Dan a hug, Dan said, "What did you have to do with this?"

"Mom told me last night she wanted to move out of the house. I had absolutely nothing to do with any of this." Annie had a feeling Donald may have had a part in her mother moving to the apartment over the garage, but she was not quite certain what it was. She made a mental note to find out.

After all the excitement quieted down, Stella said, "Well, I do want my clothes and a few personal effects." Stella then turned to Annie, "Annie, would there be some space in the garage for me to place boxes in storage?"

"I think we can find adequate space for whatever you need to keep." Annie looked at Donald and back to her mother and said, "There is the workshop and I think a small room off that area. We can figure it all out when you get back from Disneyland."

"Wait a minute," Dan injected. "That is a great workshop. What if Donald and I wanted to use the workshop for projects around the houses?"

"Since when have you or Donald ever set foot in a workshop?" Annie asked.

"We are not exactly unfamiliar with tools," Dan said to Annie. "The workshop will be a perfect place to develop new hobbies. Am I right Donald?"

Donald finished chewing the forkful of food he put in his mouth. He lifted his coffee cup and took a sip. Setting the cup down, he said, "As a matter of fact, I had a hobby making leather belts in my Dad's workshop. I would not mind a place to do that here."

"There you have it," Dan announced. "The guys get the workshop!"

"Okay," Annie said. "But only until Mom, Marie, Lizzy, or myself find a reason to use it. Then it will be for everyone."

Dan looked at Donald, "Should we wager how long it will be before any of them use the workshop?"

"Don't put me in the middle of this." Donald picked up his plate to take it to the kitchen sink. "I want to continue to live in this house."

At this point, everyone began picking up their dishes and clearing the table. Stella ran hot water in the sink to rinse the dishes and place them in the dishwasher. She placed a detergent pod in the door of the dishwasher and closed the door. After pushing the start button, she grabbed a towel and wiped up the counter.

While everyone was talking about the upcoming trip, Dan signaled Annie to follow him to the front door. "I need to discuss something very important with you right now before you leave." Dan suddenly became serous. He knew he did not have a lot of time before Annie, Donald, Stella, and Marie left for California.

"Can it wait until I finish packing my suitcase?"

"No, it is about the case." Dan announced to the group that he and Annie needed to discuss something and they would be outside for a few minutes.

Donald looked questioningly at Annie as Dan escorted her outside. Annie shrugged her shoulders. Everyone stopped talking and watched the two walk out the door. As they walked, it dawned on Annie that Dan may be asking Annie if he should marry Lizzy. Yep, she told herself. That could be the very thing he is wanting to talk to her about. He has a job, and now a house. He was all set to make a permanent commitment. Annie was getting excited and had a hard time containing her happiness. But Dan said it had to do with the case, Annie thought. Dan crossed the street and Annie followed him.

"Dan, what's this all about?" Annie asked, getting a bit nervous.

"I wanted to get out of ear shot of everyone." Dan stood looking at Stella's house and again ran his fingers through his hair and shaking his head in thought. He turned his attention to Annie, who was standing next to him in front of the white picket fence gate. "Annie, some disturbing details came up in the case when I interviewed Ronnie last night. I wanted you to hear it from me first."

"I do not understand. What is so disturbing that we do not already know about?"

Donald sighed and turned to once again look at Stella's house. "Annie, I became a police officer because it seemed like a challenging and exciting job. As with any job there are the downsides. Delivering bad news has never been at the top of my list of favorites. Sometimes, as an officer, we find out disturbing details about a case which is often difficult to explain to the person involved."

"Dan, what is it? Just tell me." Annie was now getting concerned. She had no idea why Dan was stalling with this information.

◆ ◆ ◆

"It is Eddie's reason for blackmailing the Harpers." Dan began to tell Annie that Eddie found out Helen had a baby boy. Helen gave the baby to another couple who were not able to conceive."

Annie thought about the baby photo and the framed baby clothing in the vault room. Helen had kept a secret all these years. Who was this baby and why would she give up her baby?

Dan continued, "Helen was permitted to see the child under the guise that she was his aunt." Dan stopped talking. He was waiting for Annie to connect the dots.

"Donald!" Annie said in a soft voice as she sat down at the curb of the street. She remembered the beautiful ring in the photo. It was Helen's wedding set. She remembered it being the very set that was given to her mother after Helen died. Dan had handed it to her when he stopped by the shop. That is why she thought it looked familiar. Then she remembered what Eddie said last night...' if you want to keep the information quiet from your boyfriend'..." That is what he meant, the Harpers were being blackmailed to keep the information from Donald!

Dan sat down next to Annie. "Are you going to tell him? It will come out in the court case. He will hear about it eventually."

"No, Dan, I am not going to tell him...you are. It is your case and you uncovered the information." Annie turned and looked at Dan and softly said, "It will be better if you talk with him."

Dan somehow knew he would be the best person to talk with Donald. He stood up just as Donald was walking out the front door of Annie's house. Dan offered a hand to Annie to help her stand up. They walked across the street, and as they climbed the stairs to the front door, Dan asked Donald if he could talk with him for a moment. Donald glanced at Annie, looking a bit concerned. Annie nodded for Donald to sit with Dan and hear what he had to say. She continued inside the house and closed the front door. Annie really wanted to be with Donald, but he needed to hear this from Dan alone. She was not sure how Donald was going to take the information. Annie leaned with her back on the door. She was deep in thought when her mother called out to her.

"Annie!"

Annie looked up and noticed her mother walking up to her. She stood up. Stella asked if everything was okay. Annie replied it was fine.

"You do not look fine."

"It is not me, Mom. Just the case. I cannot talk about it."

"Oh, okay." Stella was silent for a moment and then said, "Would you like me to help you pack for California?"

"No. I can finish myself." Annie began walking up the stairs and then turned to look out the living room window where she could see Dan and Donald sitting. Donald was bent over in his chair with his elbows on his knees and hands supporting his head. He sat up and continued conversing with Dan. Annie turned and continued up the stairs.

Just as Annie was zipping up her fully packed suitcase, Donald entered the bedroom. Annie was still. She did not know what to say. She walked over to Donald and hugged him. He hugged her back. They clung to each other for several moments.

"Well, that was not news I was expecting. So many things going through my mind right now."

"Do you want to talk about it?"

"I will, but not right now. I am not even sure I want to tell my parents I know at this point. They have been my parents all my life. I knew of nothing different. Having a biological mother come into the picture now is not going to change that my mom is nothing but my mom. It just does not change anything."

Annie liked the way Donald was taking this whole situation. She knew he had to be alone with his thoughts for now. They had an hour before the town car was arriving to pick them all up and head to the airport in Portland.

Annie began to pick up her carry-on luggage when Donald stopped her. "I will bring that downstairs for you." She grabbed her tote bag and stuffed her purse inside. She gave Callie hugs and kisses before setting her down on the bed. Callie nestled into the throw blanket draped across the bed and was soon asleep.

Annie found everyone at Stella's house when she walked through the front door. "We need to get luggage out front and ready to go when the town car arrives. I left instructions on the counter for care and feeding of Callie. Lizzy, give her lots of hugs and kisses."

"I will. She will probably sleep with me and..." Lizzy stopped and realized she was just about to say something she was not ready to say just yet. She quickly said, "Dan and I might trade houses"

Annie leaned into Lizzy and whispered, "Whatever house you and Dan stay at, please make sure Callie is taken care of and well loved." Lizzy nudged Annie and the two of them laughed. Annie could see how smitten both Dan and Lizzy were with each other. Were she and Donald like that? Was it always obvious that she and Donald were attracted to each other from the beginning?

Lizzy and Dan migrated out to the patio in the backyard. Dan seemed still in shock over inheriting the house. It will hit him soon, Annie thought. Annie took a bottled water from the refrigerator and waited for her mom and Marie. Marie wanted to hear all about Disneyland and the research of activities that Stella had done. They chatted excitedly as they walked to Stella's bedroom to retrieve her suitcase.

As Annie sat at the breakfast bar in the kitchen and looked out the window, she watched Dan and Lizzy talking together, spied the morning sun sparkling on the ocean waves, spotted the occasional spouting from whales, and began to think about the last two weeks. It was barely two weeks ago when she discovered that Helen had passed away. In those two weeks she became a guardian to Marie, met the man she was now going to marry, became reacquainted with her 'brother' after so many years, and inherited a house and business property, and most of all solved the mystery of who killed Helen and Robert Harper.

Then there was the budding relationship between Lizzy, her best friend, and Dan. As she sat in the kitchen of Stella's house, the very house that her mother would now be turning over to Dan, Annie realized that Lizzy will be the one sitting in this chair and looking out over the ocean in the mornings. Maybe she should not jump to conclusions just yet, but she had a feeling they were going to be together soon.

Annie stood and looked around the kitchen. This was the house where she spent most of her life, except for a few years at college and on her own before her father passed away. This was her place of security. She was glad that Dan would be moving in and taking care of the old house. She was not sure she could bear seeing anyone else in the family home.

Dan and Lizzy walked hand in hand to the kitchen. The three walked to the front door and out to the sidewalk without saying a word.

◆ ◆ ◆

The sun was shining and the day seemed to turn out beautifully. Annie was hoping the trip to Portland and the flight to San Jose would be uneventful. She was looking forward to seeing Donald's house in Palo Alto and meeting his parents. Donald had told her of the remodeling his parents had done recently. He was a bit sad to move from the house, but knew it was not logical to keep it just for the occasional business trip to his office. He could always stay at his parent's house anytime he wanted when he had to fly to California.

The group stood on the sidewalk in front of Stella's house waiting for the town car to arrive. Their luggage was all lined up and accounted for. Donald had brought over Annie's bag and a small bag for himself. He advised Dan that he had locked up the house and checked the garage, apartment, and cottage to make sure they were all locked up. He then turned to Annie and told her that he saw Callie downstairs in the kitchen eating and drinking water.

Annie was happy to hear that Callie was getting used to her new home. It was going to be an adjustment, but Callie was making the effort. Her litter box was in the laundry room. Annie made sure to list the instructions for cleaning the box in the list she left for Lizzy. Lizzy had never had a cat before, so Annie was a bit worried that Callie would not get the attention she was used to getting from Annie. Cat people worry about their furry babies.

Donald told Dan and Lizzy that they would be back by Wednesday, and that Stella and Marie would be back by Saturday. A town car was all arranged to take them from the Portland Airport back home on Saturday. Donald had planned out Stella and Marie's trip for them, and made sure they had extra spending money for souvenirs and food. Stella tried to refuse the extra money, but lost in the end. Stella had never had the luxury of anyone making all the arrangements for her. She and Marie were really excited to be making the trip to Disneyland. Marie had secretly wished they could go straight there and not stop in Palo Alto.

There was a lot of chatter between everyone when from behind a short hedge separating Millie's house from Stella's house, walked four senior ladies. Millie was in the lead, followed by LaVerne, Elsie, and Lorraine. The ladies all greeted the group as the town car arrived. Donald spoke to the driver as they both loaded the luggage into the trunk of the vehicle. Stella and Marie hugged Dan and Lizzy as they were the first to get into the back seat. They left a spot for Annie who was saying good-bye to everyone.

"Now you have a good time in California. Do not forget to come back!" Millie said. "It will be so lonely here without you."

"What do you mean 'lonely'? Lorraine asked Millie. "There are four of us living here now. You will not be lonely."

"What?" Dan asked Lorraine, "You ladies all live together in the house next door?"

"Yes," answered LaVerne. "We moved in to help pay for the taxes and utilities. It can get expensive for us seniors on our limited income."

"We are like the Golden Girls on TV!" Elsie exclaimed.

"Except we like to call ourselves the Silver Senior Sleuths, because there are men in our group now," LaVerne informed Dan.

"Just think, Detective Surely," Millie spoke up, "We are all close by to help you solve your cases! You only need to give us a shout over the fence and we will come running."

"You running, Millie?" LaVerne questioned loudly. "More like a slow shuffle."

Annie hugged Lizzy good-bye. She attempted to hug Dan, but he was distracted by the Silver Seniors talking. Donald guided Annie to the vehicle and closed the door once she seated herself. Annie rolled the window down on her side of the car. Donald made his way to the passenger side front seat. He took one last look at both houses and climbed into the vehicle.

Dan stood on the curb dumbfounded. Annie could see a pink color appearing in his face. He was not going to like his new neighbors. Annie laughed as Dan poked his head through Annie's opened window and growled, "I am going to be living next door to the Silver Snoopers?"

– Available in 2020 –

GLUED TO SEE YOU

Die-Cut Mystery Series

Book 2

Thank you for reading SCORED FOR LIFE.